FAE BONDS

THE KENZIE CHRONICLES, BOOK THREE

GENAVIE CASTLE

ISBN: 978-1-962047-04-3 Print

ISBN: 978-1-962047-08-1 Ebook

Cover design by: CRey-ative Designs

Edited by: EPONA Author Solutions

Printed in the United States of America

ABOUT THIS BOOK

Everything about this book is completely fictional. This is a why choose romance novel containing graphic sexual content, some violence and explicit language suitable for mature audiences only. Proceed with caution.

INTRODUCTION

This is book three of The Kenzie Chronicles. It picks off right where book two ends thus it'll make more sense reading the first two books in the series. On that note this book explores an entirely different world, one I couldn't ignore. It may seem like a different story line altogether. New characters are introduced and our old favorites reappear. Hope you enjoy this installment of Kenzie's story and thank you for reading!

CHAPTER 1

KENZIE

I landed on solid ground with a bone-rattling thud. Pain shot through me, wrenching a harrowing scream from my throat. I lay completely still, unable to move a muscle. Each breath was pure agony.

My magic blazed through my body, healing what had to be broken bones. It repaired my injuries inch by inch, a slow and excruciating.

To distract myself from the pain, I reached for my mate bonds. The powerful strands of love and magic connecting me to my mates – Stellan, Caid, Erik and Brody – were barely a sliver. My heart ached at their absence, and tears streamed down my face. Unable to move, I let the tears fall while I recalled what had happened before landing in the abyss. My mates and I had been tracking the Rogue, a nefarious mage who had been responsible for conducting deadly experiments on humans and the supernatural. The five of us and Gunnar, a family friend, had confronted the Rogue in an abandoned warehouse. We were outnumbered but had taken out his guards. He had escaped via a portal and returned to the warehouse with four mages.

The four mages incapacitated my men with magical bindings. Stel and Caid used the daggers I'd given them and cut through the magical silver chains. And that was the last time I'd seen them. Fury rose within me, turning aching loss to anguish.

The Rogue teleported, taking Gunnar and me with him. Fucking Rogue.

After some time, breathing became more manageable, and the sharp pains subsided to dull aches. My magic was nearly depleted after repairing the nearly fatal damages. It would take some time for it to replenish. In the meantime, I needed to get moving if I wanted to see my mates again. I wiggled my toes and fingers, took a deep breath, and exhaled. My eyelids fluttered open. Darkness and silence greeted me. *Where am I?*

I turned my head swiftly toward the sound of a grunt nearby. Nausea engulfed me. The movement, too quick and too soon, had made me dizzy. Definitely not combat-effective. Fuck. I stilled, gathered my bearings, and breathed through the fogginess.

I spotted a prone figure a few feet away from me. With agonizing effort, I forced my achy body to sit upright. *Breathe, Kenz.*

The figure continued to groan. Slowly I rose and hobbled toward the person. Immediately, I recognized his face and those awful robes. Great, not the person I had hoped to see.

My eyes squinted as I scanned the darkness. Several feet away, Gunnar lay on the ground, completely still. I ignored the pain in my body and forced myself to walk toward him. My movements, which had been graceful and swift, were sluggish, as though I lumbered through several feet of snow.

I knelt next to Gunnar and breathed a sigh of relief. He had a pulse. His face was bruised from the beating he had endured by the Rogue's guards. He gasped when I nudged his arm.

"It's me, Kenzie," I said to him. "Anything broken?"

"Kenzie?" He said. "What the fuck happened?"

"Not sure. The Rogue teleported us somewhere," I looked around but couldn't make out much in the darkness. "Can you stand?"

"I need a minute," he said. "The Rogue?"

"Over there, groaning," I gestured with my chin. "I'll go check."

"Are you armed?" Gunnar asked me.

Shit, I'd forgotten to check. I patted my pockets down and found my dagger, a magazine for my gun but no gun, and a couple of vials of restoration tonic. I took one and gave one to Gunnar. "Drink it; it will help restore your magic."

He downed it, and I went back to the Rogue.

He was still breathing. I wanted to kill him. He had dislocated his shoulder. His foot was bent at an odd angle, probably broken. I didn't care. He had a bullet wound above his knee. I was mad at my poor aim.

I found my gun conveniently behind his back. It was empty, though. *Ha! Fucker thought he could shoot me with my gun.*

"You awake?" I smacked his face. He grunted out a "Yes."

"Hey, are you awake?" I slapped him a couple more times. He grunted again and muttered. I slapped him again and again.

"Kenzie." Gunnar stilled my hand. "I think he's awake. I want him dead just as much as you do, but we need some info."

He was right. But I smacked the Rogue again. Gunnar gave me an exasperated look. "What? I was just making sure," I said.

"Hey, where are we?" I said to the Rogue, smacking his face this time. He didn't answer. He groaned out something about being hurt. This time I bitch-slapped the asshole. "I don't give a fuck. Where the fuck are we?"

"How dare you! I'm injured!" the fucker dared to say to me. "What kind of monster are you?"

"I'm the kind of monster that will cut off body parts and sell them off if you don't start talking." I held my dagger against his chin.

"The Dark Realm," he muttered.

"What the actual fuck?!" I slapped him again, just for the hell of it. "Get us the fuck out of here!"

"I can't!" he shouted. "I can't, we need a demon to get us out, or we need to get to a gateway."

I was going to cut the bitch.

"One cannot simply teleport in and out of The Dark Realm. The only way in and out of the Underworld is by having a demon connection. I have a relationship with Mammon. I need him to send me — I mean us — back, or we go through a gateway. Gateways are few and still require access in and out. You need a relationship with a gatekeeper. And I don't know where the closest is because I don't know where we are because you shot me when I teleported us, which brought us here," he continued in a defiant tone.

He dared to make this about me. I was ready to stab him when an arrow whizzed by my head. *Shit!* We had company and not the good kind.

"Teleport us to your demon." I shook the Rogue.

"I can't!" he insisted.

"Liar!" I screamed at him.

The sound of footsteps rushed toward us. An arrow whipped by and barely missed the Rogue. That got him moving. He teleported us to another location. The Rogue was on his feet, well, foot. He hung on to Gunnar and me for dear life.

"My magic is trying to heal my body. I cannot teleport as readily," he stammered.

Well, fuck on a stick.

I looked over at Gunnar.

He shook his head. "I can't teleport at all. My magic is not working right. You try."

I had just learned teleportation and was not all that confident in doing so. But these were desperate times. I went through the lesson Erik, my magic man, had taught me. Nothing.

Another arrow whizzed past my head. One stuck in the Rogue's leg.

The Rogue screamed and teleported us into a pit of snarling demons. We must have crashed a party, because they were not happy to have intruders. They came after us. Gunnar and I fought for our lives. The Rogue cowered behind us, which only got in our way. But still, we weren't ready to let him die, and we needed him to get us out. Thanks to all that was holy, Gunnar and I were combat mages. So, we fought for our lives.

CHAPTER 2
STELLAN

My brother and I teleported back to Jameson Castle, Kenzie's ancestral home. Our mate had been gone for three days. Being without her was driving us nuts, Brody and Erik included. We were anxious to get her back, and today was the day. Well, technically tomorrow, but the demon had said three days, so we decided to arrive early.

The last time we had been here, I'd been so focused on finding Kenzie that I hadn't looked around much. Now that we were here again, I took in our mate's ancestral home. Caid and I had arrived via the tech portal at the edge of the Jameson property and surprisingly walked right through the wards. Mr. Jameson must've given us access. We followed the rough stone path, which led to the castle entrance. The closer we got, the more beautiful it became. It was an ancient medieval castle straight from the fifteenth century. Maybe older. We continued up the stone path through the outer wall. Back in the day, it had served as the castle's defense. I wondered if there were old cannons perched up there. We continued through the gate-house, which was the main entryway to the castle itself.

"Good evening, boys," Granny greeted us at the front door. "There were four of you." She glanced over our shoulder.

"The other two should be," Caid said as Erik and Brody flashed into view, "right here."

"Hello, Granny; good to see you again. You look radiant as always." Brody kissed Granny's hand.

Erik, my brother, and I rolled our eyes.

"Charming," Granny smiled. "Follow me."

Like proper boys, we followed the Jameson matriarch, staying on her heels. The interior had the same gray stone walls as the outside, with dark stone flooring throughout. It was well-illuminated with electrical lanterns and seemed to have every modern convenience throughout the place. A roaring fire lit up the room, providing warmth from the bitter cold outside.

We exited the castle proper through a side door, crossed a small courtyard, and went through an entrance to a separate tower. I glanced around the area, familiarizing myself with where we were.

"This is newly renovated," Granny said with a wave of her hand. "I had it all rebuilt so that you and my granddaughter would have some privacy."

We ended up in a long hall connected to a tall tower. The bottom floor had a bathroom, a living area, a small dining area connected to a kitchenette, and a fireplace that lit up as soon as we walked through the doors.

"I hope you will be comfortable here. Come upstairs." She teleported.

Granny was always showing her speed. I chuckled as we took the stairs two steps at a time.

To the left of the entryway was a winding staircase that went up thirty feet. At the top of the stairs was a large room with a stone fireplace and a large bed draped with pelts of fur. It looked like a giant, yet cozy bird's nest.

A side door opened to a medium-sized closet. On the opposite wall, an archway led to an impressive inside-outside bathroom. The bathtub extended outside, which overlooked the sea.

"Kenzie will love this," Caid muttered while staring at the view.

"Good, I'm glad you approve. Settle in; dinner will be served in thirty minutes." Granny vanished again.

The four of us unpacked the few things we had brought, and thirty minutes later, we assembled in the dining hall. It was massive. The dining room table itself could easily seat forty people. The table was hand-carved out of one solid piece of wood. It was nicked and scuffed up in places bearing witness to the countless guests that had sat at this table for centuries. I ran my hand over the table, admiring the craftsmanship. Despite the damage, it was a masterpiece.

Mr. Jameson entered, looking as worn out as we all felt. The last three days had not been easy on any of us. After Kenzie had disappeared, her father had done some spell casting, which revealed she had been teleported into The Dark Realm, thanks to the Rogue. The Jamesons were owed a favor by a demon they'd summoned three days ago. The demon said he'd bring her back to us today.

"Good evening, gentlemen. You're early. Any news on your end?" Mr. Jameson asked, looking at me.

"Nothing good. Our aunt wasn't all that helpful. She has the gift of foresight, but when we saw her, she wasn't coherent. Our parents are keeping an eye on her," I said as he poured whiskey for us.

Erik took a swig of whiskey and said, "I spoke with one of my mentors, who gave me the coordinates on two potential gateways. He had said only someone with great magic could walk through and survive. The other option is to go through with a guide. Not that it matters; we'll get our Kenzie back tomorrow." He drank the rest of his whiskey and picked up the bottle to refill his glass. I kept my eyes on him, wondering if that was a potential problem.Brody was eyeing Erik as well until Caid cleared his throat.

We all had separate tasks in locating Kenzie, and Brody was going to speak with his med mage.

"Kenzie asked Doc Higgs to research demons that may have helped the Rogue, and he gave me this." Brody pulled out some papers from his satchel and passed them around. Photocopies of pages from a book and drawings of a demon called Mammon. "This demon can enhance powers for a short time on his own. Doc thinks this demon's blood could enhance the spell the Rogue used in the experiments." He looked over at Erik, who had finished his second glass of whiskey and poured his third. "Will this help reverse the spell?"

Erik took a closer look at the information Brody provided and nodded. "Off the top of my head, I'm not sure. But I'll research this on my end."

"This is good work. Kenzie will for sure take care of the Rogue in The Dark Realm. I don't expect him to make it back alive. But it would be good to have these experiments called off for good." Mr. Jameson stared into his glass of whiskey. "I owe all of you an apology. Well, I owe Kenzie the biggest apology, first and foremost, and I will make amends when she returns. But I owe you an apology as well. If I had gotten involved from the start, perhaps she'd be with us right now. I haven't been the best father, and you," he pointed at us, "have been affected by my failures. For that, I apologize."

Brody, Erik, and I were shocked and speechless. But not my brother. Caid looked him dead in the eye and said, "Save it. Save your apologies for the person you wronged in the first place. Save it for Kenzie."

The serving staff had appeared out of nowhere, bringing out platters of food. We all must've been starving because we ate greedily and in silence.

Later that evening, Granny came to our tower and asked us to join her in the workshop where they had summoned the demon. The salt circle was in the middle of the floor with runes scribbled around it.

"The demon arrived at exactly nine fifty-three P.M. less than three days ago. I expect it to reappear no later than that precise moment. This here is an alarm of sorts. The bell will toll when he appears, and the circle will bind him in place. When you hear the bell toll, make haste to meet here. And as a reminder, in case you four forgot, do not go into the circle and do not make a deal with the demon. Am I clear?" She gave each of us a stern look until we acknowledged her.

I was too anxious to sleep, so I left the tower and followed my senses. I found Kenzie's childhood room and was about to make myself comfortable on her bed when I heard a whimper.

It was nearly midnight, and I thought everyone would be asleep, so I checked things out.

Down the long hallway, I sensed Bear, the boy Kenzie had traveled from Vegas to Germany to rescue. His family had been abducted, and Kenzie, with the help of Gunnar, had gone searching for them. Kenzie had found Bear, who the Rogue had taken. She reported the family missing while she was in Germany, and as of yet, we hadn't found Bear's mother or sister. Bear had decided to stay with the Jamesons in hopes she'd return soon.

I knocked on his door. "Bear, it's Stellan. May I come in?"

I heard him shuffle toward the door.

"Is Kenzie home?" he asked as soon as he opened the door.

"Not yet. Are you ok? The Jamesons treating you well?"

"Yeah, Granny found me a tutor, and I've been working with Clay remotely." He flopped on his bed and I entered his room and sat on the floor.

Clay was Kenzie's tech mage and he had been mentoring Bear. The kid's magical tech abilities were emerging and he needed guidance.

"You're welcome to come home with us. To the ranch in Texas. Unless . . . you have family you'd rather stay with," I said to the boy.

He shook his head. "I'll wait for Kenzie. She's all I have now."

I nodded. We had done some research, and other than an elderly grandmother in Mexico City, he didn't have any blood relatives. I wasn't sure if he'd rather be with his grandmother. He never mentioned it.

"You have me, too. And the other guys. We're your family. You'll like living on the ranch. We have a school on pack property, and there are a lot of kids your age."

"Ok, when Kenzie gets back." He fought back the tears. The poor kid needed mothering, and Kenzie wasn't here. She was a natural at nurturing.

"Bear, you've been through so much. If you ever need to talk, man-to-man, I'm always available. You have my cell, right?"

He shook his head and pulled out his cell phone.

We talked for some time until he started to yawn. He was intelligent and would become a great man if appropriately mentored. After leaving his room, I vowed to take the kid under my wing and went to fall asleep in Kenzie's old room.

The next morning, I shifted and went out for a hunt. My wolf senses told me Caid was on the hunt as well. I went after him and found him nearly eighty miles from the castle. His chin dripped with animal blood. "She must return today. I won't survive without her," he told me.

I nodded my wolf head, then pointed with my muzzle toward the castle, asking him to turn back. He wiped his mouth, which just smeared blood all over his face. I huffed and started back to the Castle. He strode up beside me and walked a few paces, then said, "Race you. I'll even give you a head start."

I bolted, and he laughed behind me. My brother was fast, but I had worked hard all my life to keep up. We ran flat out at top speed, creating a rush of wind in our wake. By the time we got to the border of the Jameson property, I had beaten my brother by a nose. Literally. My nose touched the Jameson border before he could reach out. I shifted back and rolled on the ground laughing.

Caid was on the ground beside me laughing, "I needed that."

"Me too." We hadn't had much to smile at in Kenzie's absence. It felt good to smile a little even though I ached all over from not having her near.

Caid and I bolted upright at the same time. "Was that?" he asked. It sure was. The bell tolled, and I shifted mid-stride and ran for my life.

My brother and I arrived in the workshop at the same time as everyone else, save Granny, who already stood in front of the circle. No Kenzie in sight.

I shifted immediately, catching the attention of the demon void. The demon appeared as a blue flame like it had the last time. It had a masculine voice. We had no name, not one the Jameson's shared.

"Speak, demon," Granny said.

"I haven't located a Jameson or her companion in The Dark Realm."

"You LIE!" Mr. Jameson shouted.

"I have no reason to lie, father of the lost. Perhaps you would join me in my search. You share the same blood." The void said, "Unless there is another with a stronger blood bond." It felt like the demon void shifted its focus on my brother and me.

"I'll go." Caid and I said at the same time.

"You're not a Jameson, though, neither of you. Pity. One favor is owed to a Jameson. I am willing to make a deal, though." The greedy void said.

"No. Take me," Mr. Jameson said. "You owe us a favor and have failed to deliver. The favor is still owed to my line."

The asshole demon laughed. I was beginning to hate this entity.

"For the two that have bonded with the Fae, the cost is your first-born, both of your firstborn children," he said to Caid and me, deliberately ignoring Kenzie's father. But Mr. Jameson wasn't about to be disregarded.

"NO! I will go." He stepped in front of us, then turned to face Caid and me. "My daughter will not want you to give your child's life for hers. I will bring her back."

The demon hissed, "Fae bonds are stronger. Such a shame. Fine. The father's bond with his daughter will suffice to locate her. I'll return both of them to you in due course."

Mr. Jameson nodded at his mother, took a few steps back into the circle, and disappeared.

CHAPTER 3
KENZIE

"Kenzie?"

Someone said my name, but whoever it was, seemed so far away. I strained against the crusty seal that had formed around my lids to open my eyes. It felt like I was rubbing my eyes with sandpaper. Everything was blurry and dark. I breathed deeply through my nose and then exhaled, coughing. My mouth was dry, and my throat felt raw.

"Dad?" I asked, my vision still a bit blurry. "What are you doing here? Am I home?" I rasped.

"It's me, Gunnar. Kenzie, please wake up." He nudged my shoulder.

I focused on the man in front of me and could have sworn it was my father. I reached out to touch his scraggly beard, and he moved his head. The dim light revealed coppery hair instead of my father's brown locks. The resemblance, though, was uncanny, or perhaps I was hallucinating.

"Water?" I whispered.

"Here." He pressed something to my lips, and I took deep sips. Too much. I started coughing. "Slowly, Kenz."

"Where?" I asked, my voice scratchy and weak.

"Somewhere in The Dark Realm," Gunnar replied.

I leaned back to regain my strength as the events since the Rogue had teleported us came back to me. My first impression of The Dark Realm did not disappoint. We were dropped on a solid unforgiving surface, which according to the Rogue, was my fault because I shot him. The pain shocked his system, causing his magic to go all wonky. The asshat had teleported us into a fighting pit. If I didn't know any better, I'd say he was trying to get us killed.

The fighting pit was like the Dungeons back at The Majestic in Vegas. The Majestic was a condo hotel catering to supes. Located in the bowels of the hotel, The Dungeons hosted fighting events with no rules. I had seen fights there a time or two, but what we experienced here was all sorts of hell. We fought countless demons with everything we had. It was insanity.

While we fought through the hordes, we kept the Rogue close. Being injured and in the middle of the pit made the Rogue frantic, causing him to teleport us from one fighting pit to another. Like a coward, he hid behind us when trouble came. And thanks to his manic teleporting, all three of us were exhausted, injured, and bleeding.

Gunnar and I were left to deal with hordes of imps and lows. We fought for what felt like days upon days; my body was beyond depleted.

How we had ended up in this cave was beyond me, I must've passed out. The brief rest was necessary since my magic had been depleted from the fall. It took over then to save me from dying. And then again, to heal anything broken. And a final time, it flared around me as I fought for my life.

I searched for my magic now that I was rested; it was strong and compliant. I focused my energies on my sore rib cage and let it go to work.

"Talk, please," I whispered again. I needed a distraction from the achiness in my ribs and the entire messed-up situation.

Gunnar looked weary, but seemed unharmed.

"We're in a cave, one the Rogue seems familiar with. He's severely injured but managed to get us here. We fought for who knows how long until we ended up here. You fought like a champion. Strong and tireless. Your family will be so proud. I'm somewhat better. My injuries were minor compared to yours, but I promise, I'll get us out of here," he told me wearily.

"Where is he?" I asked. I was still exhausted, but breathing became easier.

"Right outside. Chanting."

That can't be good. *Think Kenzie.* The Rogue had been using dark magic with the help of a demon to conduct his evil experiments in the human world. Stupid Rogue. Why would he make a deal with a demon? Unless the demon owed him a favor. I doubted it, but I had to be sure.

"Listen to him. See if a demon shows," I said to Gunnar.

Gunnar moved away from me. I needed to get up. I started by flexing my feet, bending my knees, then drawing them to my chest. I wiggled my fingers, flexed my hands, wrists, and elbows, then wrapped my arms around my knees. Nothing was broken, which was a win. Still, I slowly turned on my side and then rolled upwards. Ouch. Bruised but not broken. How many times was I going to find myself bruised all over? I could deal with this. I'd been dealing with this. This shit was getting old.

"What are you doing up?" Gunnar asked. "Lie back down. You need to rest and gather your strength."

"I need to know what we're dealing with." I leaned on him. He supported my weight and helped me hobble to the cave's opening. I released him and stood without his help, testing my limits. Good, but could be better. I needed sustenance.

The Rogue was kneeling prostrate, chanting away.

"How long has he been doing this?" I asked Gunnar.

"Thirty minutes. Maybe longer."

"You should rest. I'll keep watch," I said.

Gunnar nodded and closed his eyes. In mere moments, he was out, breathing deeply. He had probably stayed awake while I was resting. I was grateful to have him with me.

The Rogue kept chanting non-stop. I sat on the floor, listening and recuperating while we waited. I wanted to know if the Rogue had made a deal or was owed a favor. A deal would put the demon in control. A favor was something else entirely.

There was a family legend about my Grand Sire, who was owed a favor by a demon. According to legend, the demon was about to be erased from all existence by my Grand Sire. However, the demon was spared and sent back to The Dark Realm, making a vow to assist my Grand Sire or someone in his line when the need arose.

I found a carafe filled with water and drank while keeping an eye on the Rogue. I missed my guys. If Stel and Caid were here, they'd rip the Rogue to shreds and have me out of here in no time.

CHAPTER 4

KENZIE

A loud rumble got my attention and woke Gunnar. I placed my hand on his shoulder to calm him. He nodded, and we watched the scene with the Rogue and his demon unfold.

A billow of smoke, black and green, coalesced in front of the Rogue, who didn't stop chanting. A demon appeared in the middle of the smoke, which he sucked back into his body. He slithered around the Rogue. From the waist-down he had the lower half of a rattlesnake. The rattle shook at the tip of his tail. His round belly jutted out like he wore a floating tube used by novice swimmers. He had a furry chest and four arms waving about with pinchers where fingers should be. His head was smallish in comparison to the rest of him. Yellow rotted tusks protruded from a snarling mouth. He had a snout and black slits for his eyes. He had no hair, just two curled horns on the top of his head.

I'd never seen a demon up close before and hoped I never would again.

"You dare summon me, mage?" the demon said in a rough voice.

"We made a pact! I need you to heal me now!!" The Rogue demanded haughtily.

The demon huffed and circled the mage. "The pact did not include healing, mage. Why would I bother healing you? Your soul is mine. Your premature death feeds me sooner than I hoped. Why would I do anything for you now?"

"I will give you two mage souls in addition to mine. For healing me," the Rogue persisted.

Of course, he would offer Gunnar and me up for his selfish gain. Asshat.

"Ha! You think I'm a fool. You bring me two unwilling souls. One of which belongs to the Fae. I should kill you where you stand for the insult." The demon stopped his circling to spit at the Rogue.

"I need healing now," the Rogue begged.

"Go find a human healer. And get the Fae out of here before it's too late. And do not summon me again. I will summon you when I am ready to claim your soul," the demon sneered, then vanished.

The Rogue needed help, and we needed to get out.

Gunnar and I stood. The Rogue rose from his kneeling position and limped toward us. He better have a solution to getting us home, or else.

"Ready to get us out of here," I asked, with strength I didn't feel.

"I barely have any magic left. You shot me, you bitch," the Rogue scowled.

"Aww, the big bad mage has a booboo. You deserve worse for all the people, shifters, mages, and vamps you've killed."

"I am in no mood for your snark." His body leaned against the wall near me.

"Well, you're in luck. Get us out now, and you'll never have to deal with my snark again."

Gunnar and I circled him. If he was going to teleport, he was taking us with him.

"If I could've teleported, I would've by now." He waved us off.

"What the fuck?!" I threw up my hands, frustrated.

"I'm injured. My magic is keeping the infection at bay." His voice lost its usual condescending tone.

"Show me?" I asked, not believing him. I had shot him in the dark. If I'd hit something vital; he'd be dead by now.

He lifted his robe showing a massive gash on his calf. Not a gunshot wound, then. He'd been bitten during one of our many skirmishes. The injury was considerable, and the infection spread rapidly. I didn't think a human hospital could save him at this point.

"Is there anything here that we can use to fix you up?" I asked.

He shook his head.

Exasperated, I started looking around. There had to be something here. I had only bothered to look at the cavern then. Aside from a cot, work table, and a few baskets, there was little to see. The Rogue had been working here. I rifled through baskets, and all I found were empty syringes, vials, and a few small alcohol swabs, which wouldn't help to clean his wound. *We can't be stuck here.*

"Is there another way out?" Gunnar asked.

"It's right behind you, fools," the Rogue responded with a pained expression.

What a dick-face.

Gunnar looked around and called out. "Here. There's a tunnel."

"Where does the tunnel lead?" I asked the Rogue

"Gateway, in the desert. Middle East," the Rogue responded.

"How far?" I asked him.

"How far what?" The Rogue's question was purposely annoying. I was going to kill him with my bare hands.

"How far to the gateway?" I ground out.

"Fifty miles or so," the Rogue said.

Fuck my life. "Let's go."

There was an antiquated water system, which Gunnar used to fill up carafes full of water.

He took the thin blanket off the cot and turned it into a sack to hold the carafes. I gave him a small smile appreciating his brilliance. Fifty miles was a long way.

I did one last search of the area to see if there was anything else helpful and came up with nothing. I checked my pockets; my phone and my daggers were still on me, as well as my gun. No bullets, though. During one of our many skirmishes, I'd fired my gun and emptied the only magazine I had on me. At least my magic simmered within me. The brief rest I'd had replenished my magical reserves.

"Ready, Kenz," Gunnar said to me.

"You coming with or will you stay here and die?" I asked the Rogue.

He grabbed a few things out of the baskets, along with a long stick which he used as a cane, and followed us out. I probably should've left him, but damn it, he could prove helpful.

CHAPTER 5
KENZIE

As we searched for the nearest gateway, we ran into more demons. And, of course, they weren't the friendly types. Gunnar and I fought to keep us safe, including the Rogue, who was not faring well. After the fifth battle, we skirted around villages and did our best to avoid demons. It was exhausting, and not one demon offered any help or directions, even when the tip of my dagger pierced their neck.

The Rogue's wound bled continuously. And judging by the putrid scent wafting from his person, the infection was spreading. His last days, if not hours, were counting down, but that didn't change his attitude. He did not repent, and his assholeness did not subside.

"You think this will die with me?! You have no idea how many people want this just as much as I do. I had billionaires, politicians, kings, and queens, all wanting what I have. The cure to level the playing field. The ability to control vampires and shifters, to drain mages of their magical powers. I have this, and they all want it. I will be the richest, most powerful mage on earth," he ranted.

Geez, narcissist much?

"Did you not see the infection spreading all over your body? Or the trail of blood you're leaving behind you? And have you forgotten where you are?" I gave him a flat stare. "You're weak, and you are stuck in The Dark Realm. You're far from being the richest and most powerful anything."

"What he meant was he will be the richest in bullshit and have the most powerful delusions," Gunnar added with a smug smile.

I laughed at Gunnar's statement. The Rogue didn't find it funny and hobbled away in a huff. After everything we'd been through because of him, I wasn't even sorry.

We were afforded a slight reprieve from running for our lives, which allowed me to take in The Dark Realm. There wasn't much to write home about it.

Everything in our surroundings was bleak, barren, and with varying shades of gray. The ground we traversed was rough gray sand, similar to shards of broken cement. The rocks, plant life, and even the building structures we had passed were all shades of gray. It was as though we walked through a black-and-white movie.

It was impossible to know how far we had gone. We kept going, stopping only when we needed to rest. It felt like we surpassed the fifty-mile mark, but I was never good at estimating distances.

For all I knew, we could have been walking in circles. The Rogue wasn't much help. He said he'd never had to use the gateway, so he wasn't even sure we were going in the right direction. We had asked the demons as we came upon them, but they were no help at all.

The concept of time was also challenging to determine. Like the landscape, the sky was gray. There was no sun, no moon, to guide us.

After a long while, the sky changed to a dark thunderstorm gray, indicating that time was moving. We passed an unfriendly village and kept hoping to find a suitable resting place.

The sky darkened quickly, casting our surroundings in an inky black. Each of us had mage sight, but we opted to conserve our magic. Thus we lit one torch and made haste to a rock formation not too far in the distance.

Less than a mile from what we hoped would serve as shelter, a loud earth-shattering screech pierced the night. Instinctively I ducked, and Gunnar did so as well. The Rogue shouted, "Run!" And he scampered away as quickly as his injured body would take him.

Gunnar and I caught up to him with ease.

"What is that?" Gunnar asked the Rogue.

"Drekavac. Malicious and powerful, it feeds on souls. We cannot defeat it." The Rogue responded while limping as fast as he could.

"Great," I muttered.

I turned around looking for this Drekavac and saw nothing at first. Then out of the darkness came two enormous glowing eyes. It had to be a giant, or it was flying because the bright glow in the dark eyes was a good fifteen feet in the air. The Drekavac came upon us quickly, moving extraordinarily fast for a one-legged creature. Shit.

The Rogue was falling behind, his injured leg not holding him up very well. Gunnar looked at me; we'd either have to carry him, leave him, or turn around to fight. Decisions, decisions.

We couldn't run forever, so I pushed the Rogue out of the way, motioning for him to hide behind a rock. Gunnar and I turned at the same time to face the oncoming demon. It barreled between us in his hulking form. I dodged out of the way right before it lunged. I pivoted to my left to hamstring the demon's leg with my dagger. The Drekavac staggered and screeched again. The dreadful sound brought me to my knees, and I covered my ears, trying to muffle the noise. It turned, latched onto my jacket, and yanked me into the air. With my arms flailing about, I swiped my dagger across its claw. Black blood doused me as I dropped to the ground.

Gunnar was dealing with the demon screaming something at me. My ears rang; I couldn't understand what he was saying. He swung a sword at the demon, his movements agile and oddly famil-iar. He seemed to be doing fine, so I took a moment to recover.

Gunnar delivered a killing blow, and the demon went down screeching. Again, with the damn screaming; I had a perforated eardrum, indeed.

Back on my feet, I asked Gunnar. "Where'd you get the sword?"

"Stop yelling." His voice sounded muted in my head. The sword winked out. Nice trick. My father had taught me the same spell. I had been too busy to practice it.

"Hey asshole," I called out to the Rogue. "You can come out now."

The Rogue hadn't been in his hiding place, of course. We searched, but he was nowhere to be found. The asshole had lied about not being able to kill the flying demon just so that he could teleport away.

CHAPTER 6
KENZIE

Without the Rogue, we picked up the pace. As much as we tried to avoid demons, we were constantly attacked. Every time we got a reprieve, another attack came. I'd have gone mad or died if Gunnar weren't with me.

We should have made it to the gateway by now. Perhaps we were lost. *Nope, not going there.* I immediately kicked the negative thoughts out of my mind. It seemed as though we had been walking for hours, days, maybe weeks, or months. There was no way to tell. It was gray all the time. There was no sign of the Rogue. Gunnar and I would rest when we could, taking turns to keep watch. We were both weary. The water had run out long ago. And we were both bruised and bleeding. We were silent most of the time. It was too much effort to speak. But the sound of his breathing was comforting. There was so much I wanted to know about him, but I didn't have the energy to ask.

I thought about the guys a lot. I wondered how Stel and Caid were doing with their baby mamas. It had taken some prodding, but they had finally embraced becoming fathers. To see them gush over the ultrasound photos increased a longing deep in my heart.

Brody was always steadfast and diligent with his work. Finding the Rogue had become an obsession. The Rogue had been elusive, showing up here and there and then disappearing for days. How could anyone have predicted the Rogue was romping around The Dark Realm? Brody would be happy to know that he wasn't losing his mind.

Erik and I had an intimate relationship in its early stages. He had been my most outstanding teacher and had shown me so much about my magic in such a short time. I loved the way Erik challenged me and kept me on my toes. Plus, he was incredibly romantic when we were alone, and we experimented once with what I called sex magic. It was all kinds of hot and an experience I'd like to repeat.

I tripped over my own feet. The darkness weighed on me, and I was exhausted.

"We need rest, Kenzie." Gunnar was tired too. His speech was slurred, and his movements sluggish. He looked like a sad drunk. Maybe that's what I looked like too.

We stumbled upon a village. The empty muddy streets had wooden structures crowded together. Lanterns provided dim lighting, for which I was grateful. At least it wasn't pitch black.

As much as I had wanted to avoid asshole demons, we needed the break. Storm clouds brewed in the distance, and the temperature cooled dramatically. We needed shelter. We walked through the rustic village quickly. The oppressiveness weighed heavily on my limbs.

A cool draft snuck up on me, making me gasp. I shivered and wrapped my arms around myself. We kept walking. Shadows seemed to come alive the further we pressed into the village. The draft stuck with us as we trudged along. My teeth chattered.

"Welcome, halfling," someone or something whispered in my ear.

I whirled around, looking for the voice, and found only shadows.

"You're not worthy. You're broken. You lured your mates to their deaths."

"NO!" I shouted. My mates weren't dead. Were they? They couldn't be.

A shrill laughter pierced the air. I swiftly turned toward the sound which had been behind me.

"Kenzie?" Gunnar said beside me.

"Did you hear that?" I asked him.

He paused for a moment listening, then shook his head.

A resounding wail broke the silence.

"That I heard." Gunnar searched the darkness just as I had. "We need to get out of this place."

Soon, a steady drizzle came down on us. A heavy droplet landed on the top of my head and then my shoulder. Before too long, I was drenched.

We kept moving in search of shelter. There was nothing, not even a ceiling or ledge, for us to stand under for a brief respite. And all the while, the wails got louder and closer as though it was coming toward us, or possibly for us.

"Broken Fae, stay with me," a ghostly voice purred on the wind.

"Come with us. We'll make you whole, barren Fae," another voice cajoled.

"No! I'm not broken," I shouted and picked up the pace.

"You will never have children of your own. Your mates deserve more."

"Stop it!" I spat out.

Laughter permeated the air.

"They will leave you, if not now, then soon. Why bother going back? We accept you as you are."

"No one here cares if you are barren, halfling."

"We can make you whole. Stay with us. Come to the darkness."

The voices taunted, crowding my head with doubts and fear.

Icy claws raked down my spine, and I ran. I wanted to outrun the voices in my head.

Gunnar chased after me, yelling, begging me to stop.

I couldn't stop, though. The voices in my head would not relent, and I was determined to outrun them.

"Poor halfling, so alone. Always alone."

"Not anymore. We'll keep you here, with us . . . forever."

"Don't run. There is nowhere for you to go. Soon you will see, this is where you're meant to be."

The faster I ran, the louder the voices became. Tears streaked my face. Despair bloomed in my belly.

"We accept you, broken Fae. No one else will."

"We accept your barren womb. Childless Fae."

I kept running.

The voices in my head repeated vile words, highlighting every insecurity I had ever had about my body. About my relationships. About my worth. I ran as fast as my arms and legs would carry me.

Gunnar grasped my hand and tugged on me to follow. He led me to a bridge a few yards away, and we picked up the pace. The voices followed, cackling as we ran.

"Poor little broken Fae."

"Childless Fae, lonely Fae."

"They will leave you, just like your husband did. You are worthless."

I sobbed as we ran. My chest was heaving from the physical exertion and the pain in my heart. They were right. I was worthless. Two of my mates had babies on the way. They had families of their own. My other two mates wouldn't want me. I couldn't give them the greatest joy all men wanted, children of their own.

"We will ease your suffering. Stay with us."

"There is no one for you now. Your mates have already moved on. They have their children now, their family. You are nothing."

"You belong to us!"

I fell on the mud-covered street, scraping my knees and elbows. I stayed on the ground and sobbed. I can't go back. I have nothing to go back to. I wanted to give up.

A sharp sting slapped across my face. *Oww.*

"Snap the fuck out of it, Mackenzie Jameson!"

Gunnar had just bitch-slapped me.

I blinked at him. Water filled my eyes, impairing my vision. He wrenched me off the ground with a harsh tug, and I followed him blindly.

We ran for miles until we reached the bridge's underpass. The bridge was a small pedestrian bridge providing a walkway over a murky green river. On both sides of the river was a walkway about three feet wide. It was difficult to make out anything in the darkness, but from what I could gather, it was devoid of any demons.

Within minutes the steady drizzle turned into a deluge by the time we made it under the bridge shielding ourselves from the oncoming rain. We were standing on the ledge about a foot higher than the river. If the downpour didn't stop, the river would overflow. When it rained, it poured.

"Are you ok?" Gunnar asked.

I nodded and looked back the way we came. Something out there knew my deepest darkest fears. I bent over at the waist as the pain of loss clenched my heart. The only solace was the rain, which blended with the rivulet of tears that streaked my face. And the voices in my head were blessedly silent.

"Hey! Stay with me, Kenz," Gunnar demanded. Then he softly added. "There's something amiss here. It's not . . . right. Don't give into the lies."

Were they lies, though? A big part of me wanted to succumb to my insecurities and wallow in despair.

"As soon as the rain stops, we'll get out of this wretched place," Gunnar said, grounding me, keeping in the present moment.

I wiped my face with the hem of my shirt and took a couple of steps backward to slump against the wall, away from the river, eager to sit and rest for just a few minutes. But as luck would have it, my back didn't hit a wall. Some unknown force sucked us into a dark tunnel. The solid surface I had been expecting wasn't there, and I tumbled into the unknown, unable to reach out to Gunnar. He caught my foot and held on.

We slid through the tunnel, traveling downward, twisting and turning at a speed roller coasters would envy. My ears popped, and my eyes squeezed shut. I was completely disoriented. Many voices bombarded my mind, but I couldn't make out what they were saying. Some whispered, some shouted, and some even laughed. Someone screamed, or maybe that was all me. I couldn't tell. I was losing my mind. It went on and on until, finally, I surrendered and passed out.

CHAPTER 7
CAID

Several days after Mr. Jameson had gone to The Dark Realm, I met up with the other three guys at our house on the ranch. The four of us had gone our separate ways. We all needed to deal with Kenzie's absence in our own way.

I had spent most of my time at Scarlet, my blood lounge, looking after my seethe. I had appointed a second-in-command as my assistant and didn't need to be there as often as I had been, but being there kept my mind busy from missing Kenzie.

Brody was already in the kitchen, waiting. My brother and Erik were nowhere in sight.

I gave him a curt nod and went straight upstairs to change out of my blood-covered clothing. With Kenzie gone, I was more vicious than usual. If I wasn't careful, I'd lose myself to blood rage, and Kenz wasn't here to save me.

I went to the kitchen, and Brody handed me a beer.

"The other guys not here yet?" I asked him.

"Stel's out back. And no Erik yet," he said as Erik popped up behind him, causing him to spill his beer.

"Dude, wear a bell." Brody scowled at him and tore off a paper towel to wipe up the mess.

"Kenzie said the same thing to me once . . . on our date," he said with haunted eyes. Then he pulled out a flask and took a swig.

Erik was a good man, but I didn't know him well. Thus I didn't know how to handle his excessive drinking. He was hurting. We all were. I gave him a side glance as he sat on a bar stool at the kitchen counter. Fuck, I had to try something.

I sat next to him and patted him on the back. "Still hitting the whiskey, I see? You may want to go easy with that."

Erik answered me with a glare.

"Seriously, you look rough. We all do, it seems," Brody added, handing him a bottle of water.

My brother came into the kitchen from the back patio. He was wet, as though he had hosed himself down.

"Did you take a shower with the water hose?" I asked Stellan.

He gave me a wry look in response. He had been in his wolf form again, which was troubling.

We weren't dealing with Kenzie's absence well. I was spending too much time around vampires. Erik was drinking too much whiskey. Stel was spending too much time as a wolf. And Brody . . . he looked like a taut string ready to snap.

Yep, he was pissed. He hadn't shaved in a while and sported a full-on beard. He tugged on his already unruly hair and slammed his beer bottle on the table.

"Alright, let's get this meeting over with. We need to get our shit together. Erik, yeah, you need to ease up on the drinking. Stellan, you need to get some sleep; you look like shit. And take a real shower. I can smell your wolf, and I don't have supernatural senses. Caid, what's with all the blood? We need to keep it together for Kenzie's sake. She'd be pissed at the sight of us." He took a swig of beer, snatched the flask out of Erik's hand, and took a swig of the whiskey.

He winced and continued. "I am getting reports of missing supes all over the country. Has anyone else heard anything?"

"I haven't been in touch with anyone. I . . . I apologize. I'll get my head in the game," Stel said, rubbing his chest. He and I shared a blood bond with our little half-Fae. Her disappearance had affected us on a level neither could explain.

"Supe disappearances, that means what? The Rogue is back? Without Kenzie?" Erik scratched his head.

"Stel and I would feel her if she was back. But if he's back without her . . ." I took Erik's flask and drained it.

"Or . . . someone else is doing the experiments without him," Brody said.

The gravity of the situation finally hit us all at the same time. The tension in the room soared. Stel cracked his neck and gripped the solid granite countertop. The big lug could break the granite stone slab with his bare hands. Erik got up and started pacing, and Brody sat back and scowled.

Rage crawled up my spine. If we were dealing with someone else conducting the Rogue's experiments, we were fucked.

"I've been tracking the disappearances. There is a pattern that is different from what we were looking at before Kenzie was taken. It may not be the Rogue, but we have to stop it either way. And as far as Kenzie goes," he paused. "Any ideas?"

"I'll talk to my sire," I offered.

"No." Stel, Erik, and Brody said at the same time.

"No fucking way. He'll bind you into another heir situation, and Kenzie will be pissed. Just no," Stel added. "I will have a group of shifters look into the disappearances and spend more time with Aunt Mimi."

"I'll do the same with the vamps," I added.

"I'll do the same with the mages," Erik said.

"Good, let's get back together in two days with your respective teams and get them to work together. If we can have all three factions working on this stuff, we can focus on getting into The Dark

Realm," Brody said as though he was back in the military, delegating the troops.

"Ok, two days. Meet back here at nightfall to accommodate the vamps," Stel said. He turned to face Brody and shook his hand. "Thanks, Brody, for staying on top of things."

"Get some sleep, bro," I said to Stel.

"Stay away from Scarlet," he replied before grabbing a beer bottle from the fridge.

"I agree with your brother. You spend too much time there. Have your second do the daily shit. Kenzie is not here to bring you back from the blood rage again," Brody told me.

They were right, so I didn't argue.

Brody and I turned to Erik, who swiped a hand across his face. "I know, I know . . . I'm not dealing with her absence well. I love her. I've never loved anyone. Without her near, I can't think straight." He stared at the empty flask, then glanced at the bottles of whiskey on the counter.

I gave him a hard stare, and he shook his head. "I don't want it. I think," Erik, the mage, shook his head again.

"Hey, I'm here to help you, brother. Just say the word, man. You don't have to go off alone all the time," Brody offered.

"Yeah, I agree. We should all be staying here. We built this place for all of us," I patted the mage on his back. "Kenzie would want us to be together."

Before we could all make a decision, the doorbell rang. The four of us looked at each other and shrugged.

"Did someone order a pizza?" Erik asked and went to answer the door.

"No, it's a wolf. One of mine," Stel said.

Brody, Stel, and I gathered behind Erik as he opened the door.

"Yes?" Erik asked.

"Umm . . . is Mrs. Reese home?" the girl stuttered.

"Who are you, and what do you want?" Stel practically barked out.

"I'm Cristela. I wanted to speak with Mrs. Reese, if she's available," the girl replied with a tremor in her voice.

"What do you want with the Alpha?" I asked.

"Umm, no, not the Alpha. Mrs. Reese, your wife." She kept her chin tipped toward the ground and took a step backward.

Like idiots, we stood there for a beat until it dawned on us that she was asking for Kenzie.

"What do you want with our mate?" Stel growled.

She was on the ground, kneeling in the front entryway, shaking like a leaf.

We were such brutes. How did Kenzie put up with all the raging testosterone?

Brody moved around Erik to save the day.

"Hi Cristela, I'm Brody; this is Erik, and I am sure you know Caid and Stellan. Why don't you come in and talk to us about what you needed Kenzie for?" He helped Cristela rise and ushered her into the house, leaving the front door wide open.

No wonder Kenzie loved the guy. He was the only gentleman out of all of us.

"Oh, I remember you. You're the nurse taking care of Carlos. Is he ok?" He smiled and gave her a genuinely concerned look.

"He's fine. He said I should come to speak with Mrs. Reese. Umm . . . I have information that she might be interested in, but it's ok. I'd rather come back." Cristela stared at the floor while she spoke to us.

"Come in and sit down, wolf, relax. The lady Alpha is on her way," Stellan said in a somewhat gentler tone.

Moments later, our mom, the lady Alpha, walked into the house through the backdoor. Her cheeks were flushed, and stray strands of hair floated around her face. Other than that, she showed no other signs of shifting and running over here. Stel must've told her it was an emergency.

"Cristela? Honey, are you ok?" Mom knelt at her side to comfort her.

"Umm, yes, Alpha. I meant no disrespect. I was hoping to speak with the beta's wife." Cristela kept her head low.

"Come inside, Cristela." Lila helped her up and led her inside to sit on the nearest chair. "Is something wrong? Perhaps I can help you?"

"No, it's just . . ." she sat down, looked up at the Alpha, then started biting her nails. She was a scared little rabbit, and it was grating on my nerves.

"Cristela. Calm yourself and talk to me." Mom's voice was maternal yet had the authoritative edge of an Alpha.

"Well, I'm a nurse, and my cousin is also. She used to work at the clinic here at the ranch." She swallowed, and her voice got softer. "And umm . . . she was forced to make some changes to a report."

She fidgeted in her seat. The four of us loomed over her.

"Sons!" Mom snapped at us. "All four of you need to relax. Have a seat at the very least."

Like good boys, we took seats farthest from Cristela to give her some breathing space, but close enough to hear every word.

"Go on, honey," Mom encouraged her.

"My cousin, Serena, she . . . she was threatened to change it, and she felt so bad she quit. Now she doesn't have a job, and she keeps getting threats. I'm helping her with her kids, but she's afraid, and I thought it's not right and so, Mrs. Reese was always nice to me, and Carlos recommended I come to talk to her. Maybe she could help Serena."

Her voice was barely a whisper. Mom stiffened in her seat.

"Which reports and for whom?" Lila asked in a clipped voice.

Fuck, Mama was pissed.

"Just bloodwork and an ultrasound . . . for Christine Simpson," Cristela said. Her body was visibly shaking again.

Oh shit.

Stel clenched and unclenched his fists while I got up and paced back and forth, furiously running my hand through my hair. *That bitch!*

Brody and Erik were staring at the meek wolf slack-jawed.

Stel started to growl. He was making the poor girl nervous.

"Son! Calm yourself. I will handle this," Lila commanded. Then she turned toward the nurse and spoke in a soothing voice. "Thank you for this information. I will handle this and get your cousin her job back, ok? Is there anything else I should know?"

"No, Alpha, but here." Cristela took an envelope out of the bag slung over her shoulder. "Here is the proof. The original report and a video of the threats."

"You did the right thing. Thank you. You may go now." Lila got up and escorted the nurse out.

"Do you want to look at this now?" Mom asked Stel once Cristela was gone.

"Of course," he growled.

The reports were paternity tests saying Stellan wasn't the father of Christine's child. It also showed that Christine was farther along than she had said. And they got a video of Christine threatening Serena at a coffee shop owned by one of the pack members. Fuuucckkk.

"I'm sorry, son. I'll take care of this." Lila placed a hand on his shoulder.

Stellan rolled his neck and paced. Then with no warning, he punched a hole through the wall and went upstairs.

Fuck me. We needed Kenzie home more than ever.

CHAPTER 8

KENZIE

When I came to, I was disoriented. My vision swam, and my stomach rolled. Nausea overwhelmed me, so much so I had to vomit, but nothing came out except water and bile. I hadn't eaten in days. Gunnar was a few feet away from me, hurling as well. We were quite the sight.

Once my stomach was empty, nausea settled.

"Are you ok?" Gunnar asked.

I nodded. "Seem so. What the hell was that place?"

He shook his head. "Not sure, but it seemed to be messing with our thoughts. I was so concerned with you that it didn't bother me as severely."

My body shuddered. The town we had just come from was a severe mind-fuck. "I don't want to go back there again. Ever."

I forced myself to get up and look around. We were in another cavern. The black rock formation surrounding us was covered with white luminescent barnacles that glowed and illuminated the dark space. The black walls moved, rising up and down in random places, almost as though it was breathing. Curious, I reached out to touch it, and the rock formation pulsed back at me like it wanted to reach for my hand.

Gunnar slapped my hand away before I could make contact and shook his head. He was right. I shouldn't go touching a rock that was practically breathing.

Unsure of where we were or where we were going, we took the only path forward. We continued for a good hour, and the rock walls around us continued to pulse rhythmically. The distraction served to keep us alert. Both Gunnar and I were running on empty. We needed to find food and water soon.

Bright lights greeted us at the end of the pathway. Hope sparked in my belly. We exited the cavern and stepped into a vast village unlike anything we had seen in The Dark Realm. I glanced at Gunnar, then back at the town, then turned toward the way we came.

I gasped. There was no cavern and no tunnel. The path leading us to the brightly lit village had disappeared, and a beautiful garden was in its place. Rows of fully bloomed roses in every color stretched into the distance. Their cloying scent hung heavily in the air, tickling my nose.

"What the . . . ?" Gunnar took a few steps and spun in place.

I had no words. We certainly wouldn't be leaving via the cavern we had just come through.

"Well, I suppose we're stuck here . . . for now. Shall we?" Gunnar waved his hand forward, and we went exploring.

Gunnar and I meandered through the village. The cool night air was refreshing. It was a busy night, and demons strolled through the town. Some were in demon form, while some looked like humans for the most part. They had pointed ears or tails, and some had wings. It was hard not to stare. Despite our bedraggled appearance, most passersby were practically friendly. They nodded in greeting, and some even smiled.

The tension knotted in my neck slowly unraveled. Although we were lost and stuck in The Dark Realm, I sighed in relief. This place seemed civilized, and I was sure we'd be able to find someone to help us locate a gateway. We kept walking in disbelief. This place seemed to be the rich part of the realm. I smelled food and freshly baked bread before the food cart came into view. My mouth watered, and my belly rumbled in sync with Gunnar's.

The vendor of the bread cart had appeared human aside from his six arms. And his voice was a melodic soprano, which took me by surprise.

Gunnar pulled out his wallet in an attempt to barter with the vendor. I was going to shit myself if the vendor took Euros or even a credit card. The demon didn't speak English, but he understood a little Gaelic. And so did Gunnar.

He had been able to communicate with the demon and told him we didn't have the local currency but were willing to trade for a piece of bread. The demon looked at the state of Gunnar and me and offered to help. He gave us complimentary bread, which was delicious, and two carafes of water. And as a kicker, he pointed to an inn where we could stay for a night. He was also sure that someone would be able to assist us in finding the nearest gateway. It was probably not the best decision to trust strangers, but we were beyond caring.

We gave the innkeeper the vendor's name, and the innkeeper didn't hesitate to show us to a room. The room was quaint and clean and had two beds with a tiny bathroom equipped with plumbing. After what we endured the past few days, it was downright luxurious. I wanted to take a bath, but exhaustion won over cleanliness. I immediately dropped onto the bed and passed out.

Something niggled at the back of my mind, and I bolted upright in bed, my heart thundered in my chest. The room was still dark and silent, aside from Gunnar, who snored on the bed beside mine. Perhaps, losing my mind had been a side effect of being in The Dark Realm.

Fatigue pulled at me hard, I needed to sleep, but my gaze was affixed on the stone ceiling, and my rambling thoughts blared in my ears like a fog horn. Too restless to go back to sleep, I went to the bathroom and eager to get the muck from the last few days off me. At least this part of The Dark Realm seemed habitable. I turned on the faucet in the shower, then heard a thump coming from the bedroom. I peeked out the door but found nothing, and Gunnar was still asleep. I took a few steps into the room, felt a sting on my neck, and then dropped to the floor.

CHAPTER 9
KENZIE

I woke with my wrists and ankles tied, lying on a beautiful, yet cold, black marble floor with shimmering gold flecks. There was no Gunnar in sight.

"You're awake." I sat upright and searched for the voice. There was nothing; it was dark all around me.

Footsteps approached. "Apologies for the dramatic introduction. We don't get many Fae here," the voice continued. A tall, hooded figure approached me. Lights flashed on with every step. He was tall, well over six feet, with broad shoulders. His face was hidden, making it impossible for me to see who, or what, I was dealing with. Fuck.

"Where's my brother?" I asked. I wasn't sure why I called Gunnar that. It just seemed right.

My kidnapper knelt before me, and with a wave of his hands, my restraints came undone. "Gunnar is fine. He's resting. Why are you here?" he asked me.

"I don't know where here is," I said.

He tilted his head, "In The Dark Realm. Why are you in The Dark Realm?"

"Why did you kidnap me?" I narrowed my eyes at him.

He laughed. "You are in my town, and you are trespassing. As the overlord here, I will do with you as I please." He paused. "Now, answer my questions. Why are you here?"

"Drugging people and kidnapping them clearly indicate you are untrustworthy. So fuck off with your questions," I said.

I was tired and hungry, and I missed my guys. Perhaps this was the wrong way to ask for help, but this arrogant asshole was being a bully. I'd fight my way out before rolling over to meet his demands. Also, a part of me was pissed off that I had let my guard down and gotten myself into this situation.

Whoever this overlord was, he was powerful. I sensed his magic. It was dark and heavy, unlike anything I had ever encountered.

"Defying me won't help your cause," he tsked.

"Listen, I am tired, hungry, and filthy. I have zero patience. If you want to fight me, fine, let's get that over with so I can be on my way," I said wearily.

"Well, you have a shit way of asking for help." He got up and walked away.

"You know what, fuck you. I have been beaten and attacked ever since I touched foot in this damned place, so forgive me if I'm not being polite, your lordship," I spat out.

He turned back to face me, and I flipped him off. He walked away and said to someone in a nearby corridor, "Get her cleaned up. NOW."

I hung my head. Yeah, maybe I wasn't handling the situation right. I couldn't think straight, apparently.

A demon helped me to my feet. "Come. It would be best if you didn't anger the Master. He will not take kindly to being refused."

"Master can kiss my ass," I muttered.

"What's your name?" I asked as I followed behind the creature.

"I am Cerai," she told me.

Cerai was beautiful. She was tall with a tiny waistline, pale skin, and dark blue wings that were almost black, just like her hair.

"My name is Kenzie," I whispered behind her. We continued

down a long dark hallway. It was dark and cold. The walls were black onyx with specks of glitter sparkling in the dim lighting. I kept track of our whereabouts, committing the layout to memory.

"Where are we?" I asked Cerai.

"This is Serpentine Manor. The epicenter of the Fourth Circle." She lifted her chin with pride.

Huh? None of it made any sense to me. So I asked more questions.

"Fourth Circle? Are there more circles?"

"Six. But we are the most prosperous of all Circles, thanks to the Master," Cerai replied.

"What is in the other Circles?" I asked.

She stopped and looked at me as though I was daft. I shrugged. The Dark Realm wasn't taught in any classroom I had ever been in.

"The Sixth Circle is very violent, meant to keep trespassers away. The Fifth Circle is where lost souls drift. Our warriors frequently go to the Fifth and Sixth circles for combat. The Fourth and Third circles are where we conduct trade. The Second is where the lord of The Dark Realm keeps his precious things. Children, pets, and so on. The First is where our lord resides."

The Rogue had probably teleported us into the Sixth Circle, and then Gunnar and I stumbled into the Fifth Circle. Well, that was better than landing in the First Circle. I had no desire to meet the Dark Lord of Hell. Nope, nuh-uh.

We came upon a large door that opened on command for Cerai. I followed her into what looked like a sitting room with a desk and a small sofa. Like the hallway, everything was black, the flooring, the walls, the drapes. The furniture, though, had different purple hues, so dark it was almost black. Sconces adorned the walls and provided mood lighting. It had a sensual vibe to it.

Cerai pushed me to stand on a platform in the middle of the sitting room. As soon as I got on it, it spun in a slow circle. After one revolution, she grabbed my hand to help me off the platform, and the platform disappeared. I arched an eyebrow at Cerai.

"Just measurements," she said and led me into the bathroom.

I was about to ask for what, but I decided to save time and ask the important ones first. "Where's Gunnar?"

"Down the hall." She gave me a stern stare. "And no, you may not see him until Master says it's ok."

"Where's the nearest gate to the human realm?" I pressed her for info. That was what we needed.

She laughed. Her laugh sounded like a horse neighing. It was unfortunate for such a beautiful creature. "Miss, you cannot leave until the Master says so. And besides, I do not know, somewhere in the Fifth or Sixth Circle."

She led me to a bathroom, which was posh. It reminded me of my bathroom at The Majestic. The most significant difference was everything in this bathroom was black onyx, just like the rest of the Manor. It would be pitch black in here if it weren't for the many sconces and lanterns along the walls. A large jacuzzi tub sat at one end, with a separate shower. The countertop had a black glass sink with pewter faucets and a large ornate mirror right above it.

Cerai tried to help me undress. I stepped away and shook my head. "Thank you, but I don't need assistance undressing."

She nodded and said, "The Master will want to dine with you. I will bring you a change of clothes and those." She pointed at my clothes. "Those can be burned."

"No, please. I want to return home in these." I wrapped my arms around my middle.

She gave me a confused look, then nodded and left.

I didn't feel safe, but I needed to formulate a plan. Under the hot running water, I let the grime and blood run off me. I scrubbed and scrubbed until my skin was raw.

Instead of coming up with a plan, the only thoughts running through my head were about the guys. I missed them fiercely and knew I needed to get home. Someone here would know; fuck the Master or overlord or whatever he wanted to be called. I was leaving as soon as I was good and ready. And at the moment, I wasn't prepared. I was too weak, and wandering around The Dark Realm aimlessly wouldn't help at all. We were utterly lost out there. Gunnar and I were tough, but we couldn't have survived much longer on our own.

I sat on the tub's edge, toweling off my wet locks, and glanced at Brody's armband on my ankle. A stab of longing pierced my gut. He had given me his family heirloom the last morning I had been in the human realm. I placed my foot on the ledge of the tub and reached out to run my finger along the magical metal. My skin wasn't red or irritated as I would have expected it to be after wearing the heirloom under my combat boots for so long. I had nearly forgotten all about it.

Sighing, I got up, swiped the fog from the mirror, and looked at my reflection. Yikes. I needed sleep and nourishment. There were dark circles under my eyes, and my face was gaunt. I unwrapped the towel and gasped. I could count my ribs, and my hip bones protruded a bit. How long had we been gone?

A tear ran down my cheek. I needed to get my wits about me. I caught a glimpse of Caid's mark on my neck and traced the puncture wounds with my thumb. Caid had drunk from me a few times since then, but those bites didn't leave a trace. I turned to gaze at my bare shoulder and Stel's mark. I raised my shoulder and kissed the mark. My lips lingered on my skin. *I miss you, all of you. I'm coming home.* I let that thought sink into every part of my being.

The bathroom door suddenly opened, and I scrambled to cover myself with the towel. I expected Cerai, but it was the overlord himself.

"What the fuck? Ever try knocking first?" I snapped.

"Little girl, you are in my domain. I take whatever I want whenever I want," he sneered.

"Get the fuck out."

His heated gaze roamed my body from head to toe. "I brought clothes for you. Get dressed, little girl."

"Don't call me that. And learn some fucking manners, asshole."

He threw a small bundle of fabric at me and stomped out. "Don't keep me waiting, little girl."

Great, he didn't have boundaries. Damn it, if I didn't need his help, I'd shove my dagger so far up his asshole. How was I supposed to play nice with the overlord when he was a royal prick?

CHAPTER 10

KENZIE

I went into the sitting room to secure the lock only to find there wasn't one, of course, not that it would've mattered.

Back in the bathroom, I strapped on my dagger and cast a concealment spell over it. Erik would be so proud. My gun had no bullets, but I hadn't tossed it. For now, I hid it under the pillow. Next, I unfolded the small bundle of clothes brought to me and sneered in disgust. The material was silky and very small.

Begrudgingly I put on the small material that was supposed to be a dress. It was a black mini dress that barely covered my ass cheeks. The top portion had two narrow pieces of material connected to the skirt and ran up over my breasts, barely covering my nipples and exposing my torso. It went over my shoulders like a halter top, but instead of tying off at the nape of my neck, the two strips of material connected and formed a braid starting at my neck, down my spine, and attached to the back of the skirt. Quite honestly, it was hot. I loved it. I'd love to wear it on a date with my guys. But not tonight. It was way too revealing and inappropriate.

The small bundle didn't come with panties, so I decided to wash what I had been wearing in. After that was done, I looked at the rest

49

of my crusty and smelly clothes. I planned to leave wearing them, so I filled the tub to wash what I had.

Cerai walked into the bathroom while I was submerging my clothes in the tub.

"Mistress? What are you doing?" she asked me.

Before I could answer her, she shook her head, "No, no, we will clean those for you if you insist. You must be ready for the Master."

She pulled on my hand and made me sit at the vanity. I shrugged out of her hands and said, "I'm not leaving this room in this." I waved at the dress, which was threatening to expose my nipples. "It's inappropriate."

"You are stunning. The Master chose it. He will be pleased."

"Master can fuck off," I said. Cerai gaped at me.

"CERAI!!" A loud, angry voice shouted from the sitting room.

She ran out of the bathroom only to be rebuked by the arrogant ass.

"Where is she? I do not like to be kept waiting," I heard him yell. Cerai was stammering. And I had heard enough.

I stepped into the bedroom just in time to block a whip aimed at Cerai's face. I caught the whip with my right arm and twisted it around my forearm; that's when I realized it wasn't a whip. It was a tentacle of magic, black, like tar, and had barbs all over it which dug into my flesh. My magic flared around my body, protecting my skin.

"What the fuck is your problem?" I sneered at the overlord.

His eyes went wide when I intercepted the hit, then he sneered back. The fucker didn't even call back his magic. *Ok, we're playing this game, are we?*

"Don't ever hit another female. Ever." I stared him down.

"You don't rule here." He held my gaze and tugged harder on the tentacle. The barbs pricked my skin and drew blood. My magic was waning, my body too weak.

We stared at each other for a few seconds, neither of us willing to give in. Then, his eyes dropped to my breasts, where my nipples were fully displayed. Fucking dress would not work without double-sided tape.

Standing this close to the so-called overlord, I could make out his features. The most notable being his mismatched eyes; one light blue and the other a honey brown. Heterochromia iridium, hmm . . . intriguing. His black shoulder-length hair framed a sharp nose and a strong jawline. His sneer was almost seductive, but I was pissed and too tired to care. I called on my fire magic and started to burn his tentacle.

He didn't notice at first. Then his tentacle started to singe. He jolted backward and recalled his magic.

"Why aren't you at the dining table, little girl? I don't like to be kept waiting," he snarled.

"I'm not going anywhere in this." I fixed the dress. "It's indecent." Then stalked into the bathroom. He grabbed my arm, which was bleeding, halting my steps. I turned around and fixed him with an impatient gaze.

He looked at my arm, which had already healed. Then a whisper of magic traveled down the length of my body. It was unlike Erik's magic, which was curious and playful. This one was dark and hot, and it pulled at me. I narrowed my eyes. His fingers trailed down my arm when he released me. A light, wispy fabric replaced his hand.

The tiny indecent dress I had been wearing pooled at my feet, and my body was covered in a lightweight, black delicate fabric. A long black skirt hung low on my hips with a high slit that came up on my left thigh. The black long-sleeve top was cropped short, exposing my belly, and the round collar showed off my cleavage. Still sexy but a smidge classier.

"Happy?" he said in a flat tone.

I rolled my eyes.

"Hurry, little girl. Our dinner is getting cold." He stalked out the door, and I flipped him off behind his back.

"Miss?" Cerai whispered behind me. "Your shoes." She handed me a pair of black stilettos that fit perfectly.

I slipped on the heels and followed behind the demon.

CHAPTER 11
KENZIE

Dash stomped down a long, dark hallway, with me trailing behind him. He turned into an intimate dining room, where Gunnar was already sitting. My travel companion also had a shower and wore a perfectly tailored suit. He hadn't shaved, though, and I swore under my breath at how much he resembled my father.

Gunnar stood to greet me with an awkward hug and pulled out my chair. He eyed the overlord suspiciously, then asked me, "Are you ok?"

I nodded and sat, wearing a fake smile.

"Your sister was being picky with her wardrobe," the overlord said. "Little girl will find herself bare-assed and bent over my knee if she continues to defy me."

Oh, fuck this! I unsheathed my dagger and slammed it on the table in front of me. "Stop calling me that." I sneered at him. "Calling me 'little girl' and making sexual innuendo makes you sound like a creepy pedophile. And that makes me stabby."

The overlord sat next to me and glared. We had a Mexican stare-off for a few tense seconds, then he tipped his head back and laughed.

After he composed himself, he said, "Mackenzie Jameson, I am going to enjoy having you here. Let's start again, shall we? Forgive me. I will find another term of endearment that you will find more suitable. Please, put your weapon away."

I gripped my dagger harder.

"My name is Dash. I apologize for the way you were brought to me. My people are cautious of strangers. This Circle is very secure for a reason. I mean you and your brother no harm."

I glared at him, still clinging to my dagger.

A human-looking demon brought in food, breaking the tension. The server appeared human aside from his pointed ears and the tail swishing behind him. I had completely lost my mind because I stared at him much longer than what would be considered polite.

"Kenzie, sis? Put your dagger away." Gunnar patted my arm.

Hearing him refer to me as "sis" took me off guard and made me smile inside.

I slipped my dagger back into its sheath and whispered the concealment spell as the server ladled steaming hot broth into our bowls. I picked up my soup spoon and stirred it around. It looked like bouillabaisse. The overlord ate, and after a few bites, so did Gunnar. I didn't touch it. The two men spoke to one another, and I tuned out their conversation entirely.

"Eat, Kenzie. It would help you regain your strength," Gunnar muttered.

"Listen to Gunnar. I won't poison you," Dash said between bites. "You have an intriguing story. Maybe I can help."

I sipped on the broth. Warm liquid touched my tongue, and savory flavors exploded in my taste buds.

The soup warmed my insides, but the cool temperature of the room and the thin fabric of my dress caused my exposed skin to prickle. I crossed my left leg over my right knee and absently ran my hand from my thigh to my calf.

"Excuse me. I'll be right back," Gunnar stood and walked out of the dining area.

I continued eating while running my hand over my leg and completely ignored Dash until he placed my leg on top of his. His hand slid over my skin.

"Hey!" I sputtered. "What the fuck are you doing?"

"What are you doing? You've been touching yourself all night." He frowned at me.

"I was not touching myself; I was trying to warm my leg. It's cold in here." I pulled away from him, but his hot hand had a firm grip on my leg.

"Why didn't you just say so?" he asked.

"Give me my leg back," I snarled.

"You just said you were cold. I'm a demon; I run hot. I am and have been trying to care for you, Mackenzie. Stop defying me." He continued running his hand up and down my leg.

I had to admit; the warmth of his skin on mine felt amazing. But it was too weird.

"You don't need to do that. I am quite capable."

He ignored my request.

"Is this normal behavior for you?" I asked.

"No, I am not myself." He squinted at me as though I was a puzzle he needed to solve. "I am never kind, let alone caring."

He massaged my calf and then my thigh.

I should have been annoyed, but my body betrayed me. My muscles relaxed, and the lovely pressure on my thigh made my sex desperate with need. I wanted to feel those hands all over my body. Wetness saturated my folds, and I knew there would be a wet spot on my chair.

"Are you a sex demon?" I blurted.

Dash laughed and leaned in close. "If anyone is guilty of emitting sexual magic, it's you."

"I don't have sex magic," I told him.

"Of course you do. You have pussy. Females in the human realm haven't figured that one out yet?"

I didn't have a witty comeback for that one.

"Besides, I can smell how wet you are right now," he said in a sex-saturated voice.

My hips rocked, and his hand slid closer to my core.

"No. Nope." I shook my head and placed my hand over his preventing him from traveling any further.

Dash gazed at me with a curious glint in his eyes.

"Stop it." I glared.

"Stop what? I'm not doing anything right now. You're keeping my hand in place," he challenged me.

Fuck. Dash was right. My body and mind were on two different planets at the moment. I released his hand, moved my leg off his lap, and sat straight as Gunnar returned to the table.

"Where'd you go?" I asked, hoping my cheeks weren't red with embarrassment.

"To the bathroom. Are you ok? You look flushed." Gunnar's brow furrowed.

Damn it.

"Just tired." I hung my head.

The men continued talking, and I shivered, missing the heat from Dash's hand.

I reached for a glass of water, and the tentacle softly slapped my hand away. I smacked it back and grabbed the glass. The tentacle seemed to slump and shy away from me as though I hurt its feelings. It burrowed under the edge of my plate and hid. I glanced at Dash; he was busy removing his jacket and speaking with Gunnar. I focused on the tentacle, and like a crazy person, I felt terrible. I whispered, "I'm *sorry*." The tentacle unfurled itself from its hiding spot and perked up. It was a part of Dash, yet capable of acting independently.

This place was so odd. Or perhaps I was having a bizarre fever dream.

I drank some water and placed the glass back on the table. The tentacle brushed against my wrist almost shyly. I smiled, and it wrapped itself around my hand. Earlier, when the tentacle was wrapped around my forearm, it was heavy and had sharp pointy barbs. Now it was soft like silk, and there were no barbs. It wound its way around my hand playfully; it was almost ticklish. It traveled up my forearm and blended in with my sleeve. Faint wisps of magic rose from the fabric and slid down to my hand. I watched it with fascination until I felt something drape over my legs.

Dash had removed his suit jacket and settled it over my legs to keep me warm. I was shocked and grateful. Yet, I couldn't bring myself to say thank you.

"You're not done eating, are you?" He pointed to my soup bowl. "You've barely touched your soup. Is it not to your liking?

"It's delicious. I'm full," I replied.

My tummy must have shrank. Usually, I'd have eaten the whole thing and more, but I couldn't stomach anything further.

The staff placed dinner entrees in front of each of us.

"It's sea bass, Kenz. It's delicious. You should have some," Gunnar told me.

I gave him a small smile and picked up my fork but didn't take a bite.

I was too tired and wasn't hungry anymore. The fork was removed from my hand, and I didn't care.

"Open." Dash held a fork full of food against my lips, and my mouth opened. A morsel of tasty fish entered my mouth. I savored the flavors and swallowed.

"What are you doing?" I pushed his hand away as he tried to spoon-feed me again.

"You need to eat, Kenzie. I know you're tired. But you need sustenance. If you're not going to feed yourself, then I will do it for you."

I glared at the demon, took the fork out of his hand, and forced myself to eat. It was delicious. After a couple more bites, I'd had enough.

Gunnar frowned at me.

I shook my head. "I'm done. Any more, and I'll be sick."

Soon after, the staff removed our plates and brought in the dessert.

"Lemon tart with a shortbread cookie crust," he said as he slid a slice of the tart onto a plate and placed it in front of me.

"Thank you," I said, and his cheeks flushed as he smiled.

I nibbled and wanted to eat the entire thing, but my tummy started to gurgle.

"Thank you, Dash, for all of this. We needed the break, didn't we, Kenz?" Gunnar said.

"Umm . . . yes, we did," I replied, making an effort to participate in the conversation for the first time that evening.

"Of course. I will do what I can to get you home. For now, take as much time as you need," Dash responded to him.

"Dash was telling me the gateways are guarded, open for short periods, and the location changes," Gunnar said to me.

I placed my face in the palms of my hands. That wasn't the best news.

"How can we find out where and when the next gateway will open?" I asked.

"I will work on it first thing in the morning. There are a few demons in the village who monitor those things," Dash replied.

"At what cost?" I was sure the overlord here wasn't doing any of this for free. There would be a price to pay.

"There's always a price, Mackenzie. I didn't become the overlord of this prosperous Circle by not being business savvy. You know this; Gunnar here tells me you're an entrepreneur. Perhaps we can discuss this dilemma you're in, business owner to business owner." He was leering at me as though I was dessert. It made me uncomfortable. "But not tonight. Eat, then rest. We can talk tomorrow."

Here we go. Demons and their damned deals. The delicious food soured in my belly. Was there ever a time when someone would help a stranger without expecting something in return? I surely hoped so, but we were in The Dark Realm. I was certain demons played by a different set of rules. Fuck. I drank the rest of my water.

Gunnar had been happily eating his dessert and drinking wine. Dash stared at me, and I knew he wouldn't give up any information until he was good and ready. And I needed a few hours of decent sleep before I was in any position to negotiate.

I placed my hand over my mouth, covering a yawn.

CHAPTER 12
KENZIE

ash stood. "Excuse us, Gunnar. I am going to escort your sister to her room. I'll be right back."

I shook my head and said, "I can find my way back."

"Stop defying me, Kenzie." Dash extended his hand to me, presumably to help me up. I handed him his coat and stayed put.

"It's ok, Kenz, get some rest. I know where your room is. I'll come and check on you," Gunnar assured me.

That made me feel better, so I bid him goodnight and followed Dash.

He pointed out a few things as we walked down the hallway.

"Why all the black? Wait, let me guess; it matches your personality," I teased. Sleep deprivation turned me into a wiseass.

Dash chuckled and pointed out things as we walked down the hall.

"The kitchen entrance can be found behind the dining room we just left, should you need food or drink. Someone is always there."

He pointed to the right. "This here is a spare bathroom, should you need it. Down this hall are my office and the library."

We went straight, then turned left. "This is Gunnar's room." He opened the door, and I peeked inside. It was similar to my room.

We continued down the hall. "This is where I . . ." The door opened before he could finish his sentence, and a tall blonde woman with reptilian skin stood in the doorway. She wore a sheer gold dress with a deep plunging neckline that extended well past her navel and was fastened with gold gems around her crotch. From there, it opened up and flowed around her legs. It was fucking hot. I wanted that dress.

Another female came up behind the blonde and wrapped her arms around her while she slid her bare leg against the blonde. She had red hair with horns that protruded from her temples. And she was completely naked.

"Dash, we've been waiting for you," the blonde cooed.

The red-haired woman stared openly at me and said, "You brought us another playmate. She's stunning and smells divine."

The blonde licked her lips, "I bet she's delicious."

"She's not for you. Keep each other busy." Dash glared at the woman and slammed the door close.

I wasn't sure how to feel about that exchange, so I kept my mouth shut. Dash opened the next door, which happened to be the room I was assigned. His room was right next to mine; too close. *Ugh!*

I walked into my room, and he followed me, closing the door behind him. "Get out." I narrowed my eyes at him.

"I have a question." Dash stalked toward me, and I backed up, wanting to escape the domineering male.

"No. Ask me tomorrow." I glanced nervously at the bed. He kept stalking me until my back hit the wall.

"I have asked you many times to stop defying me. I kill people who defy me, Kenzie. But you . . ." He grabbed my hand and placed it on his crotch. "This is what happens every time you say no. I have shown incredible restraint even when I know your pussy wants to be fucked, but you keep pushing me. So, again, stop defying me."

"Then stop asking me for shit." I snatched my hand away from his enormous, hard length.

He smirked, then got on his knees and raised my leg, the one exposed by the thigh-high slit in the fabric. His gaze held mine as his hands caressed my thigh and down to my calf, and then he placed my foot on his chest.

"No!" I tried to pull my leg away from his grasp, but he held me firmly. I quickly rearranged my skirt to place it between my legs, covering my bare pussy.

"Kenzie, if I wanted to fuck you, I would have done it by now. But I don't, and I won't. Not yet, anyway. You're too fragile, and I'd ruin that sweet pussy." His gaze dropped to my ankle. His warm hands slid up and down my calf as he stared at Brody's gift.

"Where did you get this?" His fingers brushed over the armband Brody had given me while we were in Germany looking for Bear and his family.

"One of my mates," I replied. "He gave it to me the last morning I was in the human realm."

"Ah yes, you brother mentioned you have four of them. Tell me about this mate of yours?" His finger traced over the gift my human had given me.

"That's none of your business."

His grip tightened on my leg. I pulled away from him, but his hold started to hurt.

I pushed the heel of my stilettos deeper into his chest, sinking my magic into it.

Dash tipped his head back and laughed.

"Do you seriously think you could kill me with your heels?" His eyes twinkled.

"It was worth a try," I muttered. "My mate is a sweet, gentle, caring man. He's human, and this was a family heirloom. Why does it interest you so much?"

"Human? Hmmm . . . very interesting." He looked up at me. He leaned into my body, my heel pressing into his chest while his hand traveled back up to my thigh and ran over my concealed dagger.

A shimmer of magic skimmed over my skin, and my dagger appeared. He'd just undone my spell.

"How . . . how did you do that?" I gasped.

"I'm a spell-breaker. One of my many gifts." He unclasped my holster and threw it with my dagger on the bed.

"Hey!" I tried pulling away from him and nearly toppled over.

His tentacles caught me and held me upright. I fixed my skirt, ensuring my pussy was hidden from his lustful gaze.

"You must understand two things about The Dark Realm, Kenzie. One, we do not have rapists. Demons love to fuck. If you don't want someone to fuck you, slice their throat. Two, we don't have murderers. Only the strong survive. That being said, never hide your weapon. Ever. It would be best if you carried a sword. Do you know how to wield one?"

"I've had some lessons," I replied. Swords weren't my weapon of choice. This was an interesting change of topics.

He nodded while his hands glided over my bare leg, leaving light tingles on my skin. His magic pulled at my skirt, trying to expose my core. I slapped it away.

His tentacles wrapped around my wrist and pinned me to the wall.

"No, Dash." My tone firm.

"Why not? I think you'd rather like having me between your legs. Your juices have been leaking out of your sweet pussy since dinner. Even your skirt is all wet." He toyed with the hem of my skirt.

"Nope. Not even the slightest." I said, even though my body was betraying me.

At the dinner table, Dash's tentacles were soft and playful. Now they were domineering like my demon host. Determined to be free of them, I called on my fire magic. The heat I produced wasn't even warm, and the small effort expended too much energy. My shoulders sagged.

He kissed the inside of my left knee. "If I didn't know any better, Kenzie, I'd say you were part demon. You like to stab things. You lie. And you like to fuck."

"Who said I like to fuck?"

"Of course, you like to fuck. You have four mates."

He had me there. Damn it, this wasn't going well. I needed to rethink my strategy, or I would end up having demon sex.

If bad ass bitch didn't work, go with damsel in distress.

"Master Dash, I'm exhausted. Please let me rest," I said in a tired voice.

He dropped my leg as he stood and came closer to me. His body mere inches from mine, so close but not touching.

I bit my lip.

"Not tonight. But soon." He adjusted his erection and then turned around and left.

Alone and left wanting, I had fully intended on rubbing one out. But I was too tired. I fell on the bed, not even bothering to get undressed. And dreamt.

There was nothing in the darkness except a veil made up of cobwebs in the distance. I rushed to it, curious. On the other side of the veil, Stel slept peacefully. I ran and jumped on top of him.

CHAPTER 13
DASH

The little half-Fae was captivating. Kenzie was practically starving to death, injured, and sleep-deprived, but still, she had a ferocious attitude. Covered in muck and blood, she'd held her chin up and met my gaze with unwavering confidence, and I couldn't help becoming mesmerized by her. And she had powerful Fae magic. I couldn't believe she wrapped my shadow limbs around her arm and didn't flinch as it dug into her skin. She was not afraid of me at all. It was refreshing.

Everything about her was seductive. I was anxious to learn more about her, but she was utterly exhausted.

Kenzie was unlike any female I had ever met in my life. Females of every species gave themselves to me willingly. But Kenzie would not succumb to my charms. She was clear on what she wanted, and that was to get the fuck out of The Dark Realm. And I couldn't blame her. She had been raised in the human realm, so this was foreign to her. With her power, she could easily rule this place by my side. I'd have to keep her hidden as best I could before someone else claimed her.

I had noticed the armband around her ankle and had to know

how she obtained it. It wasn't a trinket, and its magic was still active. Her human mate had given it to her. He either didn't know what it signified, or he was truly in love and had willingly bound his life to hers.

Fortunately for me, he'd affixed it around her ankle. The perfect place for me to slide my hands down her creamy leg. And thanks to my refusal to provide undergarments, I got a sneak peek at her hairless sex. So beautiful and wet. My member swelled in my pants. It seemed I was always hard around her.

After leaving Kenzie's room, I went to speak with Gunnar, who was still in the dining room. He revealed more about her. She was intelligent, strong, and business-minded. Not a wilting flower. She was checking off all the boxes on the perfect mate list. I didn't know I'd had such a list. Sure, I had my standards, but this was a new experience. During our meal, Gunnar had mentioned that she had four mates, which intrigued me. A woman who had four mates had a voracious sexual appetite. I liked it. A lot. Her four mates were a wolf, a vampire, a mage, and a human. Quite the eclectic mix. He didn't know much more than that, which was disappointing. I wanted to know everything about her. It frustrated me that she would choose mates who could not protect her. She was here after all, and from what her brother had told me about their abduction, her mates could have prevented it. Not that I could complain because it had brought her directly to me. I wouldn't force her to stay, but I was confident in convincing her.

I sent my shadow to watch over her while Gunnar regaled their time in the Sixth and Fifth circles. Their trek through the Wailing City and how they stumbled into the Fourth, my domain. Just my luck. He went on to ask me the whereabouts of the nearest gateway. I wasn't ready to divulge that. It wouldn't have mattered anyway; neither were in any shape to cross a gateway, let alone traverse the many miles to one. They needed time to rest. And I was more than happy to give them all the time they required, all while getting to know his sister much better. I convinced him they both needed time to heal; thus, he finally gave up his quest to coerce me into helping them leave in the morning and went to bed.

As soon as Gunnar left the dining room, I checked on my bedroom companions. I was a full-blooded demon, and my appetite for female company was insatiable. The two females in my bed were engrossed with one another and didn't even notice my presence. I watched them for a moment and felt . . . nothing. This was a first. Usually, writhing naked flesh and soft moans made me rock hard. I stared for a moment longer, waiting for my body to react, and nothing happened. *What the fuck was wrong with me?*

I exited my room, stood in the hallway, and summoned Devon, one of my household staff members. He appeared moments later and bowed. "Master?"

"Get rid of my guests." I tipped my head toward my door.

"Yes, Master."

I turned around and walked into Kenzie's room. My shadow form merged into my skin as I entered and reported a complete account of what Kenzie had been up to since I left her, which was not much. She snuggled under the sheets, fully dressed, and had fallen fast asleep as soon as her head hit the pillows.

Kenzie slept like a babe. Her breathing was deep, and her heart rate was slow and steady.

I hovered around the bed, looking closer at her beautiful face. Her long eyelashes fanned the top of her cheeks, and her plump lips had a lovely pink tint. With my shadow, I reached out and moved a stray strand of hair away from her face. She didn't move, so I let my shadow linger on her silky skin. I had never seen a creature so beautiful. And I had been everywhere, even amongst the humans and in the land of the Fae. My cock twitched. *Oh, so, now you want to play.*

Kenzie rolled to the side, and I quickly called my shadows back and melded into the wall. I stood there, concealed by darkness, and stared at her peaceful form. I was proud to have given her this respite. She needed it, and in a way, I had already vowed to care for and provide for her every need.

After some time, Kenzie stirred, then started removing her clothes. The temperature in my abode was always on the cooler side, but perhaps her clothing was uncomfortable. Or maybe she liked sleeping in the nude. I should have averted my eyes as her naked flesh came into view. But I was a demon, the farthest thing from being a gentleman.

She wriggled out of her top, freeing her full breasts, her nipples pink and taut. And then she shimmied out of her skirt. I could feel myself hardening as the fabric slowly revealed smooth, creamy legs and a hairless pussy. My mouth watered as I focused on her nakedness. I wanted more. I wanted her legs to spread farther apart, allowing me to see that sensitive nub between her folds and tight entrance. As though she knew what I wanted, one knee slowly bent and then the other. I was about to get my one wish when she pulled a sheet over her torso, covering her pelvis area simultaneously.

I sighed in disappointment.

Still, I stayed in my shadow form, hugging the walls while she slept. I was perfectly comfortable in this form and could remain here all night. I continued to drink up her appearance and thought of how I would make her mine and keep her happy. I would teach her the ways of this realm and how to grow her Fae power by giving her some of my demon magic. True mates could do that if they so choose. And for her, I wouldn't hesitate. Were we true mates? Perhaps we were. Only time would tell, but something in me said I had finally found the one I had been waiting for all my life.

Kenzie had purred in her sleep. Or perhaps it had been a moan. I couldn't be sure it was so soft. I focused on her beautiful face, intent on hearing everything and anything that came from those sweet lips.

She groaned a little louder this time. The sound was unmistakable; she was aroused. The heady smell of lust oozing from her pores confirmed it. Oh! Well, this was a nice turn of events. I smiled as she played out her sex dream.

My demon hearing picked up her quickening pulse. Oooh, she was exquisite. Her moans had gotten louder, and her skin reddened as though feverish. She rolled over onto her stomach, the sheet falling away from her flesh, exposing her firm bottom as she pumped her hips. I was incensed. I had to get a closer look. It was a risk, but so worth it.

She spread her folds and exposed her tight exquisite entrance. Her skin glistened with her sex juices. I licked my lips. She massaged her swollen clit, and I gripped my cock. Her moans became louder and more frantic, her breathing ragged. Then her entire body tightened, and she screamed, "Stel!"

That should have been my cue to leave and give her her privacy. But I stayed rooted right where I was as her moans of pleasure slowed . . . then picked up again. Oh! She wasn't quite finished yet. And even better, she turned over on her back and spread her legs as far as possible. I got closer to the bed.

A sheen of sweat covered her body; she massaged her breasts and tugged at her hard nipples. Her back arched as she surrendered to the pleasure her body so desperately craved. Her moans grew louder and louder. My eyes roamed all over her naked flesh, taking in every inch of her. And then I fixated on her drenched and gaping pussy. *What?* I got even closer, not believing my eyes. It was as though . . . something invisible was filling her up. And whatever it was, it was thick and stretched her tightness. Kenzie was thoroughly enjoying it. *What kind of magic fuckery is this?* I sniffed at the air, and there was nothing aside from the smell of her arousal. I opened my demonic magic and sensed nothing unusual. Kenzie was getting fucked in the dream realm, and she loved it. My gaze remained fixated on her pussy being hammered. Kenzie's full breasts jutted out, and her hands clenched the sheets. She panted, and her toes curled. Her climax was not far, and neither was mine. I stroked myself harder and faster as I imagined impaling her with my cock while she was getting fucked in her dreams.

She screamed with pleasure, calling out for Stel while she climaxed. I came with her, spilling myself all over my fists. Her beautiful pussy dripped with her cum, and her breasts heaved with every breath. She was magnificent.

I was so enthralled with her arousal that I hadn't realized I was fully exposed. My shadows were behind me, and I stood in my human form at the edge of the bed, breathing hard and staring at her. A deep, menacing growl startled me, and I shrunk back into my shadow self, merging into the walls once more.

Was that her wolf? Did he sense me? How was that possible? How was any of this possible?

CHAPTER 14
STELLAN

Fucking Chris. What a lying bitch. From the minute she had revealed she was pregnant, I had been sure I wasn't the father. The damn test proved I wasn't, but the manipulator found a way to falsify the results to her liking and forced a lower-ranked shifter to do her bidding. I was frustrated more than anything. The entire situation had hurt Kenzie, my mate. All those tears and heartbreak for nothing.

Overall I was grateful the kid wasn't mine. It was one less thing to worry about. But that bitch would be dealt with some other time. She was not a priority, and I was glad to have her out of my life — more than anything, I needed to get my shit together for Kenzie's sake.

I stomped upstairs, leaving Kenzie's other three men in the kitchen. Brody was right; we all needed to focus. While Kenzie remained in The Dark Realm, he had been doing all he could to stay on top of things. If it weren't for him, Caid, Erik, and I would be lost entirely. Fuck we needed to get her back. Without our mate, my wolf was a bloodthirsty bastard. I should reign in more control, but the ache of her absence was no less painful in my human form.

Kenzie's scent permeated our room. She had an exotic scent, a mix of coconut and just a hint of spicy cinnamon. I missed her something fierce. Everywhere in this house reminded me of her. In many ways, it was a comfort, and in some, it was torturous. I couldn't help but think of her naked flesh as I stood under the stream of water in the shower. My body responded to the memories of taking her in this shower. I groaned.

I quickly soaped up and rinsed, not wanting to give in to the desire to touch myself. It didn't feel right to pleasure myself without her. It felt hollow.

In my wolf form, the only thoughts running through my head were hunt and blood. It was easier to remain a wolf, but I knew the consequences. The longer I walked on four legs, the harder it was to return to two. I tugged at my scraggly beard. That needed to be shaved, but not right now. My brother was right; I needed sleep.

Kenzie. Where are you? I flopped onto our giant bed and nuzzled my face into the pillows where her scent was strongest. Her father was still in The Dark Realm searching.

Erik was our connection to the mage world, yet he was practically useless. Shortly after Kenz had gone missing, he'd hit the sauce hard. Whiskey was coming out of his pores. I could hardly throw stones; I wasn't coping any better.

Aunt Mimi hadn't helped as much as I'd hoped. She babbled, saying, *"The dark one will return her."* No one knew what that meant or who was the dark one. It was frustrating at best. The first few days, my wolf circled her, unwilling to go too far just in case a coherent thought formed. The longer I stayed near her, the more bonkers she seemed to get, so my mother shooed me away. I checked in often with my parents, even in wolf form, but so far, nothing.

At this point, the only avenue we hadn't explored was seeking counsel from Sebastian, Caid's sire. Fuck, that would suck. But what choices did we have? Kenzie would be pissed if we struck another deal with that psycho. She would forgive us eventually. I'd rather have her here kicking my ass than be lost where I had no clue if she was okay or not.

Kenzie. God, I missed her. I focused on the image of her and closed my eyes.

I felt her fingertips trail over my arms and down my chest. She was exploring my body as though memorizing every plane of muscle. My skin prickled under her sensual touch. She cupped my cheeks and ran a thumb over my lips, and I kissed her finger. Her exquisite scent was laced with arousal. My cock was fully engorged as she continued exploring my body, her hands eagerly tracing my stomach. Her hair tickled my leg as I felt hot breath fan over my cock. My body stiffened. I desperately wanted to open my eyes and find her with me, gliding a finger over my cock, but I didn't want to break the spell. This dream felt all too real, and I wanted to stay here in this dream forever.

Her hands moved back up over my stomach, then my chest. I felt the weight of her body straddle mine, then her face tucked into the crook of my neck. Her lips trailed kisses from my neck to my jaw, then my lips. Then she called out my name, and her tongue parted my lips and delved into my mouth. Her soft tongue was warm and wet and needy.

I love you, Stel. I miss you so much, she said in her sleepy voice.

Kenzie, I moaned.

Her pouty lips were so soft and delicious. I needed more. Hesitant to wake from this all-too-real dream, I reached up and made contact with her skin. Silky smooth, just as I remembered. My hands slid up her thighs to her round hips and over her firm ass. Her hot core rubbed against my stomach, and she moaned against my mouth. I kneaded her ass and glided a finger down her crack until I made contact with her wet folds. She gasped and tangled her hands in my hair. She rubbed against my stomach while I rubbed my finger along her tight entrance. When I slid a finger in just halfway, she came with a shudder breathing hard.

This dreamlike state felt impossibly real. I was not going to waste another moment of it. I flipped her over, trapping her small body beneath me. I kissed her lips and her throat while massaging her tits. *Oh, Kenzie, how I've missed you.*

I missed you too, Stel!

I almost opened my eyes but didn't dare. Kenzie threaded her hands into my hair, forced my lips to hers, locked her legs around me, and flipped us over again. Oh fuck. Her lips grazed my neck and down to my chest, all while she told me how much she loved me. I wrapped my arms around her and squeezed her tiny body.

Look at me, Stel.

No. I wanted to stay in this dream forever.

Stel, look at me.

I refused to open my eyes.

Then I felt her teeth graze the top of my chest and sink in. The pain startled me, and my eyes snapped open. I looked down at my chest to see dark hair and a small body on top of mine. Her mouth was pressed to my chest, feasting on my body.

Kenzie?

She gazed at me; blood painted her lips red from the little bite.

Stel! She crashed our lips together, the coppery taste of blood on her lips now on mine.

I rolled us over again and impaled her with my cock. Her pussy was wet and so tight. It must have hurt a little to thrust into her so harshly, but I didn't care. If this was just a dream, I wanted her to wake sore from my hard cock. She spread her legs wide for me, allowing each thrust to delve deeper into her body. Her moans of pleasure incited me. I moaned with her and fucked her like a beast. She clawed at my arms and my back.

Your cock feels so fucking good, Stel.

I fucked her harder, almost sure I was going to break her. But she didn't break; she wanted more, and I wanted to give her everything. Her lips were stained with my blood, which gave me an idea. If this were the waking world, this would have been a bad idea because it would hurt, but here in this dream, it didn't matter. She arched her back, her nipples sticking straight up. I leaned over her body, driving my cock in deeper, then bit over her right breast, marking her again. She screamed my name and held my head fast to her tit. I drank my fill of her while I pummeled her pussy. After a moment, her body went taut, every muscle clenched. Her pussy gripped my cock and gushed like a dam being broken. I kept thrusting, not wanting this to end, but her cunt tightened and squeezed as though she were milking my cock, greedy for my seed.

I growled like a wolf when I came and crumbled on top of her. Her body was slick with sweat, and I laved over the new mark on her breast. The bleeding had already stopped, it was raw, and if this were real, it would hurt in the morning. I savored having her in my arms, moving strands of hair plastered to her face and kissing her everywhere.

Kenzie. I love you.

I love you too, Stel. I want to come home, she whimpered . . .

I looked at her face closely and ran a finger around her eyes, nose, and lips. Then a tear dropped, and I chased it with the pad of my thumb. Wet. What the actual fuck?

Are you okay, sweetness?

I miss you and the guys, and I want to come home. I'm trying Stel. I'm trying.

Shhh. Sweetness. hhh. Don't cry. We're trying too. I love you. We all love you. How did you do this?

I didn't do anything. Please, I want to come home. Bring me home, Stel.

I know, I know, sweetness, we're working on it. I'll do . . .

Before I could finish my last thought, my nostrils flared. There was a foreign smell in the room. It was masculine and very close. I growled and looked over my shoulder to find nothing except the sliding door to the balcony of our bedroom.

CHAPTER 15
KENZIE

I woke with the feeling of being watched, and the hair on my arms stood on end. Using my magic, I lashed out at the intruder with my fists and connected with soft flesh.

My intruder grunted, then overpowered me. He threw me on the bed and restrained my arms above my head, his big frame pinning me under him.

Dash didn't see me coming, but he was powerful and had me beat by at least a hundred pounds.

"What the hell are you doing here?" I snarled.

"I was just checking on you." His voice was gravelly. "You attacked me. I, I liked it. A lot."

He shifted his weight, and I became aware of my lack of clothing and his swollen manhood.

"You need to learn boundaries, demon. Get off of me." I bucked and kicked, which made him groan with pleasure.

"Mmmm . . . fuck, Kenzie. You have me so hard right now." He rolled his hips.

"Oh. I thought you had a pencil in your pocket."

He shook with laughter. Mirth ran through his body. It was a genuine laugh that made me smile.

Dash ran a fingertip over my lips. "That's the first smile I've seen from you since you got here."

"I'm glad you're amused. Now get off me." I wriggled under his body weight.

"Keep moving like that, and I'll have to stab you with my pencil." We both laughed.

"Seriously, Dash, get off me. You weigh a ton."

He slowly rose from the bed, bringing me up while holding my hands. His eyes traveled the length of my body. I wrenched my hands away from his and covered my lady parts.

"I've already seen it all, Kenzie." He moved my hands away from shielding my body. "You are perfection."

I shoved him away from me, and he landed in the chair near the bed. "Thank you, but you need to learn boundaries, or next time I'm breaking your nose." I hurried into the bathroom, slamming the door behind me.

The interaction with Dash left me confused and a little aroused. That was just wrong; I should have been pissed off.

Annoyed with my reaction, I stood under the shower, allowing the water to wash over me and clear my thoughts until Cerai knocked on the shower door.

"Mistress, I am here to help you dress," she called.

"Hi Cerai, I can dress myself. There's no need for you to wait on me." I turned off the shower and reached for a towel.

"I insist, Mistress. Lunch is almost ready." Cerai held out a robe and motioned to a chair in front of the vanity mirror.

I slipped on the robe and sat as directed. Cerai wrapped a towel around my hair, absorbed the water then began brushing through the tangles.

I took stock of my reflection while she worked on my hair. My skin color was paler than usual, and the dark circles had receded. I was far too thin, and food would be a good thing. Both of my marks looked more pronounced, which I had guessed was due to the weight loss and pale skin color. There was tenderness over my right breast, and the skin was pink. I traced the sensitive area with my fingertip and quivered. Pleasurable tingles ran through my body.

The dream I'd had of Stellan came back to me. It had felt so genuine. My eyes closed, remembering the feel of his skin, the taste of his lips, and the coppery tinge of his blood. I licked my lips as though his taste still lingered. He had bitten me over my breast. The intense pain of his bite and the exquisite pressure of his hard length moving in and out of me had felt so real. Had it been just a dream?

I traced over my marks, the one he and his brother had left, and the tender skin over my breast. My body quivered again, and a moan escaped me. My breathing became shallow, and my heart rate quickened.

"Mistress? Are you unwell?" Cerai asked, interrupting my daydreams.

I hugged the robe around me and noticed my dark hair was now in a stylish updo.

"No, no, I'm fine. This is nice, thank you." I patted my hair.

"I will help you dress. The Master is waiting for you." Cerai motioned to the bedroom.

She opened an ornate armoire and pulled out outfits. I frowned at the options she held out for me. Every clothing item was white. The color change was different, but that was the least of my clothing issues. Each item was delicate and beautiful and a little too slinky. The dresses and skirts were either too short or long with scandalously thigh-high slits. The tops were cropped or had low necklines revealing way too much cleavage. And there were no pants to speak of unless you considered bell-bottomed leggings that had cut-out patterns on the side, running from the hip area to my calves, exposing too much skin. I asked Cerai for the clothes I had worn when I arrived, and she said they were still being cleaned. I didn't quite believe her, but I didn't want to argue over it either. With a sigh, I slid on the most conservative dress available. It was a backless long-sleeved number with a round collar that sat low across my chest. The asymmetrical skirt flowed down to the floor in the back, and the front skimmed the middle of my upper thigh. The white material was soft and almost sheer. It was beautiful. I didn't dare ruin it by wearing a bra, that wasn't an option. Undergarments hadn't been provided. I slid on a pair of heels, and Cerai guided me to meet Dash and Gunnar.

"How long have you worked here, Cerai?" I asked the winged demon.

"As long as I can remember, Mistress," she replied as she glided down the hallway.

"Please call me Kenzie."

"No, Mistress, the Master will not approve." She motioned for me to follow her again.

"You Master sounds like a real asshole," I muttered.

"He's not so bad, Mistress. There are many lords and ladies that would not treat their servants as kindly as he has treated me."

"You like him?" I asked out of curiosity.

"Yes, he is a fair Master, but no." She pulled a sour face. "I do not wish to mate him. He is far too powerful and not for me." She whispered the last bit.

We walked down the corridor and took a few turns until she opened a door that led to a terrace.

Dash and Gunnar were seated at a table covered with food. But the view beyond the terrace drew me in. The sky above was purple and blue with streaks of pink clouds. A majestic mountain was surrounded a bright turquoise body of water. The air was crisp, and a cool breeze ruffled my hair, making my dress billow behind me. I went straight to the railing, ignoring the men, and marveled at the picturesque landscape.

CHAPTER 16
KENZIE

ash came up behind me and wrapped his arms around my waist for a brief hug.

"Boundaries, demon." I pushed him away from me and noticed his eye was purplish and swollen. *That had to hurt.*

He grinned at me. "Are you proud of yourself?"

I bit my lip to keep from smiling at my handy work. "Do you not heal?"

"Yes, but I kind of like it." He shrugged. "No one has ever been lucky enough to get a clean shot at me like this."

"Nice work, Sis." Gunnar pointed at Dash's black eye.

I smiled at him, appreciating the new nickname.

"How'd you sleep?" I sat in the chair Dash held out for me.

He nodded and bit into a slice of fruit. "I slept well, not as soundly as you did, but I am recovered."

"Where are we? This doesn't look like the village we entered," I asked Dash.

"This is the Fourth Circle. The same Circle you entered through. Requiem Square is where the villagers live and conduct business.

This," he waved his hand around, "is my private residence. It spans from the village down to the Sovereign Sea."

"This is beautiful. Who else lives here?" I asked the demon.

"Just me and my household. I like my privacy," Dash kept his eyes on me and continued, "I don't have any wives or children."

"He's a bachelor, just like me." Gunnar grinned.

Oh my, the two were bonding.

"How nice for both of you. But, before you two start planning to hit the town, can we talk about getting to the gateway?"

Dash chuckled. "Of course. Let's finish our meal, and then we'll head to my library. It will be easier for me to explain everything there."

I looked at the spread and hesitated.

"We have the same foods as in the human realm Kenzie. Cows, chickens, fish, everything. It's all the same," Dash waved his fork. "We have more exotic foods, but I thought this was more to your liking."

I was ravenous. The food smelled delicious and wouldn't have mattered if it was mystery meat. I loaded my plate.

While we ate, Dash told us more about his home and business. The more he talked, the more similar it was to home. In the human realm, he would be considered an entrepreneur. He ran all of the import and export businesses in the Fourth Circle.

After our meal, Dash showed us around the terrace. Large trees, which looked like white dogwood trees, provided plenty of shaded areas throughout the verdant garden. Fluorescent flowers of every color neatly framed the stone pathway leading to the Sovereign Sea's white sandy beach.

"Why is this so different from the Fifth and Sixth Circles? Is this an illusion of some sort?" I asked.

"No, Kenzie. This is not an illusion. The Fifth and Sixth Circles are meant to be bleak. Those two circles were specifically designed for lost souls. And deters wanderers. You have to be strong to get through those Circles to get this far. The other Circles have similar landscapes as this."

Dash led us back inside, down a long corridor to a large seating area. It was dark like the rest of the house; dark walls, flooring, and furniture. Immediately, I was anxious to go back outdoors. Why does this man live in a dark ass cave when he has a beautiful beach all to himself right outside?

Across from the seating area was an extensive library like the one at Jameson castle. This one was less organized, though, and had no fireplace. He went around a desk covered in parchment. I peered at the papers as he shuffled them around. The writing on them looked like hieroglyphics. I didn't understand a thing I was seeing.

He rolled out a colossal parchment which he explained was a map of The Dark Realm. It was huge. As Cerai had described, there were six circles. Gunnar and I got thrown in the Sixth and Fifth Circles, the dodgy poor Circles where there were no rules and no civility. Demons fighting and killing one another was commonplace.

And, of course, the gates to get home were all located in those circles. They were challenging to find and even harder to get through unless you had a demon guide. The Rogue had in-and-out privileges only because a demon owned his soul. That was not going to help Gunnar and me. Fuck.

"Ok, let me get this straight. Finding a gateway is challenging, but even if we found one, we wouldn't be able to walk through without a demon guide?"

"Correct." Dash gingerly touched his black eye, which was already healing.

Gunnar immediately asked, "Would you be willing to guide us out or know of someone that might?"

"Me, no? Another demon, perhaps. I've already made some inquiries. But, just be warned, you will need to make a deal."

"What kind of deal?" I asked.

"Depends on the demon, Kenzie. If you're lucky, you'll find one that will guide you for a favor. The thing is, only higher-level demons will be able to take you. And only a few are willing to deal. I will inquire for you, though, and see if there's another way. Some portals are open on occasion. Not often, but it does happen. It usually correlates with the moon cycles here and back on earth. I have my staff looking into it."

I massaged my temples, suddenly feeling very tired. This was the worst news possible. A deal with a demon was the last thing I wanted to do, but I was a businesswoman. I just needed to find someone to negotiate with.

"I appreciate all you've done for us, but I have to ask for one more thing. Can you set up meetings with demons that can guide us through?" I asked Dash, hopeful.

"Dealing with demons is not advised, Kenzie. They don't deal in money; they deal in souls."

"We must get back. There must be a way." I refused to accept defeat, and then it dawned on me. "My family is owed a deal. That must be enough."

"Your family is owed a favor from a demon?" Dash's eyebrows shot up to his forehead. "Do you know the name of the demon?"

Fuck. I shook my head. Neither Granny nor my father had ever mentioned the demon by name. I knew the deal was drawn on demon skin and written in blood.

"I'll see what I can do. In the meantime, rest and gather your strength." Dash said as I walked out of the library, Gunnar behind me.

"Follow me, Kenz. I'll show you around." Gunnar guided me down the hallway.

We walked for some time before either of us said anything. I wasn't paying any attention to where we were, which was stupid. I needed to get a better understanding of our surroundings. This wasn't the time to get lost in thought, or I'd be in this darn place forever.

Gunnar pulled me into a room and held a finger to his lips, telling me to keep quiet. I waited for a moment while he made a few arcane gestures. I imagined he was creating a shield to keep our conversation private. Damn it, I missed Erik. I needed to work on my magic.

"Shield," he confirmed. "One can never be too careful. I've wandered around this place while you were asleep. It's massive. Keep your guard up, Kenz; I don't trust Dash completely. He seems nice, but I am sure he has ulterior motives. Gather your strength and practice your magic; we'll need it."

Gunnar made more hand gestures and peeked out the door. He was right about everything. I needed to put on my game face.

He led me around, ensuring I learned how to navigate the place. Serpentine Manor was massive, and I was glad he had done some exploring.

I was grateful to have him with me and determined to get my shit together and get us home somehow.

CHAPTER 17
CAID

I had spent most nights at Scarlet, keeping my vamps in line. It was tedious work, but it kept me busy. As soon as I stepped into the house, I knew something was different.

My nostrils flared, and I ran upstairs. I sniffed the air. Stel had slept here. But it also smelled like Kenzie. Her scent had faded over the last weeks, yet it was slightly more potent. It was faint, as though she had been here days ago instead of weeks. I was going mad.

With my vamp speed, I searched the house. It was empty, and then I went outside on the back patio. No one was there either. Then I heard their voices and met them at the dock by the lake.

"Where've you been?" Brody asked.

"Spent the night at Scarlet," I replied. Stel raised an eyebrow at me. "Yeah, I know. I won't go back for a few days."

"Where's Erik?" I asked. Brody and Stel shrugged their shoulders.

"Well, it's been weeks, and we've got nothing. I am going to see my sire," I told them.

"No," They both said.

I threw up my hands. "What then? I need her back."

"We all do. We should head to Granny's when Erik gets back.

Maybe she'll have some ideas." Brody skipped a stone across the lake.

Stel picked up a rock and did the same; his stone went farther, earning him a glare from Brody.

I picked up a rock and found the process distracting and almost soothing. We skipped stones until Erik hollered at us from the house.

"Sorry I'm late," Erik said as we entered through the sliding door leading to the kitchen. "I had to get some tonics to deal with my hangover."

I nodded at him and said, "Something seems different here. Has anyone noticed anything . . ." I cut off mid-sentence as Stel handed out beers to everyone except Erik. The movement opened up his hoodie, and I noticed a mark on his chest. He caught me staring.

"What?" Stel asked me.

"What's that?" I pointed at his chest. He looked down at his hoodie.

"Not there," I tugged on the zipper of his hoodie, revealing the red mark on his chest, and pointed. "There."

He looked down, and his eyes got big. He went to stand in front of a decorative mirror hanging in the living area. The three of us stood behind him.

"Fuck, this can't be," Stel said, his finger hovering over the red mark.

I turned him to face me and examined it. "That looks like teeth marks. Did you let someone bite you?" I leaned closer and sniffed.

"Explain Stel." I took a few steps back and tugged at my hair. "What the fuck is going on? I sense . . . Kenzie. How is that possible? What the fuck happened?"

Erik and Brody wore bewildered looks on their faces. And Stel shook his head.

I started pacing. "Stel, I'm about to lose my shit. Start speaking."

"I had a dream. Of Kenzie. She bit me." Stel glanced at Erik and asked, "is this possible from a dream?"

Erik looked pinched like this was too much information, and he needed a drink. "Dream walking is possible. Rare but possible. Kenzie has strong magic. If anyone could do it, she could. Fuck. I need to make some calls. Give me a second."

He sat on one of the leather chairs in the front room and pulled out his phone.

This was shocking news. If Kenzie could dream walk, we at least had a connection and could get a location that may help her father find her and bring her home. I was optimistic.

While Erik made a few calls, Stel gave Brody and me the abridged version of his sex dream. I was jealous. Kenzie hadn't visited me. But again, I hadn't slept much. I couldn't. I tossed and turned most nights. None of us had gotten any sleep since she'd been gone. And now we wanted to shoot ourselves. Perhaps Kenz had reached out, and there had been no one there. I was sleeping tonight. We all were.

"Well," Erik said, "my mentor said he read about dream walking that described the benefits of Fae bonds. He thinks that it is certainly possible since we are bonded to her. This is good news; we might have a way to communicate with her. He doesn't have the book, but he told me where I might be able to find it. I'll head there and get it. I'll meet you back here, but it may take a couple of days."

"What's the name of the book? Maybe Doc Higgs has it in Montana, and I could ask him to look. And maybe Granny can check her library," Brody said.

Erik gave us the info, and we all went to work on it. Stel called Granny, Brody called his Doc, and I called one of my vamps, Richard. He was as old as Dad and had old-world connections. I'd made him my number two. He seemed to be reliable and not at all hungry for power. I asked him if he wanted to run the seethe, and he'd given me a definitive no. He did not want that much responsibility, nor did I, but he insisted that he was not the right person to make hard decisions. He had little interest in being my number two, but I appointed him anyway. So far, he was doing a good job.

"Richard," I said when he answered my call, "I need to track a book called "Fae Bonds." Can you put some feelers out?"

"Of course, sir, but if I may, your father is rumored to have the largest vamp library. He might have it," Richard said.

"Can you make inquiries, discreetly?" I rubbed my forehead.

"Certainly, I know a scholar in that area. I'll make the call," he replied.

After he hung up, we all packed up and headed to Scotland.

Thanks to Brody's savvy business brain, we all had plenty of tech gadgets to teleport at will. He worked out a deal with an info mage who specialized in engineering. Stel got Carlos, billionaire genius, and his big bucks involved, and we added Clay's special touch with tech magic, and voila, teleporting chips made especially for us four. We needed it. With Erik only able to teleport one person at a time and his troubles with alcohol, he needed it too.

We found Granny in the library, looking through stacks of books. "Finally," she said, not even bothering to look at us. "I need help going through all these books. I've already gone through this entire wall." She pressed a lever, and the wall panel tipped to the left, then slowly slid back out of view, and another wall of books took its place. "There are twelve of these shelves; just hit this lever here. Every notch will reveal a new wall of books. Most of them are in Gaelic and priceless. Be gentle with everything. It is late, and I am old. I need my rest."

She vanished. And the guys and I went through the stacks and stacks of books.

By morning, we had only gone through four walls of books. We pulled the ones that had anything to do with the Fae. And Brody enlisted Bear to help. He was now Granny's ward until Kenzie returned. The kid seemed in good spirits when we arrived. Granny and Clay, his tech mage tutor, said he was doing well with his studies but showed some signs of depression. Poor kid; we needed to get in front of that problem soon.

Erik took off to the Mage Emporium in Switzerland, which served as archives for all things magical and was the world's only magical university. It wasn't huge from what he had said. Only select individuals were admitted, and he was an alumnus. They did have the most extensive library. Hopefully, he would find something. His contact said the book was rare, and only a few copies printed.

"Get some sleep, Caid," my brother said with his back turned to me. I made a face at his back.

"Stop being childish, Caid," Stel said as though he saw me. "You haven't slept since whenever and maybe . . ." he turned and looked at me, "you'll get a visitor in your dreams."

Kenzie. I put down the book I was holding and went to the tower Granny had remodeled for us.

"Sweet dreams," Brody called out, and I flipped him off. He chuckled.

CHAPTER 18

KENZIE

It took me a couple of passes through the many hallways of Serpentine Manor until I could commit the layout to memory.

Once I felt confident enough to navigate my way around, I left Gunnar at the doorway to his room and decided to explore independently. There were areas of Dash's residence that were forbidden. One corridor, in particular, had a ward so strong when I pushed against the invisible barrier, it nearly burned the skin off my hand. It was just as well; we needed a gateway home, and I felt whatever he was protecting wasn't it.

I returned to what Gunnar had said was the entrance to the village. The double doors rose twenty feet in the air and were solid metal. I wasn't sure if they were iron or steel, but they looked heavy as all get out. There were no handles or door knobs, so I placed my hands on the metal and pushed. Magic hummed against my skin upon contact. I studied the patterns on the metal, looking for symbols, alphabets, or something that would help me solve the puzzle. There was nothing of the sort. The design was a lovely scroll pattern that was etched into the metal.

"Have you solved the puzzle?" Dash's voice startled me.

I turned toward the sound of his voice, but there was nothing. The entryway was dark with its black walls and nearly dark furnishings. The tall stained glass windows and the chandelier hanging from the cathedral ceilings barely provided any light. I squinted in the darkness as shadows approached.

Out of the shadows, Dash appeared, then the shadows retreated into his body. I tilted my head to the side. Very interesting.

"It's warded to keep people out," he said.

"And people in," I finished his sentence.

Dash smiled. "No, you and your brother are not prisoners. You can leave anytime you want. However, I don't recommend it. At least not unless you have someone with you."

The doors creaked as they opened, and I had to take a few steps back to avoid getting hit by the heavy metal. The process was slow, and not very convenient if you wanted a quick exit or entrance. The unsaid message was clear; escape would not be easy, nor would it go unnoticed.

He stood next to me as I watched the doors swing fully open.

"Shall we?" Dash motioned with his hand toward the outdoors.

Outside his home was a lush garden surrounded by a wrought-iron fence. Like the landscape behind his terrace, this garden also had large trees and vibrant unknown flowers.

Dash led me out of the garden and held open a gate. Before stepping away from his residence, I turned and marveled at Serpentine Manor. The colorful garden made the Gothic architecture seem less ominous.

The demon waited with a patient smile as I admired his home, and then I followed him through the village.

The air was cool, crisp, and dry. The village we walked through was as I had remembered when Gunnar and I had stumbled in days ago. It was clean, like outdoor shopping malls in affluent neighborhoods at home. Demons were out and about. Some were in human form, most in demon. There were many shops and eateries. Demons bowed to Dash when we passed by. He smiled as we kept moving.

And I did my best to keep my footing. Not an easy feat with five-inch heels and uneven stones. Stupid heels.

Dash placed a hand on my arm to steady me, the corners of his mouth upturned. He whispered something then the ground under me changed. Or maybe it was my heels; I couldn't tell. But the ground seemed to have evened out under every step, although the cobblestones remained. I took a couple of steps forward and then backward, stunned at how smooth the pathway had been under my feet.

"I couldn't allow you to wobble at every step, now could I?" Dash grinned.

"How?" I asked, then waved my hand. It wasn't that important. Impressive but not an essential fact that would get me home. And, of course, he had magic; he was a demon, after all. It bothered me how little I knew about demons in general. It was never a topic I had any interest in.

We walked without speaking as questions ruminated in my mind about what he was and what he was capable of. He was successful in this realm. That would mean he was a powerful demon. But if he was powerful, wouldn't he be able to guide us through the gateway?

"You're frowning, Kenzie. Why don't you ask your questions?" Dash said. There was so much I wanted to know, and I didn't know where to start.

I released an audible breath to clear my thoughts and focused on the village.

"Where are we?" I finally asked.

"This is Requiem Square. The Fourth Circle's most affluent neighborhood." Dash stopped to shake a distinguish-looking demon's hand. He was as big as a bear with walrus tusks and wore a tuxedo. It was almost funny, but I held back my giggles and smiled at the well-dressed walrus.

"This is where you conduct your business?" I asked.

"Yes and no. I own this Circle. The demons here own their businesses, and they pay me a tax or percentage. This way." He grabbed my hand and crossed the cobblestone street and led me to a charming courtyard. His hand felt hot on my skin. I suddenly felt uncomfortable about choosing the backless dress. A human-looking demon nodded at Dash and led us up a flight of stairs. I was busy looking at the courtyard as we passed and almost missed the first step. Dash held my hand and guided me up the steps as my eyes remained on the courtyard below.

Like Dash's home, this scenery seemed too lovely to be in The Dark Realm. Or maybe I was judgmental because of my time in the Fifth and Sixth Circles. The courtyard was adorned with beds of roses, and a soothing stream ran through it. Demons sat on benches that were placed throughout the courtyard. It all seemed like a typical scene in the human realm. I was fixated on the scenery below and hadn't realized we were at a table. Dash stood beside me, patiently waiting for me to take a seat. He held my hand while his other hand rested on my lower back. I felt his finger trace my spine, sending an electric pulse through my body, which brought me back to the present.

I angled my body away from his reach. "Pardon me. I'm stunned. Everything here is so different yet familiar."

I sat in the chair he held for me, and his fingers brushed over my shoulders.

"You haven't traveled outside your realm; I take it." He pushed my chair in for me.

I cleared my throat. "Realms? No, I haven't," I replied.

Humans were just getting used to magical folk being out in the open. I don't think humans nor supes contemplated traveling to other realms. Most humans had yet to travel out of their home states.

Dash was having a conversation with a demon who seemed to be a waitress. I tuned them out completely and took in the area. Our table was near a fountain that fed the stream running through the courtyard. The spray of water was slight yet refreshing. I reached out with my Fae magic, and it fluttered like a pleasant tickle. I called a stream of water toward me and smiled. I made twirly hand motions, making the water dance. It was silly and delightful, and it made me giggle.

From the corner of my eye, I noticed Dash staring at me, including the waiter and everyone else in the courtyard. My face reddened with embarrassment. "Oops, sorry," I released the tiny stream of water back into the waterfall.

"Your Fae magic is strong. It's captivating." Dash's mismatched eyes held a mischievous glint which made me uncomfortable. I cleared my throat.

He placed a hand over mine and said, "You are safe here, Kenzie. It's ok to enjoy the simple pleasures after the journey you've had."

I nodded, not in agreement but to change the subject and to focus on getting home. He was right about the hellish journey; still, getting comfortable was not an option.

"Thank you for everything you've done for us. But I need to get home. Where would I find a demon to help guide us through a gateway?"

"I've set up meetings; the first is in two days. If I can get more, I will," Dash said as the waiter returned with a bucket of ice and a bottle. The bottle opened with a pop, and he poured a glass in front of me and a drink for Dash. The liquid was pale pink, making me think it was a Rosé. I held the glass to my nose and wished I had my magic ring from the bazaar that detected poison.

"I'm not trying to poison you, Kenzie. What would be the point? You've been the most intriguing guest I've ever had." He held up his glass and I clinked our glasses together. I took a small sip and smiled. A light fruity taste danced over my tongue. It was delicious. But I refrained from drinking too much or too quickly. Instead, I focused on the demon.

There was no denying that Dash was an attractive male. He was tall, six feet five, at the very least. His shoulders were broad but not as thick as Stel's. He was tan, not bronzy like Caid or as dark as Tristan. If he were human, he would be a mix of Caucasian and Latino ancestry. His hair was inky black, like his shadows. And those multi-colored eyes were hypnotizing if I stared into them for too long. He had chiseled cheekbones, a strong jaw, and perfectly symmetrical everything on his face.

As though I had no thought filter when it came to this male, I blurted, "Is this," I motioned toward his body, "your true form, or are you wearing some sort of glamour?"

He bowled over, laughing. After a few minutes of laughing his ass off, he finally composed himself.

"Oh, Kenzie, the things you say." He wiped away tears of laughter. "Yes, this is the form I was born with; although, I have many forms. You saw them earlier, my wraith."

"The black tentacle thing? The one that whipped out and tried to hurt Cerai?" I frowned at him, remembering what an asshole he was.

"Yes, that one. Cerai is fine. And no, I haven't hurt her or anyone else since." He smirked at me as though I was the ridiculous one for asking him not to hurt her.

"Wait, hold up. Why do you hurt her or anyone else that works for you?" I asked, ready for an argument.

"No need to get riled up. It's a demon thing. Demons respond to dominance. If I don't exert dominance, demons will want to challenge me." He waved his hand as though saying that was the end of that.

I wasn't buying it, but I could tell arguing with him about that topic was useless.

"Do you have other forms?" I asked, changing the subject.

"Yes, six," Dash said casually and poured more of the pink liquid for himself. "Demons of my rank are born with many forms depending on their lineage."

"How many forms can a demon have? The maximum?" I sipped my drink.

"Six," His eyes focused on my mouth as I licked the juice droplet off my bottom lip.

Just as I thought. "So, that tells me you're a powerful demon." I held his gaze as he nodded. "Then why can't you guide us through the gateway?"

He tipped his head back and laughed.

"I do love having you around," he leaned closer to me.

Uh oh. I shook my head. "You're avoiding my question. Besides, I have four mates."

"So, maybe if you gave me a chance, you'll find you only need one." His gaze heated, and my pulse quickened. I clenched my hand and dug my nails into my palms.

"Answer my question, Dash. Why can't you take us?" I kept my voice even.

"I could, but mostly . . . I don't want to. Traveling through gates diminishes my power. At the moment I cannot afford to do so. There are always power struggles along the border. The minute I leave my Circle, my people will be vulnerable. If there were no threat, I'd happily take you to your human realm and," he leaned back in his chair, "make myself at home there. Even then, it would take me considerable time to prepare."

Butterflies fluttered happily in my belly and pissed me off. This was not the time. Four men were more than enough. *No, Kenzie.* I took a deep breath.

"Hmm . . . you seem like a decent enough demon, but I have my own troubles. So, I guess I shall make a deal with another demon then." I finished my drink and grabbed the bottle for a refill, topping off his glass first, then mine.

"Tell me about your troubles, Kenzie," he said sincerely.

And so I did. I told him about the Rogue, baby mamas, Bear, and his family. While I talked, we drank two bottles of the pink bubbly and had a round of human-food appetizers. He was a good listener and offered sage advice. I told him about the guys, and my trouble with my Fae magic. It was as if someone had put a quarter in me, and I couldn't stop talking.

Once we finished eating, we stood to leave without paying. When I asked Dash how currency worked in The Dark Realm, he showed me what their money looked like, which was colorful, like Monopoly money. But since he owned the Circle, he didn't have to pay for anything anywhere. I asked him if the wait staff earned gratuities, and he said yes, but as the owner, that didn't apply to him. That was rude and pretentious, so I reached into his pocket, took out the wad of bills he had, and placed several demon dollars on the table, hoping it was enough.

His jaw dropped, and his eyes widened as I patted him on the chest and walked down the steps. At the bottom of the stairway, he had a big smile. "I . . . I don't know what to say," he said to me.

I placed the remaining wad of cash back into his pocket and shrugged my shoulders. He grabbed my hand and held it as we walked back to his place. Surprisingly, I wasn't wobbly on the cobblestones and didn't feel tipsy. Perhaps demon alcohol wasn't that potent. Then, I thought about it. Did the alcohol make me loquacious? I stopped mid-pathway and stared at him accusingly. "Was there something in that wine?"

"That wasn't wine, like the wine you're used to. It's fruit juice. I'll show you?"

"You took me out to give me non-alcoholic wine?" I started giggling. Of all things, that was just comical.

"I'm a demon, yes, but not a neanderthal. You are not one hundred percent healthy. Alcohol would be ill-advised until you've gained some weight back. And besides, it wasn't meant to be an official date. We'll do that another time." He ushered me through the wrought iron fence and down a path that wound around his manor.

Before I could comment about the date part, we stood in front of a large tree, so large it could have easily been a redwood tree in northern California. But it wasn't a redwood tree; it was something very different. It was a hundred feet tall and had huge pink fruit dangling from its branches. I placed my fingertips on the tree's large trunk and my Fae magic hummed.

Dash came up behind me and pressed his body against mine. My Fae magic surged inside of me.

"Your Fae magic likes it here," he whispered.

I shrugged, not entirely sure it was The Dark Realm that my magic responded to. "It's certainly stronger," I replied but didn't move away from Dash.

"We're closer to The Land of the Fae, so your magic would be. You're closer to your magic's source." His nose grazed my cheek, and lust simmered in my core.

Ooh, this was bad. I felt like a cheater. My body stiffened, and I sidestepped away from him. I turned to face him. He smiled down at me.

"This is what we were drinking, the signature fruit of the Fourth circle. Requiem." Dash held out his hand, and fruit dropped down into his palm. He extended it to me, and I reached for the fruit. It had a good weight to it and smelled sweet. The shape was very similar to a dragon fruit. "I'll have the staff make some for us tonight. As I said, it has many healing properties and will help restore your strength."

The fruit magically disappeared. Dash grasped my hand and walked me to the front door. "You are welcome to go anywhere with a guide, never alone, ok. The demons here are loyal to me and respectful, but I do have enemies, and they would love nothing more than to use you against me."

I nodded in compliance as we entered the entryway. "Thank you for everything." I walked away, needing space from Dash. It felt all too comfortable being close to him.

As I walked, I considered my options. I was nowhere near getting home, and Dash was being evasive. But we had to rely on him. There was no other choice. And that bothered me more than anything. I walked into my room and paced in the sitting area. Dash was being kind, but I didn't know enough about him to trust him implicitly. I almost wanted to leave and take my chances in the Fifth and Sixth Circles. Another look at the map could be helpful.

With that thought, I decided to find Gunnar. He wasn't in his room, so I searched for him and found myself back on the terrace.

Gunnar was nowhere in sight, and I hadn't seen another person or demon anywhere.

I stood on the terrace and appreciated the view. When I had awakened earlier, Dash said it was midday. It seemed as though time hadn't changed. The sun was still high against the light purple sky, and the air was cool and crisp. To my surprise, each step I took was sure-footed over the cobblestone path. It seemed whatever magic Dash had used was still with me. Each step felt as though I walked on even ground, and I didn't stumble at all. This would be a helpful trick to have at home.

The area I ended up in was nearly half a mile away from the terrace. I wasn't at shore level yet, but I found myself near an archway made up of white stone, which had been weathered with time. I accessed my mage sight and saw it pulsing with blue and pink magic that beckoned me.

In front of the arches were manicured hedges with yellow-orange snapdragons. The flowers were huge, the size of my palm. And they swayed hypnotically on the breeze. Their strong sweet scent was pervasive yet alluring at the same time.

At the archway, I peered at the maze. The hedges were no more than four feet tall and wound in twists and turns that seemed to go on for miles. I was intrigued and about to step in when I heard my name. I turned to face the voice and noticed a branch of flowers reaching out toward me. Curious, I raised my hand.

"No, Kenzie! Don't!" Dash cried out at the same time I grazed the flower with my fingertip. It was soft and velvety and razor sharp. I frowned at the blood that welled on my finger and slowly turned to face Dash, and then the ground rolled up and smacked me in the face.

CHAPTER 19
STELLAN

Kenzie had been missing for several weeks and everyone was at wit's end. She hadn't shown up in my dreams since the last time, which had been a few weeks ago. Admittedly, I wasn't sleeping well, nor were any of the other guys.

Erik had gone to the Mage's Emporium to gather every book he could find on the Underworld and Fae and then had brought them to the ranch. The four of us poured through the books. We hoped to learn more about gateways and the Underworld in general. And we all wanted to find out more about Kenzie's dreamwalking abilities.

Kenzie's father had yet to return from The Dark Realm. Granny continued tracking his progress, but that honestly didn't tell much aside from the fact that he was moving across the Sixth Circle. This was adding to the stress. Since knowledge of The Dark Realm was minimal we could only be patient and hope he'd return with his daughter soon.

To top that off, reports on missing supes and humans continued. There was no indication the Rogue was involved, which didn't make things any easier. I had several pack members working on it, and my brother had several vamps on the team.

I was struggling to maintain my sanity. Without my mate, I was a surly fuck. My wolf clawed at me from the inside, wanting to find her.

Caid, Brody, Erik, and I were in the living area at the ranch, reading through books about the demon realm. Erik had borrowed dozens of books from the Mage's Emporium, and we all helped him with the research. It was boring as fuck, but it gave us something productive to do until we could find a way into The Dark Realm.

Brody sat on the floor with a couple of books open, scribbling furiously on a notepad. Erik tapped a pencil on his temple, and his brow scrunched as he focused on the tome in front of him while Caid was laid out on the couch with a book covering his head. Usually, I'd be a pain in the ass and throw something at him to get him up, but sleeping was good for all of us. We had hoped Kenzie would dreamwalk again. She hadn't since our last interlude, which had been weeks ago. It made me worry about her. I hoped she was okay and getting adequate rest.

Suddenly, my brother sat upright, and his head whipped toward the front door. My nostrils flared, and I picked up the faint scent of a vamp getting closer. It was daylight still, which meant it was his baby mama.

"Fuck," he muttered.

I smirked. I was glad I didn't have to deal with the baby mama drama anymore. My mother confirmed Cristela's story with the lab directly. The paternity results had been altered, proving I was not the father. I was relieved. I was pissed, not because I wasn't the father, but because Chris put Kenzie through so much heartache. My parents had summoned her, but she had conveniently left town for personal reasons. Because she was with child, they weren't pursuing her. For the time being, there was nothing we could do. No one wanted to risk the unborn child's life to reprimand her. But she would have a lot to answer for once the baby was born, and Kenzie returned. In the meantime, I let the Alphas handle it; the situation didn't involve me anymore.

Caid dragged his ass to the front door to deal with Simone.

"What do you want?" he said as soon as he opened the door. Being polite had long left the building around here. He was all out of fucks to give; we all were.

"I want to make a deal. I help you, and you help me. Invite me in, asshole," Simone said in her heavily accented voice.

Caid led her into the foyer but no further.

Perhaps the other two guys and I should have given them privacy, but nobody moved. Erik glanced up, wearing a frown. Brody moved seats to get closer, and I pretended to be engrossed in the book in front of me.

"What do you need help with?" Caid crossed his arms over his chest.

Simone cocked her hip to the side and placed a hand on what used to be her waist. She was pissed about something.

"You're such an asshole. How your mate puts up with you is a mystery," she said.

"I don't have time for this," Caid growled.

She waved her hand in the air. "I heard your mate is in the underworld, and I know someone that could help."

Me, Brody, and Erik turned toward them. We were interested in what she had to say.

"I want to have a visitor," Simone glanced my way. "But we need help."

"What kind of help, Simone? And just cut to the chase," Caid told her. "You can have visitors anytime."

"Her name is Talia. I love her. She . . . she is my mate." Simone looked at the floor. "And she's a shifter."

Oh shit.

Caid looked at me. I scrubbed a hand down my face, not wanting to get involved, but if Talia was a shifter, specific protocols needed to take place.

Brody got up. "Simone, please have a seat. Can I offer you something to drink?"

"Finally, one polite male out of four of you." Simone sat down on a chair nearest to the door. "Thank you, I'm fine."

"Did you speak with the Alphas about this? I'm sure they would be happy to extend the pack's hospitality to your mate," I offered.

Simone shook her head. "It's not that simple."

I looked at Caid. This was not going to go well. I just knew it. Simone was from France and she hadn't mated with anyone here, thus it was likely Talia was from Europe. And some packs in Europe didn't play well with others.

"What pack does she belong to?" Caid asked her.

"Russian Federation," Simone said in a small voice.

"Fuck," Caid cursed.

I had to agree with him; the Russian Federation was the worst one of them all. The Alpha was nasty.

"The Alpha will have to petition for her to visit," I told her. "Once we have that, she is welcome to visit you."

"She's on her way. She boarded a flight an hour ago." Simone hung her head.

"Fuck on a stick, Simone. You better hope her Alpha doesn't give a shit about her." Caid started pacing.

"She's Alexi's daughter," she replied in a small voice.

Fuuucck. She was the Alpha's daughter. Could this get any worse? I pulled my phone out of my pocket and dialed my father.

"We have a situation. Do you have a minute?" I said as soon as he answered. "We're on our way," I replied.

"Dad's in the office. Let's hop in the truck," I told Caid and Simone while grabbing my keys.

We arrived at the pack office within ten minutes, and the staff lurked outside the conference room. Whoever was in there with my father had caused quite a stir.

"Alpha Sons," Helen, the office manager, greeted Caid and me. "Your father has a visitor. Perhaps you would want to wait in his office."

"Who's in there, Helen?" Caid smiled at the old lady.

"Umm . . . Christine." She averted her eyes.

I shrugged. I no longer cared about the wench.

The conference room door opened, and Chris stepped out, wiping tears from her eyes.

"Stellan, you must help me. I didn't mean to. I just wanted you to be the father," She sniveled.

I stood in front of her. "Christine Simpson, I abjure you. From this moment forward, you are nothing to me."

I shouldered past her into the conference room. Caid, Simone, Erik, and Brody followed behind me.

My father glanced at Simone, and a worried expression flashed across his face. *Yep, Dad, your two fully grown sons are coming to you with female problems.* Sometimes we were so pathetic.

"What is this all about?" my father asked after we were all seated.

"Simone's mate, Talia is on her way," Caid said. "She is the daughter of Alexi Korableva."

The Alpha growled.

"We just learned about this moments ago. According to Simone, Talia can summon a demon which may help us find Kenzie," I added.

"I'm sorry, Alpha. I miss my mate, and we, Talia and me, we didn't know what else to do." Simone kept her eyes on the floor.

My father closed his eyes, trying to calm himself. Alexi was a right bastard. This could be an all-out war if we didn't get ahead of the problem.

As if we didn't have enough shit to deal with.

"When is she expected to arrive?" my father asked in a deathly tone.

We all turned to Simone, who pulled out her phone and glanced at it.

"Her flight arrives in five hours," she replied.

"And you're sure she has a way to summon this demon?" he asked her.

"Yes, I saw the parchment myself. She'll summon the demon, no problems. We want to be together in exchange." Simone patted her belly.

"Well, obviously, her father is against your union, or she wouldn't be sneaking her way here. That being said, I cannot guarantee anything. I will petition her father, but if her father wants her back, she will return to Russia on the next flight," My father said in his Alpha tone.

Simone nodded.

"Give Helen Talia's flight info, and she'll see you get home safely."

Helen opened the conference room door as though she had been listening to his directives the entire time and ushered Simone out.

"Erik, do you have a way to soundproof a room?" the Alpha asked.

Erik made a few arcane gestures, then nodded.

"Aside from Kenzie, you two have the worse taste in women." He scrubbed a hand down his face. "You think summoning a demon would help you find your mate?"

"We can't go into The Dark Realm without a guide," Caid replied.

"Okay, I will have Talia brought here, we'll get this demon info, and then you four will go find your mate. I will deal with the Federation pack . . . after." He waved us off.

Me and the other guys sighed in relief.

"Oh, and boys, no more drama. Find your mate and get right," he added.

The four of us left the pack offices all smiles. Five hours. In five hours, we'd have a demon guiding us to The Dark Realm, where we'd find our mate and bring her home.

CHAPTER 20
DASH

My door flung open in the middle of an important meeting. I was about to lash out with my power when Cerai spoke, "Master, come quickly; the Mistress is nearing the maze," her words came out in a rush. "I couldn't keep up with her."

Fuck.

I dismissed the demon I had been meeting with and rushed toward the maze. Kenzie was there at the entrance, her hair flowing in the breeze. I was almost there. She placed one foot at the entrance, and I called her name. She paused and looked toward me. Then she looked at the insidious flowers. Oh shit.

"No, Kenzie! Don't!" I shouted.

But she did. She traced a finger along the deadly flower and frowned at her finger, then dropped to the ground.

I picked up her limp body as the poison spread up her hand toward her forearm, like dark thorny veins under her skin. I placed the finger that was pricked by the Dragon flora and sucked. Using all of my magic, I drew the poison out of her body and spat it on the ground beside me.

I repeated the process over and over again until the spread stopped. The thorny black veins under her skin stopped at her bicep. They didn't fade, though, and that scared me. Gunnar rushed to my side as I brought her back inside. Cerai told him what had happened while I focused solely on Kenzie. I took her to her room and laid her on the bed.

"Where's the healer?" I shouted. I had healing magic, but this poison was beyond my abilities.

"Here, Master. He just arrived," Cerai said.

In mere seconds, the elf appeared at Kenzie's door. "Did you suck out the poison?" he asked me.

"Of course," I snarled at Benedict. I knew he wasn't to blame, but my patience was short. I stepped to the side and let him examine her.

I did tell her not to wander around alone. Why was she so stubborn? She was also gorgeous and intelligent, and funny. I hadn't laughed in decades. But the little half-Fae made me laugh, genuinely laugh. I couldn't lose her.

"Is she going to be ok?" Gunnar asked beside me.

"Dragon flora, danger to all that comes in contact with it." Except for me, but I didn't say that out loud. Demons knew dragon flora was deadly and to steer clear. "Kenzie should be fine, I sucked out the poison, but she might need to recover for a day or two."

"Is there anything I can do?" Gunnar asked.

"Yes, stay away from the maze. If you need to go out, take Devon with you. Never go anywhere without an escort."

He nodded and left.

"It seems you have gotten rid of all the poison. There shouldn't be any residual left in her body. She should be fully recovered in a day," Ben said, then he looked at me. "Keep her comfortable and keep an eye on her hand. If the poison travels, call me. She is Fae. Her magic is strong and will protect her, but . . ." He shrugged his shoulders.

I understood what he left unsaid. My father had created these flowers, especially for his children. They were potent and deadly.

They were made to keep us safe, and that wasn't untrue. However, he'd created them to keep track of us and those around us. If Kenzie were an enemy, I wouldn't give two shits about the effects of the flower. But she wasn't; she was *mine*. If the poison had gotten deeper into her system, he would come for her, and that I couldn't allow.

After the healer left, Cerai offered to undress her. I waved her off and said I'd take care of it. Cerai refused to leave, saying it was unseemly and Kenzie wouldn't want me to. She was right, and it shocked me that she cared so much. Still, I wasn't leaving Kenzie's side. Finally, Cerai left only to return an hour or so later to bring in dinner. It sat at Kenzie's bedside. I had no desire to consume anything.

I watched the steady rise and fall of her chest. She looked utterly peaceful, but too still, as though she wasn't real. I pressed my palm to her forehead. Her temperature felt normal. I accessed my demon's sight and scanned her body. The poison hadn't receded, but it hadn't spread either. I scanned her body, looking for anything untoward, and stopped at her pelvis. I tilted my head and frowned. She couldn't bear children. I looked deeper at the issue and felt confident I could repair it. I'd have to discuss it with the half-Fae first. Scanning her body as I had was invasive enough.

She muttered something, and my gaze shot to her face. She squirmed a bit and looked tangled up in her dress. I should have had Cerai undress her. I could easily do it with my magic. But it'd be more satisfying using my hands.

Gently, I eased one sleeve down and then the other. Her nipples had been hard all day, making it difficult for me not to stare. It wasn't any easier now that her breasts were right in front of my face. I licked my lips, but ignored the urge. I covered her up with a sheet and slid the dress down past her hips, over her thighs and calves. My fingers lingered over her soft skin.

I laid the dress off to the side, then sat back and waited.

Nothing happened for some time, which was a good sign. Then suddenly, Kenzie thrashed, her body convulsing. I called for Benedict, who waited in my residence as I had instructed. He rushed to her side and said, "The poison! There must be another cut!"

He tore off the sheet exposing her nearly naked body. We turned her over as she convulsed in my arms. We didn't see anything on her body.

"Spread her legs," Benedict instructed, and I wanted to backhand him for suggesting such a thing. But he did it anyway, and he was right.

Between her legs, on her left inner thigh, just above her knee, was the tiniest trace of a cut from the dragon flora.

My heart spasmed. *How could I have missed this?*

I should have inspected her more closely. A sickly web of poison had spread from a tiny cut along her inner thigh. And it was growing.

Benedict held up a scalpel, ready to slice into her skin, but I gripped his hand and pushed him out of the way. I pressed my lips to her skin, drawing the poison into my mouth. I called it to me with my magic and pulled. Then I spat the venom onto the floor, where it sizzled on the tiles. Benedict jumped out of the way.

I repeated the process repeatedly, just as I had outside in front of the maze. The acidic poison hissed and sizzled as it hit the floor, but I didn't care. I kept at it until her blood was clean.

Benedict placed a hand on my back, signaling me to stop. "Enough, Master Dashiele. Enough. It's done. Now we wait. Her body has to fight it off on her own."

I gave him a stiff nod and glanced down at my sweat-drenched clothes. I almost felt human. The solid marble flooring beneath a bear skin rug from the human realm was in ruins. The poison had burned straight through. If Kenzie weren't Fae, it would have burned through her body in seconds. She had strong magic, for which I was grateful and concerned. He would be on his way. There was no doubt about it; the poison had been in her system for too long.

I picked her up and moved her into my private room, the only place in the Fourth circle where he couldn't break the wards. My father was coming.

CHAPTER 21

BRODY

Alpha Reese was pissed. "Find her." His voice was calm and deadly.

A group of five shifters headed out to do his bidding.

Stellan and Caid barely contained their rage, but their father ordered them to stand down. Well, he ordered all of us to stay put.

Simone's mate Talia had come to the ranch with a parchment that would summon a demon. We were excited to finally have something solid to help us get our mate back. But one minute, the parchment was there; the next, it was gone.

From what the Alpha could tell, it had been stolen. And the thief was Christine, Stellan's ex. She'd heard about our plans, snuck into Simone's rooms, and rifled through her and Talia's belongings. According to the shifters, the only scent in the room that didn't belong to Simone or Talia belonged to Christine.

The Alpha made us promise not to pursue the pregnant she-wolf. He was right to ask. We weren't in our right mind. We were too angry to deal with the matter delicately. Thus we reluctantly agreed and left the ranch, going our separate ways.

I arrived at the ranch house, our designated meeting spot, a few

110

days later. We had vowed to meet up once a week to keep ourselves in check. We needed the support. Stel was spending too much time in his wolf form, Caid was vamping out more than usual, and Erik was drinking himself to death. And I couldn't judge the others; I had my anger management issues to deal with and bloody knuckles to prove it.

Caid arrived shortly after me, and I could tell he hadn't slept. Stel in wolf form strolled in with a blood-stained muzzle. And Erik showed up staggering and slurring like he just came in from an all-night rave.

Fuck. How does Kenzie put up with us?

"You all need to sleep," I groaned and massaged my temples. This sucked. We needed Kenzie back soon.

"No, no, I have good news," Caid said and pulled a book out of a bag. It was wrapped in plastic; the leather cover was worn and weathered.

"Holy shit. Is that it? Where did it come from?" Erik slurred and reached toward it. Stel had shifted and smacked Erik's hand away from the book.

"It looks old and expensive. We need to handle it properly." Stel growled out. His voice was getting raspier, if that was at all possible. I wonder if that was a side-effect of being in his wolf form for too long.

"True, bro, too true. That's why I have this," Caid theatrically pulled out a notepad.

"Richard, my second, got a hold of this from a scholar. The scholar is a research geek and commissioned the book from my sire's library. The librarian gave it to the scholar, no questions asked and no conditions on return, which is why we now own it," Caid said proudly.

I could tell it was Caid's way of sticking it to his sire. I gave him a fist bump.

"The scholar said pages were missing, but these were all her notes. I read through it as soon as I got it, which was last night. And learned that the power of dreamwalking is a trait only known to be possible by Fae royalty. Perhaps our mate is a princess, after all. In any case, she has to be the one to reach out to her bonded. The stronger the bond, the easier for her to connect. And depending on the emotion, she can reach out physically." He looked directly at his brother when he said this.

"She did this. It happened." Stel rubbed the mark on his chest. "I'm not crazy."

"Well, I wouldn't go that far, bro. You've always been crazy." Caid smirked. "I haven't slept. I am going to bed now and will try to reach out. If we all do, we can connect at the same time, according to the text."

It was worth a shot. "You guys get some sleep. I want to read through the notes. Stel, seriously dude, take a shower." I said to them. Stel flipped me off and then went upstairs.

"Did it say anything about what it takes to be bonded?" Erik asked Caid.

"The Fae chooses," Caid replied. "There is magical mumbo jumbo that I don't quite understand. Perhaps you can make heads or tails of it." He slid the notebook over the counter to Erik. "I'm going to sleep at the Fort."

Erik hunched over and started to read the book; then, he shook his head. "I'm seeing double," he said with a lopsided grin and slid the book over to me. I nodded my head and started reading as he went upstairs to get some sleep.

The notes were a good outline of the book. As Caid described, dreamwalking was possible. That would be incredible if she could do that. The bonds were magical, something I didn't have. Stel and Caid had bonded with Kenz through their mate marks. And Erik had bonded with her through their magic.

I had to admit; I was feeling short-changed, not being magical. That was one of the things I loved about Kenzie; she never made me feel less than the others and always made me feel cherished just as I was. I went into the dining area and returned to work on the missing supes and humans. That was another shitshow. The disappearances were similar to what we had been dealing with when we'd known the knew the Rogue had been involved. Now though, the numbers were increasing. This could be a real problem if there were feral supes involved. How was that possible, though, if they needed Fae blood to do this? Did the Rogue have Kenzie hidden somewhere? Were there more Fae? The Alphas needed to get on top of this. And I would tell them so as soon as their sons were awake.

After some time, my body succumbed to exhaustion, and I passed out on the sofa and dreamed.

Kenzie laid there on the bed surrounded by white, looking as beautiful as ever. I stroked her cheek with my thumb and brushed my lips against hers.

Since she'd been gone I'd dreamed of her. This was different. Could it be a dreamwalk? No; if it were, she'd be awake right now.

"Come home Kenzie, please," I murmured in her ear.

Then her body went into spasms and she screamed in pain. I jumped back not sure what to do with this nightmare, and then an alarm went off in my ear.

I startled awake, panting and glanced at my screeching phone notifying me of an incoming message.

Granny: My son is home. Come now.

Her son was home, not Kenzie. She would have mentioned Kenzie if that was the case. I clenched my hands into fists and calmed my racing heart, recalling the nightmare.

The guys had been asleep for two hours. I decided to let them rest in case Kenzie reached out to one of them. I penned a short note, pinned it to the fridge, and teleported to the Jameson's.

I found Granny pacing in the library. Bear was sitting on the sofa, fretting. But there was no Mr. Jameson in sight.

"He's in the shower," Granny said, then she glanced behind me. "The others?"

"They needed to rest. We're hoping Kenzie makes contact," I said to her and patted Bear's shoulder as I walked by him.

Mr. Jameson showed up a moment later, so I explained what transpired with the dreamwalking and why I left them to sleep.

He nodded and said, "Good, the demon will be asleep for some time anyway."

"The demon is here?"

"Don't worry; he is perfectly contained and won't be awake until we wake him. Besides, he already agreed to rest here until we were all together to speak with him about the next plan."

Both Bear and I exhaled together upon hearing this news. Who kept a demon in the basement?

CHAPTER 22
KENZIE

The pain was so intense I passed out immediately. It started in my trigger finger, then traveled up my wrist, and then to my bicep. It seared my blood, burning my insides like battery acid, consuming every inch of me. Then, by the grace of all that was holy, it stopped.

I found myself floating in the abyss. At first, I felt nothing, no pain, no joy, absolutely nothing. *Was this what death feels like?* If I was dead, this wasn't so bad. But the absence of all sensation was empty. And I did not like it. I wanted to feel shivers of pleasure and the bite of pain again. I wanted to hear the sound of a raspy masculine voice. And feel the piercing sting of a fang bite. Or soft pillowy lips, caressing my own. Or the surge of magic that rose from my core and reached out to touch magic that was my equal.

Those sensations didn't come to me, though. The pain receded briefly, then overwhelmed me once more. It began in my leg, burning and crushing me internally. It squeezed and squeezed, and I was convinced my leg was about to be smashed into fine particles of blood, ligaments, and bone. I thrashed about, wanting to be free of whatever threatened to burn and crush me to death.

After some time, the pain reduced to a dull ache. I lay as still as possible, trying to catch my breath. The ache I felt in my arm and leg remained under the surface. Although it was no longer painful, there was something more sinister about it, like a foreign entity had entered my body and was biding its time.

Then it reared its ugly head, consuming me once again. I thrashed about, my skin feverish. The foreign presence burrowed deeper, evading my magic.

Help me! I screamed. Someone would hear me; someone had to. So I cried and called, begging for help.

Loving arms enveloped me, and soothing words were whispered into my ears.

"Shhh, love, I'm here. Shhh." Caid rocked me in his arms.

"Caid?" I whimpered. "Help me. I want to come home."

"I know, love, this is the best we can do for now. Open your eyes, love. I need you to focus. I need you to talk to me."

With a sharp intake of breath, I wriggled away from the menacing ache slowly digging deeper into me. My body tensed, and I panted.

"Get it away from me!" I screamed.

"Sweetness, look at me," Stel said in his raspy Alpha voice.

I blinked several times and focused on my wolf's handsome face. "Stel, don't let it have me. Please. It's coming."

Pain lanced at my insides as though it did not like being ignored. I wriggled free from his hold and convulsed under him.

"I'm here, sweetness. We're here," Stel said again. "Fuck, what the hell is going on," Stel muttered.

"It's either a spell or poison." Erik's voice reached my ears, but it was foggy. My eyes snapped open, and his face came into view. "I'm here, beautiful. We're here."

My guys were with me somehow. "Erik, help me. Please. It hurts."

His lips pressed against mine.

Pain scorched my insides this time. My skin scorched.

I felt something soothing reach into my core — Erik's magic. I sunk into it and reveled in his magical embrace. The sinister pain would not have it. It snapped at Erik's magic and flung him away. I bolted upright, worried about Erik.

He was on the floor of some dreamlike space. Oh fuck, I hope he wasn't hurt.

"Fuck me. It's dark magic. A demon is burrowed inside of her. We have to get it out," Erik said, getting to his feet.

"Sweetness! Focus. You are stronger than any demon, do you hear me?! Tell us how to find you," Stel said sternly.

My body spasmed.

"Damn it, Kenzie, fight it! You have to focus; tell us where you are."

I gathered my magic and screamed, forcing the dark magic back. The pain ebbed, but it lingered, waiting to attack once again. Somehow, I knew this was a brief reprieve. I only had a few minutes — if that.

"Fourth Circle." I panted and clenched my hands together, determined to remain focused on my guys.

"Good girl. Tell that fucking demon to back the fuck off; your mates are coming for you." Caid left a blistering kiss on my lips.

I was exhausted and barely coherent.

"Transfer magic," Erik said to Caid and Stel. "Pack magic and vamp blood. Hurry!"

Stel placed his lips to mine, and a flood of pack magic flowed into my body. His magic felt like a sweet elixir swimming through my veins. I welcomed it and allowed it to swallow me whole. I breathed in my wolf, taking everything he offered me.

The sinister poison receded farther, leaving my body. When I could no longer feel the wicked poison, my body relaxed with relief.

"It worked," I smiled against Stel's lips and kissed him. His lips tangled with mine. I ran my hands through his beard and his hair. I was desperate to feel him again. I missed my wolf; tears flowed down my cheek.

Stel pulled away from me and said, "Take some of Caid's blood, sweetness. It will help heal you."

I whimpered, feeling empty without him against me. But Caid took his place, branding me with hot kisses all over my lips and neck. His tongue flicked over his mark on my neck, and I moaned with pleasure.

"Drink, love." Caid pressed his wrist to my lips, which were already flowing with blood.

Caid's blood was warm, thick, and sweet like honey. I drank greedily, breathing through my nose. He kissed and licked the mark on my neck. I moaned around his wrist and rolled my hips. He settled between my legs; then he kissed down to my breast and over the tender area where Stel had bitten me in my dreams. His hard length pressed on my bare pussy. I reached down to grip his cock. He groaned and palmed my breast with his free hand.

Desperate to be connected to my mate, I drew away from his wrist and said, "Fuck me, please."

Caid didn't waste any time. He plowed into me, and I screamed his name. He pumped into my wet cunt, stretching me wide to accommodate his girth. He gripped my hips and buried himself so deep I thought he would split me in half. He latched onto the mark on my neck, and I came, shattering into a million pieces. He kept pumping into me until his seed coated my inner walls.

"I love you, Kenzie. Stay safe; we're coming for you." Then he slipped away.

No! I wasn't ready to wake up.

"I'm here, gorgeous," Erik said, lining up with my core.

I moaned against his lips. He slid inside me, nice and slow, his lips adhered to mine. He whispered he loved me repeatedly as his cock filled me deeply. He reached into me with his magic.

Our magic collided together the way it had on the beach. He pulled me onto his lap and allowed me to ride him while his magic did delicious things to my clit and nipples.

My greedy cunt squeezed his cock, milking him for all he was worth. He came hard, and I came harder. My hips rocked over and over his hard length, prolonging our climax.

"I love you, Kenz. Hold on. We're on our way." Erik crushed my body to him, then he faded away.

I slumped on the bed, feeling so alone, until the bed dipped behind me.

"You didn't think I'd let you get away from me that easily, did you?" my wolf said over my shoulder.

I leaned back and wrapped an arm around his neck. "You wouldn't dare if you knew what's good for you."

He chuckled and kissed me all over my shoulders and neck. He pushed my body forward and forced me to all fours.

"You are so beautiful, Kenz. I miss you so much," he said as he ran his fingers gently through my folds.

I looked over my shoulder to see him gazing lovingly at my cum-drenched pussy. He leaned in and licked, which was all kinds of dirty, even in this dreamlike state. But I was all for it; I rocked my hips back, pushing his face deeper into my core. Stel sucked me whole, his lips devouring my cunt, then his tongue separated my lips and teased at my entrance.

I came again, squirting all over his face. He moaned, the sound vibrating over my pussy.

He pressed my upper body to the mattress and threaded his massive cock into my tender, well-fucked cunt. I gripped the sheets and gasped. My hair was plastered to my sweaty face. Stel drove his cock into my pussy hard. I wanted it harder. I begged for more, and I moaned his name over and over. His unrelenting thrusts gave me everything I asked for.

Stel wrapped my hair around his fists, pulled me up, and latched onto the mark he'd left on my shoulder. My muscles tightened around his enormous cock, and I came again, stars clouding my vision. He continued to fuck me through my orgasm until he came with me.

We both collapsed down to the mattress, breathing hard. I held him tight. "Don't go, Stel. Please stay."

"I'm here, sweetness," Stel said and rolled to the side, his cock softening inside me.

I held onto him, refusing to let him go. "Where's Brody?"

"He's taking care of things. He loves you and misses you; we all do." Stel pressed his lips against my neck.

Caid joined us on the bed and snuggled to the front of my body.

"Where'd you go?" I asked Caid as I ran my fingers through his hair.

"Not far. Someone had to keep watch," he whispered. "It's ok, we're here. Well, except Erik. I think he might be having problems with magical stamina. And Brody, as Stel said, is dealing with a few things."

"Is this real?" I asked.

"You've pulled us into a dreamwalk, sweetness. Your Fae magic can do this because we are bonded to you," Stel replied.

"Are you all ok? Tell me everything," I said in a rush.

"Don't worry about things here. We're ok. We need you back." Stel's warm breath brushed my shoulder, making me shiver.

"We're coming for you, love," Caid said. "Just stay alive."

I nodded, with one arm gripping Caid around his neck and the other wrapped around Stel behind me. I held on tight, refusing to let them go.

Stel growled, and his chest rumbled against my back. "He's here."

Caid's nostrils flared, his eyes blacked out, and his fangs flashed. Alerted to danger, I jolted awake.

CHAPTER 23

KENZIE

I sat up in an unfamiliar bed. A cool breeze floated in through an open door, and I gathered the fluffy white comforter closer to my chest.

"You're awake," Dash said to the left of me. He sat in a chair beside the bed with his right ankle resting on his left knee. He wore pajama bottoms and no shirt. His muscular torso was on full display. His dark hair was completely disheveled, as though he had just woken up or had run his hand through it several times.

I averted my eyes away from his naked torso. "How long was I out?"

"Three days. You were poisoned by a plant. I'm not sure if you remember, but I did say not to explore alone. I wasn't suggesting that to control you or to watch your every step. I was doing that to protect you." His voice was laced with tension.

I put on my humble pie face. "You were right, and I was wrong. I had no idea. Thank you for taking care of me."

He nodded, his eyes reflecting worry. Were there side effects of the poison? I was about to ask when he stood abruptly. "You need to

121

eat. Fortunately, we were able to keep you hydrated through magical means, but you still need more nutrients. The bathroom is through there," he pointed behind me.

I glanced back to where he had pointed and asked, "Where are we?"

"My private room. Yours got ruined." He handed me a robe.

Why am I naked?

I frowned at him while slipping on the robe and then stood on shaky legs.

Dash held out a hand to support me. I waved him off, then went to the bathroom. Three days was a long time to be out. The poison must've messed me up.

This place was a nightmare; I couldn't wait to see my guys again. I thought about the intense dream I'd had. Being with them in the dreamscape felt so real. I wanted to touch myself, but Dash was right outside. In record time, I finished in the bathroom and returned to the room wearing the robe.

A sliding door opened to a veranda, where Dash was overlooking the view. He saw me approach and motioned for me to sit at the table covered with breakfast-looking goodies. His forehead was scrunched up in a worrisome frown. Something was troubling him. I wanted to smooth the lines with my fingertips. But he still hadn't put on a t-shirt, and I was naked under the fluffy robe. Physical contact was not a good idea.

He turned away from me to pour a couple of glasses with pink liquid. With his back facing me, I saw the ink on his back. Like mages back home, those tattoos looked like brands.

"Runes for various things," he said as he sat down.

He must've noticed the confused look on my face. "The brands on my spine are runes," he explained as he sat next to me.

I nodded and asked, "Did we sleep together?"

He snickered, "Yes, but don't worry, I was the perfect gentleman."

"Who undressed me?

"I did, but again, I was the perfect gentleman. I didn't even look." He grinned. "Ok, maybe I peeked."

I scowled at him and was about to give him a tongue-lashing about manners when a bell interrupted us.

"Eat, Kenzie." He stood and went to attend to whatever or whoever rang the bell.

I was starving and could tell I had lost more weight. The food he had prepared was a typical breakfast of eggs, bacon, and waffles. I ate till I was bursting. I drank more requiem fruit juice and started to feel better.

After eating, Dash hadn't returned, so I got up to take in the view. The sounds of waves crashing against the shore filled the silence. The landscape was filled with dense trees but no colorful flowers like the area around the terrace or the maze. I shuddered, thinking about that damn flower, and went inside the room.

The demon hadn't returned yet, so I searched for clothes. Dash was a clothes whore. Everything he had was finely tailored suits, which had reminded me of Stel. I hadn't found anything casual, so I pulled on a long-sleeved button-down shirt and used a tie to wrap around my waist like a belt. I realized then that my dagger was gone. Fuck. I rushed out of the closet to see Dash sitting at the edge of the bed.

"I was curious to see what you'd choose to wear out of my closet." The corners of his lips turned up.

"Sorry, I figure it would be better for me to wear this than to walk around in a robe."

"This is your room now, Kenzie." He pointed behind me to another open door, a closet with women's clothing. I saw something glint on the shelf and walked toward it. My dagger. I hugged it to my chest and sighed with relief.

"Thank you for returning this to me," I said. Fuck, I was thanking this demon a lot. And that probably wasn't a good thing.

"What do you want?" My brows scrunched together. "You've been awful kind. There must be a price."

"Very perceptive. I am a demon, after all, and we do like to make deals. It's our nature." He leaned back on the bed, propping himself up on his elbows. His gaze roamed over my body. Heat pooled in my core. *No, Kenzie.*

"Well?! Out with it. What do you want?" I insisted.

"I don't want anything; well, ok, I do. But not in the way that you might think. You intrigue me, and I want to get to know you better. However, I won't force or hold you here against your will."

He stalked closer to me, his gaze held mine, and said, "I believe in fate, Kenzie. I believe you and I are intertwined somehow. I don't have the answers yet, but those will come. I shall remain patient and assist you as best as I can. And one day, perhaps you will indulge me. But not yet. Your heart and soul are elsewhere." He placed a finger under the collar of my shirt and slid it down to my newest mark.

My breath hitched, and I stepped away from him.

He smiled at me, then said, "As much as I like seeing you in my clothes, you should probably change. But this is where you will sleep until you leave, Kenzie. The poison had to be sucked out of your body, and I spat it on the floor. That room must be renovated before anyone sleeps there again."

"That poison must be potent to cause damage to, what was it? Marble flooring?"

"Yes, on both counts. Marble flooring. And," he scrubbed a hand down his face. "The poison is lethal, Kenzie. If your mates didn't intervene, you wouldn't be here right now."

"But I'm safe here?" I tilted my head to the side.

"Of course, if I wanted to take advantage of you or kill you, I would have done it by now." He turned and walked back out to the veranda.

I dressed quickly, and Dash took me out to see Gunnar. I thought we'd be walking down long dark corridors again, but instead, he wrapped an arm around my waist, and we teleported to his library.

"Kenzie, fuck, I was worried. That plant was awful." Gunnar hugged me.

"Yeah, and I barely touched the damned thing. Sorry, what did I miss?" I stepped back from his embrace.

Dash turned me around to face him before Gunnar could answer and placed a searing kiss on my lips. My brain short-circuited, and my lips parted for his tongue.

Gunnar coughed behind me and brought me back to my senses.

Dash didn't release me immediately, though. He kissed and nipped my lips, then my jaw, and ran a tongue over Caid's mark on my neck. My knees buckled. He held me steady and pressed his forehead to mine. "I have a business to tend to. Stay away from the maze and take an escort if you leave."

I nodded, then Dash was gone.

Gunnar bopped me on the forehead. "Kenzie, I am happy you and the big scary demon are getting along, but we got things to do, come on."

I followed closely behind him to the front doors, where Devon, one of the staff members, had been waiting. He didn't look anything like Cerai or Dash. Devon had stringy, long, dark hair that touched his flat bottom. He was skin on bones, this one, with elf-like ears and webbed fingers.

Devon guided us to The Pub. Once inside, our demon guide nodded at Gunnar and went straight to the bar counter. Gunnar and I continued through the bar, passing a couple of unoccupied high-top tables, and chose a corner table that gave us privacy to speak.

Despite being empty, Gunnar kept his voice low, "Devon is very loyal to Dash, but he has introduced me to others that have been quite forthcoming. Today marks the full moon cycle when the full moon rises and sets simultaneously here as in the human realm. A portal will open nearby, and we're taking it to get home."

My jaw dropped. This was indeed the best news we could've hoped for, what we had been waiting for.

"Well done, Gunnar. Sorry for leaving this all in your hands. But you didn't need me, anyway." I gave him a small smile.

"You've been more helpful than you realize. With you laid up,

Dash was glued to your side, allowing me to make arrangements." He smiled and tipped his head in thanks as Devon delivered two pints to our table.

Our conversation halted until the demon got back to the bar.

"Please tell me you didn't make a deal with a demon," I asked eagerly.

"Didn't need to. There is a nightclub here where the portal will open. Demons go in and out this one night. We just need to get there."

"How will we do that without Dash noticing?"

"We have thirty minutes until it opens." His chin tipped to a clock that hung on the wall. It was different from a human realm clock. I looked at it sideways and wondered what was so different, and then I realized there were more numbers on this one than the clocks we had back home.

"Don't worry. I learned how to tell time here. You should try this." He took a swig of his beer and then wiped his mouth with the back of his hand.

I'd never acquired a taste for beer, so I had no intention of trying the demon variety. Then I thought about it; what the hell, how many could say they'd had a beer in The Dark Realm? I took a sip and grimaced. Yep, still disgusting. I pushed it away from me.

Gunnar chuckled. Then with a more serious tone, he said, "Kenz, Dash is not as he seems. He had to have known about this portal, but he never mentioned it. He intends to keep us here. Or you, anyway. He isn't about to let you leave, no matter what he may have said or promised."

I contemplated his words and couldn't refute any of them. I had no proof of it one way or another, but I had suspected Dash's kindness had strings attached. The demon hadn't denied it when I confronted him. Still, a twinge of disappointment sat like lead in my belly.

Acts of kindness like the one he'd shown us would have been

sweet had it been given freely. It shouldn't have mattered. Yet, it did. Although I had four men waiting for me at home, I wanted Dash's generosity to be something more. Not just another deal for the already successful and powerful demon.

CHAPTER 24
STELLAN

Dreamwalking with our mate gave us the hope we needed to hang on. My wolf was still bloodthirsty, but not nearly as much. Or perhaps I had better control. The constant ache in my chest from Kenzie's absence was ever-present. I did my best to occupy my time, and there was plenty to do.

Caid had allowed Richard, his second, to handle most things at Scarlet, which was good news for all of us. For one thing, we didn't have to worry about him losing himself to blood rage. And we hadn't needed to ask his sire for help to find Kenzie. We were working hard on other avenues to get into The Dark Realm. Nothing had worked yet, but we maintained hope.

Erik had gotten better but not great. Being with Kenzie for that short moment had knocked some sense into him. But, he had a tough time shaking his dependency on alcohol. He settled for human whiskey, which helped some. Going without alcohol gave him the shakes, so he opted for the weaker human stuff. We all stayed at the ranch most of the time, which helped us monitor his alcohol intake. Erik was often found with his nose buried in books. He was busy studying anything we could find about Fae magic, The Dark Realm, and demons. He was brainy when his brain wasn't swimming in booze.

Brody was a trouper. He missed Kenzie and hadn't connected with her, which had to sting. I felt sorry for the dude. But he pressed on, not missing a beat. We'd be lost without him. He tracked a feral outbreak in Canada. We all went up there to handle that situation and weren't needed at all. The feral vamps and shifters had turned on themselves. It was gruesome, and we'd witnessed it all first-hand.

The primary focus was getting into The Dark Realm, but we couldn't ignore the missing supe situation. We assembled a team of shifters and vamps to help us with this mess. It seemed the Rogue was behind all disappearances, but he was nowhere to be found. We had assumed he was in The Dark Realm with Kenzie, but that meant someone else was continuing his insane experiments. The entire situation had us all worried.

Mr. Jameson was back. Whatever he had gone through down there messed with his head, and he needed a few days to heal. As soon as Mr. Jameson could focus, he mapped out the details of the Fifth and Sixth Circles. He even pinpointed two potential gateways. And with the news about Kenzie being located in the Fourth Circle, the Jamesons had sent their demon to search for her. The demon had said access to that Circle wasn't freely given, but he was working on it. That didn't sit well with us, but we didn't have a choice.

Thankfully, we were resourceful.

Through my shifter contacts, I got word of a potential portal that would open up tonight at the Catacombs, a nightclub in The Majestic of all places. Once a year, on a full moon, a demon portal opened on the fifth floor of the Catacombs. We knew that floor was only accessible to demons; we didn't know it was a portal. Fucking Majestic. What the hell were they thinking?

Thanks to Bunny, Kenzie's friend, we got VIP access at the last minute.

The guys and I were often in different places, even though the ranch was our home base. As soon as I received news about this portal, I texted them the information.

Erik was at the mage library in Switzerland. Brody was in Canada, investigating some leads from the feral outbreak. I had been dealing with a supe situation in North Carolina. And Caid was at the Jameson's in Scotland. This portal situation in the Majestic was a top priority and something we needed to do together. We took care of the things we had been dealing with and used our new teleporting gadgets to get to Vegas.

How we had managed without magic tech portals before was mind-boggling. We were teleporting all over the place, managing a million different things. And today, it sure as hell came in handy. I heard about the portal midday, and we scrambled to get everything worked out. We weren't letting this opportunity slip past.

Caid, Brody, Erik, and I teleported to Kenzie's penthouse at The Majestic. The sun was setting, and I took my time looking around, soaking up the memories. The last time I was here, Kenzie had kicked us out. It wasn't my finest moment, but damn, she was fierce and sexy as fuck when she was pissed. I smiled as I took my stuff upstairs to settle in her room. My wolf got pissy if we weren't sleeping in her bed, whether here, at the ranch, or with the Jamesons. The guys weren't going to argue with my wolf, thankfully. Kenzie would be pissed if my wolf bit anyone. Her scent was more pungent here than in other places. I breathed in deeply. It made me miss her more; the ache in my chest throbbed.

I strolled downstairs to see the guys digging into boxes of pizza. None of us ate anything remotely healthy while Kenz was gone. Dudes just couldn't be trusted to care for themselves when their woman was away.

Despite bonding over pizza and beer — water for Erik, tensions were riding high and we all knew much was at stake. We were planning a demon hunt.

"Do you remember when Kenzie threw us out the door with her badass magic?" my brother asked me.

I smiled at his attempt to lighten the situation and at the memory. I nodded my head, "Remember? I can still feel it."

The guys laughed while my brother and I retold the tale of Kenzie's wrath. It was funny because she was so small and precious. Bringing up the memories made us miss her all the more. I reached for a bottle of whiskey. Erik drank a little while the rest of us drank a lot. It was human whiskey, though. It would take cases to render Caid or me useless. The other two, well, I kept an eye out. Especially on Brody. We'd all witnessed what a mess he was after he had too much of that purple wine stuff Kenz loved so much. And she wasn't here to nurse him until he sobered.

Before leaving for The Catacombs, we went over our simple plan. Find a demon to get us into the portal, take us to Kenzie, and haul ass back home. The challenge was nabbing a demon and getting him or her to comply. It was worth a shot.

The Catacombs were crazy crowded as usual. We bypassed the long line and continued downstairs. I paused on the third floor and recalled our last time with Kenzie. She was an incredible woman and so fucking hot. What I wouldn't give to have her here with me now. Caid patted me on the back and nodded. He was feeling nostalgic too. It had been an unforgettable night.

We bypassed the fourth floor, and waltzed onto the fifth floor. Demon territory.

The intel on the fifth floor was sketchy. My source was a lion shifter with a particular penchant for the dark side. Good ole Gareth loved him some succubus sex. Hey, everyone had their kink. I wasn't going to judge. He said the fifth floor was more or less a sex lounge, except for special events. The layout constantly changed depending on the occasion. Bunny confirmed this info and said the hotel had nothing to do with the special events here.

Furthermore, there were no cameras. I had Clay confirm that tidbit. He said people often tried to take videos from their phones, and the footage was deleted or completely blacked out when they replayed it.

Thus we had no idea what to expect. Typically, I'd like to have a strategy in place that included access points and exits. And backup plans in case things went tits up. But . . . we had no time to prepare for this, and the next event like it wouldn't happen for another year. Fuck that. For Kenzie, the reward far outweighed the risks.

As soon as we crossed the entrance, my supernatural senses perked up. My wolf sensed demons and was ready to claw his way out. He knew as well as I did what the goal was, so he sulked just under the surface. Sometimes he was an obedient pup.

Red neon lights flashed off and on in the dark room. A stage, or what one might call a runway for fashion shows, started at the back wall and ended almost at the halfway point of the club. It was twenty-five feet long and about four feet off the ground. Approximately eight feet from the runway were rows of booths on either side. The booths sat on a raised platform, giving patrons a higher vantage point to see the stage. Most booths were occupied, and the bar was six people deep. The place was jam-packed.

Mirrors covered the back wall, and the floor beneath it was covered in smoke. Laser lights flickered to the beat of the heavy metal music. It looked like a hokey magic show. I'd be pissed as fuck if my contact was wrong about this.

The hostess led us to a table located in the middle of runaway. A waitress sauntered to our table with a tray of glasses and a bottle of whiskey. I dismissed her after she set the bottle service on our table. We had a good view of the stage, but we'd be boxed in if things went awry. I was about to voice my concerns when the music cut out, and the place started to change.

A deep loud bass, thumping like a heartbeat, roared through the speakers. And then the chanting began. It wasn't a language I understood, but it reminded me of Gregorian Chant, perhaps Latin. The stage retracted on itself. Smoke drifted all around the club, increasing the ominous vibe. The ground rumbled, and the earth split where the runway had been. The crowd cheered and clamored toward to glowing pit in the ground. Men and women shifted into their demon forms.

Caid, Brody, Erik, and I stood in our booth, ready for anything. My wolf growled in my chest. Caid was vamped out. He flashed his fangs. Christ, he was scary. Magical sparks ran up and down Erik's arms. Brody was cool, calm, and collected. His eyes were trained on the spectacle before us. Either he didn't realize the danger, or he had utterly lost his mind. I refocused on the horror show while keeping a side-eye trained on the human we were responsible for.

My brother and I had trained together since we were boys. We fought each other and fought together, which made us a great team. We were able to track each other despite the chaos around us. We had both agreed to keep a close eye on Brody. Although the human proved to hold his own, the fact was; humans were delicate. And I had made a promise to my mate to keep him safe.

Demons shrieked and jumped into the split earth. The floor beneath our feet shook. The earthquake seemed to go on for hours when maybe it had been only minutes. Abruptly, the rumbling stopped. The hole in the ground closed, and everything went silent again.

Moments later, blinding light exploded from the back wall, making me squint. When the bright light dimmed, a silhouette stood at the center. It was a tall humanoid form with large wings at its back and horns sticking out from its head. And it spoke in a razor-sharp voice that hurt my ears,

"The portal is now open!"

The crowd roared, and the music began again, a mixture of trap music and Gregorian chant. The crowd danced as several demons passed through the flaming gateway. One after the other, they walked out of the portal.

There were so many. I anticipated a dozen at the most, but more than twice that amount came through. Worse yet, the portal would remain open for at least another ten minutes.

I poured a shot of whiskey for all of us. We raised our glasses, clinked them together, and went to work. We decided to pair off Caid, and Erik would take one side of the bar, and Brody and I would take the other. Our job was to find two or three potentials. Once we acquired our candidates, Erik would cast a spell to bind their powers. It was common knowledge that demons lost half their magical powers when they crossed through. Still, we planned to be careful.

We got a few feet from the booth when the demon yelled, "Stop!"

The room went eerily quiet.

Then suddenly, Brody broke free of the crowd and yelled, "Kenzie!"

CHAPTER 25

KENZIE

Thirty minutes seemed to go on forever. The thought of getting through a portal that would lead us home had me all kinds of anxious. My bouncing knee must have grated on Gunnar's nerves because we left five minutes early. We snuck out of the pub and left an intoxicated Devon behind.

The appointed location had an unassuming storefront. It looked nothing like a nightclub; it looked more like a convenience store. We passed aisles of packaged snacks, drinks, and various things and went toward a refrigerated section. Nothing looked familiar, and I had guessed the contents; although, it didn't quite matter. We were heading home. Excitement bubbled up in my belly, and I had to remind myself to breathe.

Gunnar opened the refrigerator door and pushed on the shelf that held bottled beverages. Once the rack was out of the way, it opened to a narrow corridor. I stayed close on his heels as he led me down a narrow pathway lit by fluorescent lighting that annoyingly flickered off and on. We walked for some time, making me nervous that we'd miss our mark. "Don't worry. I timed it so we won't miss it," Gunnar said, reading my mind.

When we finally came to a stop, we found ourselves in a tiny room filled with demons. There was music up ahead and many voices talking at once. I absently reached for my dagger with a sweaty palm. Tension rolled up and down my spine. I inhaled and exhaled slowly, trying to relax as we followed the slow-moving crowd.

The music got louder, and a bright light signified we were getting closer to the portal. I gripped Gunnar's elbow, and he placed his other hand over mine, assuring me.

I peered over shoulders and heads in front of me to see demons going through the portal. One by one or two by two, demons stepped on the platform and were sucked into the bright light. I truly hoped this was a gateway to the human realm. It would so suck if we got transported to another planet.

Almost there, I squeezed Gunnar's arm. He reached for my hand and held it tight. We were in this together, and I couldn't be more grateful. I had relied on him implicitly. How would I have survived without him?

Gunnar positioned us so we had stepped up to the platform together. Another step and were sucked into the portal. Vertigo overcame me, my stomach lurched, and my vision swam. Gunnar looked like he was experiencing the same effects, but I held fast to his hand.

"STOP!" A loud razor-sharp voice screamed and brought us to our knees. The world went quiet.

Footsteps approached my and Gunnar's prone forms. I shook my head, trying to clear the fog.

"Well, well, two humans trying to escape hell . . . isn't this interesting," the demon said.

I looked up and saw a tall demon looming over us. *Well, shit, this wasn't good.*

Gunnar and I stood simultaneously, meeting the demon's gaze. He circled us, and we circled with him, keeping him at our front.

The demon laughed, "I'm sure your demon Master will pay dearly for you two."

Fuck this. I pulled my dagger at the same time Gunnar called his sword. We were fighting our way out.

The demon tipped his head back and laughed. Gunnar and I separated, allowing us to surround him. He may have been powerful, but we had each other. And home was just on the other side of what I had noticed to be a stage.

"You think those measly human weapons will harm me?" He swiped at Gunnar with extended claws. Gunnar ducked a few blows. They exchanged swings, both of them missing. Gunnar was fast, but the demon was toying with him. Then Gunnar launched his sword right into his gut. It passed right through him as though he was nothing but air.

The demon laughed again. Gunnar swung his sword rapidly, each strike passing right through the demon. While the demon stood there and laughed, I took advantage of the distraction and got in several slices. My magical dagger hit its mark. The demon's skin oozed black, steaming blood. He looked down at his wounds and fixed me with a menacing glare. "Fae blade," the demon snarled, then launched at me.

He came at me with his claws swinging wildly. I dodged his attacks and countered, slicing and stabbing every chance I got. The demon was much larger than me and taller than any of my guys, but he was slow. My combat magic flared to life, making me faster and more agile. Each strike cut deep, causing more of his black blood to pour off his body. He launched a fireball at me at close range, which I barely managed to roll and duck under. Gunnar hit him with several spells that took the demon off his feet. The demon lashed at him with his tail and then slammed him with a force of magic, knocking the wind out of his lungs.

The demon faced me with a feral glint in his eyes and came at me with unrelenting force. I was able to shield my body while backing away from the assault, but I couldn't get in a counterstrike. Then a familiar voice shouted my name. I lost my footing and glanced in the direction of Brody's voice and saw him running to the stage. Gunnar was on his feet and had kept the demon busy . . . or so I thought.

I ran toward Brody. He was so close. I extended my hand through the barrier while he reached toward me. Our fingertips touched.

Gunnar yelled, "Duck!" I dropped to the floor, and Brody did as well, dodging a stream of fire that went through the barrier. *Fuck.* Anything from this side of the portal could get out, which meant I needed to keep the assault aimed away from my mate. He was only human, after all.

Fire came at me, and I reached into my Fae magic and sent it right back. The demon was crafty; he'd switched to hellfire. It was a neon blue flame, and my Fae magic had no defenses against it.

I ran farther from where I had last seen Brody, keeping the demon focused on me. We exchanged magical blows. The demon deflected a stream of fire, which went wide. I anxiously wasted precious moments searching for Brody when Gunnar barreled into me, saving me

from more hellfire. *Fuck that was close.*

"Oh, halfling, this has been the most interesting Moon night in centuries. I think I will keep you to myself," the demon hissed.

Gunnar and I scrambled backward, then rolled apart, just missing another stream of hellfire. I got to my feet and fired off a force of magic that made the demon stagger.

At the other end of the stage, I noticed my wolf and my vamp running full-force into an invisible shield, trying to get to me. My magic man was firing all his magic at the barrier, trying to create a hole. I could get to them, but they couldn't get to me. The portal was an exit only.

I summoned my power, ready to deliver the killing blow when the demon sent a force of magic that knocked me off my ass.

My breathing was labored, and I struggled to my feet. Gunnar helped me up. I glared at the demon who was smirking at me.

"Concede, halfling, and I won't kill your friends." A ball of hellfire hovered above his claws.

"Fuck you!" I spat and hurled everything I had at him. He met my magic with his. It was a battle of wills, and my muscles strained with effort. *Fuck, he was strong.*

An earth-shattering roar came from the demon side of the portal. Startled, both of our magics winked out at the same time.

"Your demon Master is here to collect you. And I hate that arrogant shit, so I'll kill you . . ."

Before he could finish that statement, I sent a stream of fire right at him. The quick fucker deflected my fire as though he was swatting away a fly. He sent my fire off the

stage and through the invisible barrier. I panicked and stood there, praying it wouldn't hit my mates. Thankfully it soared high into the air missing the patrons of wherever we were.

While I was distracted, the demon sent his hellfire right at me. I hadn't realized what was coming toward me until I noticed the frightened look that fell over Stel's handsome

face. Intense heat from the hellfire came straight at me and threatened to burn

me alive.

Paralyzed with fear, I watched everything happen in slow motion.

With a whoosh of air, the hellfire was redirected mere inches away from consuming me and blazed across the stage, through the invisible barrier, then slammed into my beautiful

brown-eyed human. Brody let out a gut-wrenching scream as the flames consumed

him. His flesh burnt to ash in mere seconds.

Devastated, I fell to my knees. My body heaved as I screamed.

CHAPTER 26
KENZIE

I rubbed my eyes, trying to remove the crust of tears that had formed overnight. *Brody.* Tears fell again, and I buried my head in the soft pillow. Pillow? I had no recollection of falling asleep on a bed. That should have been worrisome, but my heavy heart weighed me down.

"Hi," Dash said beside me.

I hid my face in my hands and sobbed as reality set in. This wasn't home, and I hadn't made it out of The Dark Realm. I was in Dash's bed, and Brody was gone.

"I'm sorry, Sis," Gunnar said.

"Is . . . is he gone?" I turned to face him. Gunnar nodded, and his eyes shifted to the floor.

I lay there in a fetal position and sobbed. "No, not Brody."

The bed dipped, and Dash pulled me in for a hug. I let him hold me for a moment, then got off the bed and went into the bathroom. I closed the door, turned on the shower, sat on the shower floor, and cried until the water ran cold.

Dash entered the bathroom, turned off the running water, and wrapped me in a large towel. My body shivered. My skin covered with goose flesh, but I didn't care. He carried me into another room and sat in front of a roaring fire with me on his lap.

"Kenzie." He kissed the top of my head, the gesture was kind, yet it made me uncomfortable. My love was gone, and the intimacy with this stranger felt inappropriate.

I wiggled free of his embrace, but he held me tighter. "I'm sorry for your loss. I . . . I didn't mean to. I deflected the hellfire away from you and your mate ran right into it. I'm so sorry."

Dash held me, and I relaxed against his body for a moment. "It's not your fault. I don't blame you and don't want you to blame yourself either."

He nodded, and then carried me to the bedroom where Gunnar still waited.

Once snuggled under the covers, I reached for Gunnar's hand. "What can I do?" he asked me.

I couldn't find the strength to get up or think straight. My heart was broken. With a sad sigh, I said, "I just can't, Gunnar. I don't have it in me."

"Ok, I understand. Grieve, Kenz; I will keep you safe and find us another way." The tone of his voice and the softness in his eyes were a small comfort.

I closed my eyes and let my sorrow drown me.

Sleep was a bitch and being awake was not at all pleasant, either. A constant stream of tears flowed from my eyes when I was awake. And sleep brought on the nightmares. I dreamed of warm chocolate-brown eyes riddled with pain followed by agonizing screams of torment, and then a beautifully strong body turned into ash . . . over and over again.

I flailed in bed, fighting off the nightmares, kicking and screaming.

Strong arms encircled me and cradled my shaking body. "Kenzie," Dash said in a soothing voice. "I know you don't want this, but it has been days, and this is not healthy. Forgive me."

A stream of magic entered my body from the middle of my forehead. It wasn't unpleasant or menacing, but it was hot. The fire seeped into my soul, then enveloped me as though a second skin slid over me like a glove, and then the nightmares stopped.

"Sweetness? Sweetness, wake up," Stel beckoned.

"Come on, love, open your eyes," Caid cajoled.

Their voices were so far away, I was sure I was dreaming. It was comforting hearing their voices, but I wanted them near. I wanted to feel their skin on mine.

"We're here, sweetness, but you must open your eyes." Stel's calloused hands ran up and down my arm.

I rolled over.

"That's it, love. Come back to us." Caid's lips kissed my hand. My hand? Why is he kissing my hand? I frowned, or at least I felt like I frowned.

I felt lips on my shoulder and then on my neck. I sighed and smiled.

"Kenzie. Open your eyes right now," Stel's Alpha voice said to me, and my eyes snapped open.

"Why are you yelling at me?" I muttered.

Both men let out a deep breath of relief. "I wasn't yelling, sweetness. That was just a subtle kick in the ass to wake you up. We've been watching you sleep for a long time. We thought you were dead."

"Am I home?" I asked excitedly.

"No, love, you're dreamwalking. You called us, but all you did was sleep. We woke, and then we had Erik use magic to make us sleep so we could stay with you," Caid explained while clenching my hand.

"Oh well, that sounds complicated. What . . . what happened?"

"Um . . . we um . . ." Caid started to say, but he couldn't finish his thought, and I knew why.

My gaze flickered over to Stel. And he gave me a solemn nod. I tried to stifle a sob.

"I'm so sorry, sweetness. I failed you." Tears streamed down my wolf's face.

"Not your fault Stel. Not your fault at all." I chased his tears away with my fingers.

"I promised to keep him safe . . . for you. And I couldn't," he sniffled, and my heart broke again. "I couldn't get to him in time. Forgive me, Kenzie."

I sat up, threw my arms around him, and squeezed tight. "There is nothing for me to forgive. Please. Please don't blame yourself, Stel. You did all you could, and I believe that. I knew he was human. I was well-aware that his life was short. At least we have good memories, right?"

I pulled away from him to look him in the eyes. He nodded. "Right."

"And we can't wait until you get home to reminisce with you, love," Caid said.

"Home? Fuck, I'm still in The Dark Realm? Shit. I need to wake up." I rubbed my forehead.

"That's what we've been trying to tell you," Caid muttered, then smiled at me.

I reached over to caress his jaw. Stel rested his chin on my shoulder, and I pressed my cheek against his hair.

"Not sure what's going on, love, but it seemed like you were in a magically induced sleep. Almost like you were in a coma. Can you recall anything?" Caid held my palm against his face.

"Um . . . no, I had nightmares. Then I woke here." I tried to recall what had happened, but nothing came to me.

I was curious to know what happened on their end. How did they end up at the portal? Where was the portal? What was happening at home? So many questions to ask, I didn't know where to start. With each question that entered my consciousness, different sensations made themselves apparent. I felt a breeze on my skin and heard muffled voices around me.

Stel sat up alert, "Your body is waking, sweetness. And someone is watching you. I can smell him. He is . . . concerned. Stay safe and stay strong. We will find a way to get you home. I love you, Kenzie." He left a searing kiss on my lips and then broke our kiss.

"Kenzie, love, we need you back. Now more than ever. We're doing everything on our end. But, whoever that demon is, convince him to bring you home. Please," Caid pleaded.

"I tried, Caid. He said no. But I'll try again."

"If you have to fuck him in order for him to bring you home, do it. Rock his world, love." Caid cupped my face between his hands.

"I agree, Kenz. This has gone long enough. Do whatever it takes to come home. We're falling apart here." Stel pressed his chest against my back.

"I love you, I love you, I love you," Caid said between the kisses he left on my face.

"I love you both."

I watched my wolf and vamp fade away.

My conscious pulled at me, but I resisted. I longed to see Erik. He was closer to Brody than any of us and had to be suffering.

Determined to find him, I wandered through a sea of cobwebs, lost, until my magic man came into view.

CHAPTER 27
ERIK

The amber liquid ran down my throat. There was no burn. It didn't even warm my belly the way it used to. I had drank so much of it, my body had become immune. It was practically worthless to me now. At least my body was numb . . . somewhat. My thoughts still raced around in my head.

I had fallen in love. And just like that, she had been snatched away from me.

Every book I had read gave me no answers about how to retrieve her from The Dark Realm. I searched. Lord knows, I searched. My heart squeezed in my chest.

And now my best friend, a man I considered a brother, had been taken away from me. It happened so fast. One minute he was there, and the next, he writhed in pain and then he was gone.

I drank more whiskey, waiting for him to return and give me shit for drinking again.

He wouldn't come back. He was human. Not that a supe could survive hellfire. Damn it, Brody. Of all of us, why him?

I folded my arms over my desk to rest my head in the crook of my elbow and closed my eyes.

Something soft and gentle traced my cheek, brushing my hair away from my face.

Smooth lips pressed against my jaw and trailed kisses to my ear.

Kenzie. Her magic caressed mine, silky and seductive.

I didn't dare open my eyes, too afraid I'd scare the dream away.

"I miss you, Kenz. I've been trying to find a way to bring you home. I feel worthless."

My cheeks were wet.

Feathery kisses fell over my eyes.

"And now, with Brody gone, I'm drowning in despair."

My breath hitched.

"Don't give up, Erik. I need you. I will be home soon."

I reached out and held her close, still refusing to open my eyes.

"Kenzie?" I sobbed.

"Shhh. I'm here. I'm dreamwalking, I guess. I'm so sorry for your loss. I feel it, too. But we can't lose hope, ok? I'm coming home. I have a plan, sort of."

My magic surged to intertwine with hers.

I breathed a sigh of relief.

"Erik, look at me."

She pulled away and cupped my face.

"Erik! We don't have much time."

My eyelids fluttered open.

"Hi." She smiled at me. "I miss you so much."

I smiled back. "It took us a while to figure out you could do this, and well, we haven't slept all that much."

"I heard. I love you, and I will get back. I promise. But you need to promise me something." Her thumb ran lazily along my jawline.

"Anything." I gazed into her gorgeous green eyes.

"No more drinking. We need you sharp. You're the brains of this ragtag crew we've got. And I want you to be well," she said in a stern voice, which for some reason, assured me of her love.

"Ok. It's hard. And I know better. Alcoholism is in my family. I just . . . fuck, Kenz, you not being here messed me up. And now, Brody. It's rough." I hung my head.

She held me tight against her breasts.

"But I won't disappoint you." I tilted my head to gaze into her eyes, making a solemn promise to her and myself. *No more self-loathing.*

"Hey. You're not a disappointment. Ever. This is hard on all of us. And to be honest, I'd be rather pissed if you didn't miss me." She gave me a sassy smile.

I rolled her body under me and kissed her hard.

"This feels so real. I don't want to wake up without you." I kissed her neck and laved over the mark Caid had left there.

She moaned, and her breathing picked up. "I don't want to let you go either. But my body is waking."

I kissed her everywhere, desperation in every kiss.

"It's ok, Erik. Caid gave me an idea to help me get back home."

And then she slipped away from me.

CHAPTER 28
KENZIE

My body felt stiff, and my mouth dry. I rolled over and groaned. *Fuck, how long did I sleep?*

I felt the presence of someone lying next to me. "How long?" I muttered.

"Long, almost four days. The first couple of nights, you had night terrors. To ease your suffering, I had to use my powers." Dash held my hand, his forehead scrunched with concern.

I narrowed my eyes at him. "You magicked me to sleep?"

"I didn't know what else to do. You were tormented." He brought my hand to his lips.

"Umm . . . ok. I guess. I need to pee." I sat up and quickly covered my naked body with the sheet.

Dash gave me a wry look as though I was being ridiculous. He reached behind his head, tugged his t-shirt off his muscular frame, and handed it to me. It was so hot how guys did that, and I chastised myself silently for noticing.

After pulling on his shirt, I went to the bathroom and freshened up. While I toweled off, I noted how different his private quarters were from the rest of the manor. The color scheme in his room and bathroom had varying shades of cream with accents of black giving it a masculine, yet elegant, feel. The use of lighter tones in his personal quarters, which told me he preferred softer hues to the dark colors everywhere else. That explained the white clothing he had left for me. I redressed in his shirt and strolled out to the bedroom.

Dash stood on the veranda overlooking the ocean, his back toward me. He wore jeans and hadn't bothered putting on a shirt. Most of the time, he dressed in black suits. It was nice to see him look so relaxed.

"Join me, Kenzie," Dash said without turning toward me.

"Please." He extended his hand.

I stepped forward, but was reluctant to grasp his hand. He took the decision away from me and gripped my fingers. With one arm he pulled me against his chest and breathed deeply, his nose grazed my hair.

He poured a tall glass of water with his free hand and then handed it to me. Parched, I drank the liquid in one go.

Dash guided me to my chair, then refilled my glass. His body was tense, and he had been reticent.

"Where's Gunnar?" I asked. That was my favorite question to ask him.

The demon smiled, set the filled glass in front of me, then sat beside me. "He's fine. I've already told him that you are awake. He has been spending time at the Pub. Hopefully, next time he plans an escape, he will seek my guidance before taking action."

I drank my water. So many questions came to mind. They all jumbled up in my head in a confusing mess. I didn't know where to begin.

"Eat, Kenzie. You must be starving." He placed a napkin on his lap, and I realized how human his mannerisms were, and they had always been. More questions popped up in my head.

"You're going to give yourself a brain aneurism if you keep trying to figure things out in the pretty little head of yours. If you have questions, ask," he smirked.

Did he just insult me by saying "you're going to hurt yourself if you think too hard"?It was probably an insult, and I wanted to punch him in the nose.

He laughed. "Kenzie, I can tell by the murderous look on your face that you're insulted. I promise; I didn't mean to offend you. How about we try this? I'll talk about myself while you eat." He pointed at the food.

I nodded. Anything to distract me from thinking about Brody was a win. I began piling food on my plate. There was a healthy kale Caesar salad, roasted chicken, and mashed cauliflower. My taste buds and tummy were in heaven.

Dash started his monologue by telling me about his export business, but he had already mentioned his business dealings, so I interrupted him. "You've told me that part. Tell me something different," I said between bites. "Tell me about your demon form, or was it forms?"

"Hmmm . . . They don't teach much about demonology in the human realms, do they?"

I shook my head.

"Well, most supernatural species on earth have a lineage from this realm. For example, vamps are most certainly of The Dark Realm." Dash was brown-skinned with black hair and mismatched eyes. In the blink of an eye, he transformed into a vampire, with sharp fangs, claws, pasty white skin, and black veins all over his torso and blacked-out eyes.

The sudden change in his appearance shocked me.

He flashed back to his normal appearance and chuckled. "Shifters in the human realm also inherit their abilities from this realm. I'd show you that form, but I'm afraid he'd scare you. Plus, he wouldn't fit on this veranda."

My eyes got big, and I swallowed a bite of chicken. "I'm intrigued." *I wanted to see him shift. Who wouldn't?*

Dash gave me a genuine laugh, and it pleased my ears.

"Another time. As I mentioned, I was born in this form, but only demons with great power can hold a human form."

"What about Cerai? And the other people that work here?"

"Cerai is a pixie. Born in the land of Fae and brought here by a slave trader. Devon and Neo are mid-level demons. They have enough power to hold a pseudo-human form. They are very loyal and have known me all my life. I don't have a big household. I did at one time, but now it is not needed. The manor is easily managed by the three, and staff isn't allowed here, in my personal quarters," he explained.

"If they're not allowed here, who cleans and cooks?" I waved a hand over the food.

"I do. I like it." He tipped his head to the side and paused. "I used to like my solitude and privacy, thought I didn't need anything else. And I don't trust anyone in this place. This is the only place where I am truly safe."

How could this powerful demon not feel safe? He ran an entire Circle, which was huge from what I could tell.

"What about your lady guests?" I asked remembering the two female demons in his room the first night I'd gotten here.

"Lady guests are not invited here, present company excluded." Dash looked at me over the rim of his glass.

Something in his gaze made me squirm in my seat, so I changed the subject.

"Are there many humans or Fae here?"

"Alive humans, no. I have heard of demons kidnapping humans and keeping them as slaves. But not in this Circle. And there aren't many Fae here; although, I have met a few over the years. Fae have powerful magic and they are coveted. There are those that would love to harness your powers." Dash gazed at me with a look I understood without him having to say anything.

I wasn't safe here. The demon at the portal wanted to keep me for himself. Fuck. I needed to start shielding my magic, like I did at home, and hope it was enough.

I massaged my temple.

"What's wrong?" He arched his eyebrow, then smiled. I could tell he wanted to warn me not to think too hard before I hurt myself . . . again.

I huffed and leaned back in my chair. "Every time you say something, I have more questions. And as intriguing as this all is, I am wasting my and your time. I want to go home. I understand your reasons for not wanting to leave your people, but you're powerful and have money and influence. It seems like you have the resources to get me out of here. Which either means you're keeping me here on purpose. Or you're lying to me about something."

I stared at Dash and couldn't get a read on his reaction.

"There are things I haven't told you on purpose. But I'm not purposely keeping you here. You were poisoned, and then the portal situation. Both scenarios frightened me, Kenzie. And I don't scare easily."

He turned my chair to face his and held my hands which rested on my bare knees. My legs were between his, and he propped himself on his thighs, his upper body leaning toward me. A memory flooded the forefront of my brain, and a tear trickled from my eye. Brody and I had sat in this same position when we first met at a restaurant in The Majestic. I started hyperventilating, and the waterworks turned on full blast.

Dash gathered me in his arms and placed me on his lap.

"Don't cry, Kenzie. Please. All is not lost. You'll see. Slow your breathing, Kenz. Inhale. Exhale."

He took deep breaths, allowing me to mimic the rise and fall of his chest.

"Good. One more time."

I took another deep breath in and released it slowly.

"Better?"

I wiped my cheeks with the back of my hand and nodded.

"Do you want to talk about it?" he whispered.

I shook my head and breathed in deeply again.

"I um . . . I need to get moving." I stood and pressed the balls of my hands to my eyes. "I need to find Gunnar. This was delicious. Thank you."

"You're welcome," he smiled. "I like you in my clothes, but . . . the demons out there may get the wrong idea if you walk around the village that way."

I gave him a small smile and went to get dressed.

CHAPTER 29
KENZIE

All the clothes provided fit perfectly. I'd love to take some back, but that might be rude. *Thanks for the clothes, but I'll be taking them with me now, for free.*

I was utterly destitute in the demon realm. Not that I needed anything. Dash was a generous host. We were safe, sheltered, well-fed, and clothed. And thus far, he hadn't asked for anything. He hadn't helped us much with our primary goal, but in all fairness, I had been out most of the time.

We had been in his domain for days now, maybe weeks, and I was busy playing sleeping beauty. I shook my head in disgust. *Get your shit together, Kenz.*

My heels clicked with every step down the long dark corridors. The only footwear that had been given to me were stilettos, not that I minded, since I could walk in them just fine. They weren't practical in the human realm, and I did prefer my combat boots, but those never found their way back to me. At least my dagger was always near.

From his personal quarters, we teleported to the house's main entrance and then walked into the village. A cool breeze danced across my skin as Dash led me down a street I hadn't seen before. It was pleasant in the Fourth Circle. I pushed the thought out of my head as soon as it formed.

"Ask your questions, gorgeous," Dash said beside me.

"Are you a mind reader?"

He chuckled. "No. You seem to wear your emotions on your face."

That wasn't good. I was a merc and knew better than that.

"Your face is scrunched up, which tells me you're frustrated with yourself for whatever reason." Dash gave me a small smile as he closed the wrought iron gate behind us.

"I'm not myself here, and it is frustrating," I muttered.

Truthfully, I found myself intrigued by the Fourth Circle. The weather has always been at the perfect temperature. The colors of nature were more vibrant. And one demon, in particular, captivated me in ways I wasn't entirely comfortable with.

He placed a hand on the small of my back and guided me across the cobblestone lane. I had no problems walking in my heels across the uneven ground again. And hence another question.

Lost in thought, I continued walking straight while Dash turned down an alley. I hadn't notice I lost him until he trotted up beside me and tugged my hand.

"Where are we? I thought Gunnar was at the Pub. None of this looks familiar," I asked him, not even bothering to remove my hand from his.

"We have more than one pub, and that brother of yours has a knack for exploring."

"Watch your step." He braced me with his arm around my waist as I nearly face-planted on a stairwell.

I blushed. "I thought the magic shoes were supposed to keep me upright."

"The magic was to keep your footing while walking on uneven surfaces. When there is a stairway, you climb. To do that, you place one foot up." He demonstrated. "And then the other. See?" He placed his other foot on the next step. "Now you try?"

"Cheeky fucker," I muttered and climbed the stairs passing him. He laughed behind me.

At the top of the steps, we entered a swanky wine bar. I had guessed it was a wine bar because of the many bottles like I expected for wine. There was a decent-sized crowd, and the place was buzzing with lively energy until we entered. Everyone turned toward Dash and bowed their heads. He tilted his head in subtle acknowledgment, and the demons returned to their business. He was undoubtedly the swinging dick in these parts. Why wasn't he helping me?

Gunnar had been seated at the bar and got up immediately when he saw us. He rushed toward us and greeted me with a hug.

"Kenzie. I heard you were awake. Did you eat? Are you ok?" He placed a hand on my forehead, which was cute. I was depressed, not sick. And last I heard, depression doesn't cause a fever. Or at least it hadn't happened in my case. Still, it was cute to see him fuss.

"I'm fine. Thank you." I hugged him back.

"Come this way." Dash motioned to a table nestled behind a mirrored wall.

What I had thought was a large mirror turned out to be a one-way window. We could see the entire bar.

"Security purposes," Dash said. "For the most part, I know when someone who doesn't belong enters my domain, but sometimes, a sneaky fucker gets by. This is a popular bar as it is the only place that offers wines from many realms. And sometimes, the unwanted try to sneak in."

I smiled as I sat and picked up the wine menu, which I placed back down because it was written in gibberish.

Dash tapped my menu, and the gibberish jumbled together went out of focus and then translated into English. *Whoa!* His magic was impressive. I scanned the menu. I was surprised to see wines from Napa, champagne from France, and many other wines I wasn't familiar with.

"I'm not trying to be overprotective, Kenzie, but don't you think alcohol is unwise? After all, you've been through?" Gunnar gave me a stern glare.

I peered at him over the menu, then snapped it shut. I was ready to argue my right to get drunk when Dash placed an arm around me and said, "He has a point, but how about a compromise? Requiem fruit juice first, then a glass of whatever you want."

Dash handed me the pink, bubbly juice, and I took a swig. It was light and refreshing. And it did help with restoring my strength and energy levels.

"What's that?" Gunnar pointed at my glass.

Dash filled him in, and they started talking about wine, the village, and other mundane things. I participated in the conversation only slightly. I scanned the wine bar while peering at Dash from the corner of my eye. The more time I spent around him, the more he reminded me of the guys. He had Stel's protectiveness, Caid's playful side, and Erik's intellect. And Brody. Dash reminded me of Brody's easygoing manner, the way he adjusted to any given situation or different types of people. I got misty-eyed and bit my lower lip as though that would keep the tears safely in their ducts.

Both men noticed. Gunnar fidgeted as though he didn't know how to handle a crying female in public while Dash placed his hand over mine and gave it a gentle squeeze.

"Ah, here it is. You must try this. Both of you," Dash said as a waiter brought a bottle and three large wine glasses to the table.

Grateful for the distraction, I dabbed at my eyes and focused on the conversation.

The waiter set up three glasses in a row and then opened the bottle. As he poured the thick black liquid flecked with gold into each glass, a wisp of smoke floated out of the bottle.

Dash placed a glass in front of me while the waiter did the same for Gunnar. Gunnar and I looked at each other, then back at the glasses filled with black liquid. It looked like gasoline.

"This is called Liquid Gold." Dash held onto my hand while swirling his glass. The gold flecks swirled around the black liquid. "It comes from our rarest plant, which grows on the peaks of one of the oldest active volcanoes. It won't hurt either of you. Try it. It's delicious." Dash took a sip.

I looked at Gunnar. He shrugged and then took a sip. I clenched Dash's hand. A part of me worried he might fall to his death. He placed the glass on the table, tipped his head, and then he made an awful choking sound. He grasped his throat, gasping for air, and then fell over in his chair.

I immediately knelt beside him, ready to administer CPR, when he rolled over and laughed. "Oh my God, Kenzie, your face!" Gunnar cackled.

I stood up, placed my hands on my hips, then kicked him in his ribs. "That wasn't funny, ass!"

Dash laughed, clutching his belly, so I smacked him on his arm. But I couldn't hide the smile creeping over my lips.

Gunnar got up and sat back in his chair. He was still laughing and wiping laughter tears from his eyes. Then he held out a fist bump to Dash, who said, "Classic, dude."

"I hate you both!" I said trying to hide my giggles.

"That was funny, Kenz. Admit it," Gunnar said.

Laughter erupted out of me. He'd gotten me. And that was precisely what I needed after all the tension, sadness, and stress we had gone through.

Gunnar's immature antics helped me relax, and enjoy his and Dash's company. We drank more delicious demon wine and ordered some food.

The gasoline-looking wine tasted like whiskey with a hint of chocolate, and I may have had a glass too many. What started as subtle flirting became downright obvious. Dash reached for my hand, and I never pulled away. Then he scooted closer to me; his leg touched mine. At some point, he draped his arm over my shoulders and pulled my body against his. And I leaned into his touch.

Gunnar said nothing, and he didn't make a face either. He was also tipsy, and I realized this was the first time he and I had been on a casual outing. Ever since we met, we had been on the run. First, we chased after Bear, then the Rogue, and got lost in the Fifth and Sixth Circles. And then, we stumbled into the Fourth Circle. I had tuned out a story he told us about his work as a merc, and then it hit me like a ton of bricks. I leaned forward on the table, scrutinizing the man across from me. And there it was, the same familiarity that haunted me whenever I was around him. Sometimes it was the way he held his sword. Sometimes it was the tone in his voice. Sometimes it was the way he spoke. And from this closeup, it was definitely in his eyes. He reminded me of my father. Perhaps he was my brother. Was that possible? Did my father have a son and not tell me about it?

Dash somehow picked up on the shift in my body language and decided to distract me. My top rode up a little on my torso, exposing my back. He rubbed my exposed flesh, and my skin heated under his touch.

I kept glancing at Gunnar, though. I wanted to ask him straight out, but I didn't have the nerve to do so. Maybe he already knew? Or perhaps he didn't. If that was the case, I didn't want to drop a bomb in his lap.

Then Dash kissed my cheek and hooked my chin to face him. He planted a kiss on my lips. Electricity sparked between us. "Are you ready to go, gorgeous?"

I swallowed hard and shrugged, "Sure."

Gunnar stood and held out a hand to help me stand. I grasped his, but my eyes kept shifting to Dash.

"You good?" Gunnar asked me.

"I'm a little tipsy," I admitted with a smile.

He laughed, "Liquid Gold is good stuff, isn't it? I'm glad you got to try it. Why not have a little fun while we're in hell?"

Smiling, we followed Dash out. As we traveled down the cobblestone path, I marveled at the star-studded violet sky. There was a full silver moon with two crescent moons floating beside it. It was fairytale perfection.

"This is sensational!" I spun around with my arms open wide. My skirt flared out around me.

Gunnar grabbed my arm and said, "Yes, it is, but stop spinning. You're going to break your ankle, and I'd have to carry you home."

I laughed and shook my head, "Nope, I have magic steps." I raised a foot and waved my hand over it.

"No more demon wine for you," Gunnar muttered.

"It's true. Tell him, Dash." I kept walking with my head tilted up to the sky.

Dash told him about the spell holding me up with one arm. Gunnar walked beside us.

They chatted while we walked to Dash's place. Once indoors, the demon offered more drinks and refreshments. Before I could answer, Gunnar shook his head and said, "No more for me. Thanks, Dash." The men shook hands. Gunnar pecked me on my cheek. I hugged him and whispered, "Goodnight, big brother." I wasn't sure if he heard me, but it felt right to say it anyway.

Dash slipped up behind me and wrapped his arms around my waist. In a flash, we were in his room. Candles were lit, and the sound of the Sovereign Sea lapping gently on the shore in the distance.

Dash turned me around to face him, holding me against his body. We stood there for a moment, swaying to an inaudible melody.

"You're captivating, Kenzie."

His voice broke the spell I was under, and I took two steps away from him.

"No." My head shook while my feet moved closer.

He smiled.

"I don't want to sleep with you. I should be in my room. This is . . . inappropriate," I stammered like a virgin.

He gave me a sensual smile, undressing me with his eyes. Warm and tingly sensations ran up and down my skin.

"I won't force you to do anything you don't want to." He circled me, then stopped at my back. He trailed a finger down my neck, circling Caid's mark, but not touching it. "Nor would I take advantage of you while you're emotionally vulnerable or tipsy."

My breath hitched, and I leaned toward him.

He snaked a hand over my waist again; his large hand caressed my belly. His nose grazed my jawline, and I bit my lip and groaned.

"Kenzie," his warm breath brushed against my cheek. "If you say no, I will stop."

I turned in his arms and rested my forehead on his chest. It took everything in me to calm my breathing.

Caid and Stel's request filled my ears. I was supposed to seduce the demon. The way arousal flowed through my pores, I would've given it up for free.

Dash grasped my hand and kissed my knuckles and the inside of my wrist. I raised my chin and gazed into his multi-colored eyes. I traced my thumb over his lips.

"Dash . . ." I moaned his name while sliding one leg on the outside of his and hitching it around his hip. "Is this . . . is this what it'll take for you to take us home?"

He released a deep chuckle. "Are you offering your body to me, my precious Fae?"

Dash gripped my leg and peppered kisses on my shoulder, his lips gliding over my mate mark.

I tipped my head back, giving him access to my neck. "Yes."

"I want you more than you know. I want you to want me. To crave me. But not like this. I want our bodies to merge when there are no ultimatums." His hot lips seared mine, our tongues wrestled, and I clawed my fingers through his hair.

He picked me up, laid me on the bed, and then trailed kisses down to my navel. Abruptly, he released me with a pained growl.

"Not like this, Kenzie." Dash palmed his hard cock, his eyes fixed on my body, and then he turned away.

"You will stay here. It is the safest place in my domain. Even with the doors wide open. I'll be back to check on you."

Dash transformed into his wraith form, and then he disappeared.

CHAPTER 30

DASH

I was in love with a little half-Fae who was already spoken for. Everything in me said to risk going through the nearest gateway and killing her mates. Then she'd be all mine. But . . . Kenzie had been devastated watching the one die in front of her. She would be crushed if they were all dead. I couldn't do it.

Besides, sharing wouldn't be so bad. She had a good life in the human realm. It was her home, and she wouldn't want to leave. And I couldn't leave here, not for long periods anyway. Maybe we could do a long-distance thing. That would be better than losing her completely.

Fuck, I was pathetic.

Stomping around the manor did nothing to quell the anxiousness roiling me, so I climbed the steps to the roof and jumped. I shifted mid-air and soared toward the northeast border of the Fourth Circle, searching for a fight.

My Circle was the most prosperous and civilized Circle of The Dark Realm, but we were all demons. Pent-up aggression was never suitable for our species. Thus I allowed death matches at the Den located along the border. It was lucrative, and kept my people in line.

In my shifter form, I soared high in the air, clearing my head. But bloodlust lingered on the tip of my tongue. I landed far enough away to conjure a glamour. No one would dare go against me in my familiar forms, so I donned a disguise, strutted through the Den, and went straight to the ringmaster.

"I'm next," I told him, and he signaled the referee ringside.

The ongoing bout ended soon after, and I entered the ring. My opponent sized me up. He was large, almost the size of my beast, but no match for me; this would be too easy. I toyed with him for a moment, drawing out the inevitable. He knocked me off my feet, and the hit fazed me. I shook it off, darted around the ring, and then clotheslined my opponent. He fell hard, then I climbed on top of his chest and ripped out his throat with my teeth.

I was far from sated. I signaled the ringmaster to send another. And another. And another. One by one, two by two, sometimes even five at a time. I killed every opponent until no one dared go against me. That satisfied my bloodlust, and I left the ring.

Outside the Den, I walked for miles until I was entirely out of sight, shifted again, and shot into the air.

While I soared in the sky, I imagined living here with her. She would become so strong, and she would be happy. Life alone wasn't horrible. I had gotten used to it, but after having her around for a few days, I could never return to solitude.

Then I felt him stir, far to the East. But his presence was palpable, even across the vast distance. Shit, my father was restless. And that meant he was curious about my new houseguest. I needed to mark her as mine. That was the only option to keep her safe.

I swooped down to my manor, eager to get to her.

Kenzie was sound asleep on my bed. I hadn't lied about not sleeping much, but I could rest when she was in my arms. I kissed her forehead and went to the bathroom to wash off the blood and grime.

Love made everything so fucking complicated. Sometimes I wished to be more like my father, the cold bastard.

I didn't bother getting dressed before slipping under the covers. Kenzie dreamwalked often and wouldn't notice. That didn't made it ok. Who was I kidding? I was a demon, and demons liked to push boundaries. And above all else, I was addicted to feeling her silky skin against mine.

To my surprise, Kenzie snuggled up against me and rested her head on my chest. Then she draped her thigh over my torso. I caressed her smooth skin and let out the slightest sigh.

She had my heart and soul.

I pressed my lips to her forehead and then dozed off.

Sometime later, I woke alerted to the change in her breathing. She was on her back, and my head rested right above her breast. I didn't move an inch, not wanting to wake her. She was dreamwalking again and was probably having an intimate moment with her mates.

Her knees split further apart, and her skin became feverish. My cock swelled. Her lips parted, and she moaned.

I rolled away from her and hated myself for doing so. I wanted to dip my cock into her wet folds. But I'd hate myself. She was not the type of woman to fuck and leave. She was the type you wanted to keep and spend every waking second ensuring her happiness.

My gorgeous Fae baby was a sexual being. She loved physical pleasures, and it wasn't the fact that she had four mates that tipped me off. I'd watched her dreamwalk a few times. And each time, she couldn't get enough.

Her breathing became ragged, and her hips bucked. I knew if I looked between her legs, her entrance would be gaping open from being penetrated by one of her men. Her hands roamed her body, and she tugged at her nipples. Her moans became louder.

I smeared the precum pooling on the tip of my cock and started stroking myself, enjoying the view. I wasn't sorry for intruding on her personal moment. She was in my bed, and it wasn't like I was slipping it in, even though I wanted to. Badly.

Her delicate fingers were between her legs, which made me curious. Silently, I went to the edge of the bed and watched her fingers disappear into her drenched cunt. The scent of her arousal was intoxicating. Her hips undulated in a steady rhythm, moving faster and faster. I stroked my cock at the same pace.

Kenzie moaned louder and cried out. *Yes, don't stop!*

Whoever she was fucking was one lucky son of a bitch. I imagined it was me, kissing those beautiful lips and slamming into her juicy hole. My fist gripped my shaft tighter, and I pumped harder and faster. I was on edge, my body ready to burst.

Kenzie let out a loud gasp and arched her back. Her juices leaked out of her pussy, and she continued fingering herself.

Yes, Dash! Fuck me harder, she moaned.

I shot my load at the sound of my name. My cum covered my stomach and splashed my chest. My breathing was ragged, but Kenzie continued working her pussy. I cleaned up my mess with one of the throws draped over the chair and snuck back beside her.

Then she turned over, her face buried in the pillows. Her hips bounced up and down. I wanted her to fuck me just like that. She groaned louder.

Her body tightened, and her hips did short, small pumps, and then she let out another body-shuddering moan. Her breathing slowed, and her body quivered from the aftershocks.

She said my name; I know she had. I wanted to hear her say it in that sex-drenched voice again. I lay there next to her and focused on her face. She parted her lips and moaned. I wanted to kiss her.

"Kenzie, what are you doing to me?" I muttered.

My gaze traveled up her naked form and landed on her beautiful green eyes.

I was so busted.

CHAPTER 31
KENZIE

The intimate exchange between Dash and I was troubling. My body was tired even though I had slept for days, yet I couldn't turn off my mind.

Tired of tossing and turning, I lay in Dash's bed and stared up at the ceiling. Where was he? If he was here, he could magic me to sleep. Or we could continue what we started.

I scrunched my face into the pillow. His bed smelled like him. It was a mixture of cinnamon and cloves. Spicy and a bit mysterious, much like the demon himself.

Stel and Caid wanted me to seduce him. And I wanted to, tried to. I knew it wouldn't end there, though, and that made me feel guilty. I was still in love with my four men. But there was no denying the sexual tension between Dash and me. The way he touched me had me all kinds of restless. I wanted nothing more than to fuck the hot demon, but it would make things more complicated than they already were. In some ways, I was grateful he left to give me some space.

Every time Dash entered my thoughts, I chased him away with a memory of one of the guys. That just made me hornier. I decided to give dreamwalking a try. I needed my guys, and dreamwalking was the next best option.

I lay flat on my back and began a meditative breathing technique. It wasn't easy, but slowly I shut my eyes and turned off my thoughts.

In my dream, I was all alone. None of the guys were with me, which meant they were awake somewhere in the human realm. But I waited patiently, just in case.

Dash entered my dreams, completely naked. He stalked toward me, his broad, muscular chest glistened with sweat. His big, thick hands roamed over my body and his hot lips collided with mine. He reached down between my legs and worked me up into a frenzy. And then his enormous cock plunged deep into my core, and I came hard.

I was basking in the afterglow of my sex dream, and then I heard his voice.

Kenzie, what are you doing to me?

My eyes snapped open, and Dash was lying in bed with me.

We were lying on our sides facing each other.

"Hi," Dash gave me a sensual look. "Did I wake you?"

"Umm . . . no." I was at a loss for words. As I lay there in front of Dash, my skin felt hot, and my thighs were wet from the orgasm I'd just had.

Dash knew about my dreamwalking ability, and I hadn't thought about what I looked like in the waking world. Did he see me pleasuring myself? His half-hooded gaze told me the answer was yes. He'd gotten a free show.

"I've watched you dreamwalk," he said in a bashful tone.

And there was my answer. A part of me was mortified, and another was . . . turned on. Exhibitionism was my thing, and yes, I was well aware of my issues.

"So, I'm guessing that wasn't your first time to Kenzie's Sex Show?"

"It's such a great show; I've become your biggest fan." He grinned.

His gaze traveled down the length of my body. We were inches apart and completely naked.

I covered my breasts with my arm and clenched my knees together.

He licked his lips, and I wrestled with my eyeballs to keep my gaze on his face.

"As you already know, I've seen every bit of you." He pulled my arm away from my chest and then spread my knees apart, revealing my nakedness.

"You're beautiful, Kenzie."

Gooseflesh rippled over my flesh. My heart beat rattled my chest.

"I'm making you nervous." He chuckled.

"Come here. Try to relax." He lay flat on his back and drew me into his body.

But I was too keyed up to sleep. "Tell me something about you . . . something . . . personal."

He grabbed my hand and pressed my fingers to his lips. "What would you like to know?"

"Umm . . . why aren't you married?" I angled my head to look up at him.

He squeezed my hand and exhaled. "I was. Everyone I've ever loved is dead. It happened decades ago. I had three wives and a dozen of children. They were killed, every last one of them. I . . . I could have protected them, but I wasn't here." He let out a heavy sigh.

I hooked a leg over his torso, and he ran his hand over my thigh.

"Being a powerful demon has its perks, but it also comes with arrogance. As a young demon, I felt invincible. Rules didn't apply to me, which meant I was a complete asshole. My wives and children lived here in this village. I was busy conquering the Fourth Circle . . . from my siblings."

My eyes shot up to my forehead, but I didn't interrupt, and he continued.

"Yes, it is as bad as it sounds. Our reputation is hardly embellished. As I said, demons love to fight and fuck. And we like to manipulate and wage wars. Anyway, I was out conquering the Fourth Circle because I wanted to impress my father. He rejoiced when his children waged war against one another, but that's another story." He paused and then shook his head.

"Anyway, I was out conquering and exploring and left my family here unprotected. I was strong on my own, and I had an army at my back. No one dared challenge me, so I hadn't thought much about it. Then, one of my siblings and his army ran through my village to prove a point and gutted every soul. The carnage was devastating. We were at war for some time. Once it was over, I swore I'd be single forever. Decades later, I was in the human realm and fell head over heels for a human. She wouldn't have survived here, so I stayed there for a time. After several years of living in the human realm, I made her a vampire, and then we moved here."

"We lived in peace for many years. Just her and I, and for a little while it was enough. I thought I was happy. And then I went exploring again, this time to the land of the Fae and then back to the human realm. When I returned, my father had claimed her. There was nothing I could do to save her. She was enslaved, and of course, she hated me. I tried to fight him, but he was much stronger. The war between my father and I was long, and she got caught in the crossfire. True death claimed her."

"After the battle, I focused on rebuilding the village and the Fourth Circle. I never looked back. Most of what you see in the Fourth is a combination of magic from the realm and my power. It has taken years to rebuild. But my father is ever-present; he has eyes everywhere. I've snuck into the human realm, but only for a short time. I have to leave some magic behind for protection when I am away, but it's not enough. My absence makes my people vulnerable, and I become weak as well. When I leave this realm, I don't have the same power level."

Hearing the story of his life was heartbreaking. Most of it

consisted of loss and struggle. And his family was always involved. What a lonely existence.

"Your family is kind of messed up." I stroked his hand with my thumb.

He chuckled. "Yeah, that's an understatement. I thought I was ok with my life as a single businessman, but . . . with you here, I've had second thoughts. It scares me. Here in the Fourth, we have peace and prosperity while the other Circles continue to struggle. My siblings have called a truce. But we are demons, and there is always a bit of jealousy."

"And your father?" I asked softly.

"He's as sinister as ever. He knows my power has grown, my people are loyal, and my army is well-trained. And that means he keeps a close watch." He rested his chin on my head.

"He sounds like a wanker." I cuddled into his side. "I understand why you won't take us back. And I don't blame you; there's too much at risk. The villagers all seem to love you, and this place is beautiful. You've done well."

"Thank you, my precious Fae." He hooked my chin to look up at him. "Having you here, Kenzie, has reawakened my soul. It's frightening, and it is refreshing all at the same time. I'm afraid to let you go, and I'm afraid to keep you here."

My poor sad, lonely demon. I pecked his cheek and snuggled my head into the crook of his neck.

CHAPTER 32

DASH

Kenzie had become precious to me. She listened to me retell the tales of my tragic past and hadn't judged me at all. She fell asleep in my arms, and I slept as well.

She was still asleep, so I sat and watched. A few moments later, she turned over and murmured, "It is creepy to watch someone sleep."

I chuckled, then leaned over and kissed her cheek. "Good morning, my precious Fae. I have a business to attend to. Breakfast is ready, and when you're ready to leave, the door there will lead you to the main section of the manor. You won't be able to come back here without me, though. But I'll be working in the library if you need anything."

"Ok, thank you." She burrowed under the covers.

I smiled and then shadow-walked into my library. I was working here more and more. It was larger than my office, and I'd been researching gateways since Kenzie arrived. They didn't understand that the gateways to any realm constantly changed. There was a pattern to it, and so I was mapping it out to give her the best chance I could.

A big part of me wanted to force her to stay. But another part of me, the part that wanted to be more like me and less like my father, wanted her to choose me the way I had chosen her.

"Master." Neo, my assistant, was standing in the library's doorway. "Your appointment is here."

"I need a minute," I replied.

My first appointment was with Damon del Torro. He was a demon, of course, and a bit of a busybody. He had a vast network of spies. He was the one who had told me about the portal that Gunnar and Kenzie had gone to several nights ago. And now he had come to collect his due. I was happy to pay him and get him out of my hair.

I cast a concealment spell over my desk. I didn't want him to know what I was doing, and the last thing I needed was him selling off my secrets.

"Come," I called out.

Damon strolled in, wearing his human form. Human forms were the most difficult form for demons to hold. It took a lot of power. Damon was trying to impress me, and his attempts had yet to work.

I pulled out a stack of demon currency and slipped it to the demon as he sat down. "Our business is concluded."

He tipped his head and said, "If I may, Master, there is some info that you may be interested in, for a price, of course."

I leaned back in my chair and waited for the demon to continue. If he thought I would offer up anything for info that may or may not be of value to me, he had another thing coming.

"Speak or get out," I stated.

Damon fidgeted in his seat. "It's your father, Master. He stirs in the First Circle. Rumors say he is interested in your Fae guest."

Fuck. I'd felt my father stir in that bottomless pit of his. This was not good news. I needed to implement plans to keep her safe quickly.

"You're not telling me anything I didn't already know. Anything else?" I said, which was true. I wanted to see if he had anything else to offer.

"No, Master, I will keep you apprised of any changes." He stood, bowed, then scampered away.

I wanted to pull my hair out. "Neo! Where's Jafir? Get him here now."

"Master, I have not been able to reach him."

I growled. "Find him. Send the Legion out."

The Legion was a group of soldiers in my army, most of which had wings. They were fast flyers, formidable in combat, and able to communicate with one another over long distances.

I needed to find Jafir in hopes he had good news before I ran out of time.

For the next few hours I went through the routine day-to-day tasks it took to run the Fourth. There was only so much I could delegate. And I had been consumed with the precious Fae in my bedroom the last few days. It was worth it; she was worth it.

How could I keep her safe?

I had a few options, and none of them were great. The one option that was a sure thing was to mark her. She had already been marked by a wolf and a vamp and shared magic with a powerful mage. They were bonded to her, the lucky shits. My marking her wouldn't negate those marks at all; it would be another mark that would keep her safe and amplify her powers and her mates. The downside, she would be bound to me for life. She would have to spend a considerable amount of time here. And what was mine would become hers. And that included all my riches and all my enemies. But my father wouldn't be able to touch her.

The other option was to keep her hidden in my private quarters. It was the only place completely safe from my father. I'd have to lock her in and throw away the key . . . for a little while. My father would know she was here, but wouldn't have the power to locate her. This was the riskier option.

She would hate being locked up. Even if she saw the reasoning, she'd fight me.

My hope with this option was to give her time to accept the

mark. Once marked, she would have the freedom to move between realms safely. This was the riskier option. Knowing him, he would wage war with my people until I offered her up.

Both options led to the same conclusion, marking Kenzie as my forever mate. One was to do so now, whether she liked it or not. The other was to lock her up until she accepted it. She was the first and would be the only mate for me. My previous wives weren't mate material, there was a difference. I cared for them, maybe even loved them. But it wasn't soul-deep, it was temporary. With Kenzie, I knew it was forever and I was excited to make it official. However, she probably didn't feel the same way . . . yet.

I did have one ace up my sleeve, well, two if Jafir would get his ass over here. Until he showed up, I had one bargaining chip, which I was sure would be enough to convince her. I wanted to present that as a gift. But with my father showing up, it was a manipulative move.

Fuck it. I was a demon and could manipulate with the best of them. Hopefully, I could convey how I felt and the urgency to keep her safe at all costs.

"Master, pardon the intrusion. Damon is back."

Damon came in panting.

"Sir, I just received word. Your father is about to cross the Second Circle's border." Damon's words rushed out and slapped me in the face. Time was running out.

"Your intel is appreciated. How much?" I kept the tone of my voice calm.

"Nothing, sir, I . . . I will be unavailable until the dust settles." Damon ran out.

I sat dumbstruck. My father was on his way, and he was coming for her. He was tying my hands. One look and he would become obsessed. The thought of him encroaching on my territory made me murderous. I threw an electrical surge of magic at the wall opposite my desk.

Kenzie walked in as the wall smoldered. Her eyes were wide as she looked from me to the damage I'd wrought and then back to me again.

"Is this a bad time?" She looked at me warily.

I waved off the scorched wall and motioned for her to come in.

"Sorry, precious Fae. Um, yes. Come in, please." I walked around the desk and embraced her. It was odd behavior but holding her in my arms felt right.

She pulled away from me and looked into my eyes. "Do you want to talk about it?" She cupped my cheek.

I tilted my head a bit to kiss her hand.

Here goes nothing!

"Please, have a seat." I tugged her over to the overstuffed chairs in the middle of the library. I guided her to sit and sat on the table in front of her chair.

She looked nervous, and I had to admit, so was I. There was no easy way to do this. I took a deep breath and held both her hands in mine.

"I want you to stay here with me. I will have someone take Gunnar back, but you cannot leave. I won't allow it."

The corners of her lips turned up, and then she laughed.

"That would be a definitive NO. I thought you understood that. What changed?"

"You can't go, not yet," I insisted.

She moved to stand, and I pulled her back down a bit forcibly. She narrowed her eyes at me.

"Hear me out," I squeezed her hands. "You won't have to stay for long. Maybe six months. A year or two in human years."

"My name is Mackenzie, not Persephone. What the hell is wrong with you?"

"Let me finish. In exchange, I will heal your womb. If you stay."

"Excuse me?" She pulled her hands away from me and straightened in her chair.

"While you were recovering from the poison, I scanned your

body," I swallowed hard. "You are unable to have children, yes? I can fix that for you. I need you to stay for a while and come back."

"First, you scanned my body without permission. And now you're trying to manipulate me by using my deepest insecurity against me?!"

My head whipped to the left. I felt dizzy. Spots swam in my vision. When I refocused, Kenzie was gone, and my jaw ached.

Did she just hit me? Again? I rubbed my tender cheek. *Fuck, she just hit me.*

I was about to run after her when Neo walked in. "Master, the Legion has found Jafir. He is on his way."

Thank fuck. I hoped Jafir had good news.

I found Kenzie in the hallway with Cerai. My precious Fae flipped me off.

"Kenzie, please, talk to me."

"Fuck off," she shouted and stomped away.

Cerai stood in the hallway, shaking.

"Keep an eye on her," I demanded, then went back to the library.

I replayed my proposal and realized that maybe the approach was all wrong. Too late now. I was desperate to keep Kenzie safe. My father would stop at nothing to destroy me, and taking Kenzie would do precisely that. He would follow her to the human realm to do it, too.

CHAPTER 33
KENZIE

I stomped away from Dash and went looking for Gunnar. It was time to go. Now.

Cerai caught up with me. "Mistress, I have something for you."

I waved her off, "Cerai, you shouldn't be around me right now. Just tell your boss I was pissed and locked myself in Gunnar's room or something like that."

"No, you must," she tugged me around the corner and pulled me into a small empty bedroom. "Here, I fixed it for you and kept your other items safe."

She walked over to a shelf, pulled out my boots first, and then a bundle of black with a pouch. She shoved the items into my hands. I looked down at them, dropped everything on the floor, and hugged her.

"Oh!" she said and awkwardly patted my back.

"Thank you!" I stripped out of the lovely white dress, set my dagger on the nearest table, and started putting on my undies, jeans, black top, and jacket. Not only were my clothes cleaned, but they also felt completely different. The fabric was soft, stretchy, and lightweight.

"This is different, so much better," I said as I bent over to put my socks and shoes on. The last thing was my belt which holstered my dagger, and my gun, which was in the pouch. Still no bullets, but it was comforting to have the weapon on me.

"It's not the same set you wore; I remade it," Cerai said, shyly.

"It's incredible, much better."

She nodded and said, "Spider silk. The fabric is almost impenetrable. It's sturdy and comfortable. Plus, easy to clean."

"Amazing! Thank you for this. I need to find Gunnar, and you need to pretend you never saw me."

"He was in his room. I will tell the Master that I left you with him. Follow me." She went out the door, and we hurried down the dark hallways.

I hoped Dash wouldn't take it out on the poor girl. That would royally suck. But I couldn't stay. We had to go before he locked me in forever. Everything had been going so well; he knew I wanted to and needed to leave. I didn't know what changed his mind, but there was no way I'd hang around for two months, let alone two years.

Cerai stopped in front of a door and knocked. Gunnar answered moments later. Then she hugged me. "Thank you, Mistress, for defending me. Be safe."

"You too." I hugged her back. Then she disappeared down the hall.

"Time to go," I said to Gunnar.

He didn't hesitate. Gunnar grabbed a bag, and I followed him out. He led down a hall that twisted and turned here and there, then opened a nondescript door. The passageway we entered was narrow, no more than two feet wide, and dark and damp. He had done some exploring, and once again, I found myself grateful to have Gunnar at my side.

After walking for hours, we finally arrived at a steep set of stairs.

We climbed. My legs burned from the exertion. Damnit, I was out of shape.

Gunnar stopped at the top of the stairs and finally spoke, "This will take us to the Fifth Circle. You ready?" I nodded, and he grabbed my hand as we went through a door. At first, it was nothing but darkness, then the world heaved, and the ground went out from under me. The experience was just as it had been when we stumbled into the Fourth and just as unpleasant. After the tumbling, Gunnar and I stepped aside and wretched. This time it was worse, as I had eaten a big breakfast, and now my stomach felt green.

"Up, Kenzie." Gunnar swiped a hand over his mouth. "We need to put more distance between us and that demon of yours."

I frowned and muttered, "He's not my demon."

Gunnar took a piece of paper and moved on, "He wanted to keep you, didn't he?" He gave me a side glance as we walked into the dreary Fifth Circle.

I nodded, then asked, "How did you find the passageway and whatever that is?" I pointed at the paper in his hand.

"I made friends amongst the staff and got them drunk. Alcohol made them very talkative. Plus, I studied Dash's map in his library as often as possible and drew this out." He handed me the paper, which was thicker and heavier than human paper. On it was a sketch of the Fifth Circle.

"This is where we are," he pointed to an X. "This is where we want to go," he tapped a star closest to the X. There was another star further away.

"And this?" I pointed to another star that was further away.

"Back-up, plan. From what I understand, the gateway doesn't open in the same spot. According to my intel, these are next. So I wrote them both down. There are other access points on the opposite side, but let's hope we don't have to go that far. Here," Gunnar pointed to a couple of wavy lines, "is the border to the Sixth." Then he flipped the paper over and said, "There are more access points here and here."

"Well, shit, Gunnar. You've been a busy little bee. Thank you."

He chuckled. "Don't thank me yet. We've got a long way to go."

Then we set off, keeping a steady pace. Gunnar not only had done an excellent job with the map and the passageway, but he also squirreled away some food and water. He had to have been a boy scout when he was a kid.

We didn't stop at all and kept on even when it went dark. The boy scout had the foresight to bring a flint and a few rags we used to tie around sticks to create a torch. I'd be utterly lost without him.

CHAPTER 34
DASH

Scorch marks ruined the once-tranquil landscape surrounding my terrace. The inside of the manor did not look any better. I searched every room and came up empty. Where the fuck was she?

Cerai cowered behind Neo and Devon. The three before me were once regarded as my most trustworthy and loyal. Their allegiance was now in question. All three quivered with fear as fury radiated off my monstrous demon form.

My dark shadows hovered above them, demanding answers.

Earlier, I had made Kenzie an offer. Well, ok, it was a demand. I needed her to stay to keep her safe, and in exchange, I had offered to heal her body. She didn't ask questions; she didn't even ask for time. Her answer had been a hard no, followed by a punch to the face. If that wasn't enough, she and her brother ran off.

I had guessed it was to seek a portal. But no one had seen Kenzie or Gunnar come or go. And that had been nearly mid-day. And it was well past midnight. In the human realm, that was almost two days. Three depending on the season.

Gunnar was crafty, which I'd learned days ago. After the botched attempt at the portal, I'd thought he and I had come to an under-standing. The little shit had been scheming and plotting right under the noses of my most loyal subjects.

I glowered at my staff. I wanted to hurt all three of them — even Cerai. But Kenzie would be displeased, and I had done enough of that. Thus, I took my frustrations out on my home. If these three hadn't put out the many fires I'd started, the manor would have burned to ashes. The last place her scent was the strongest was in Gunnar's room, then it disappeared. Someone had helped them. And I had a feeling I knew who it was. The only female demon here. I wanted to snap her neck, but . . . Kenzie.

My time with my precious Fae was far from over; she would be back in my arms. And I planned to keep her disgust of me to a minimum.

"Speak!" I roared. The entire village probably heard my tirade and ran for cover.

"Master," Devon bowed and then mumbled something intel-ligible.

I shrunk down to my human form, "Devon, quit your stammer-ing! I want answers. Stand up!"

In his human form, Devon looked frail; combined with fear, he appeared to be on the brink of death. Part of me felt guilty; he had been with me since I was a child. Always loyal, always honest. I had forgiven him for letting Kenzie and Gunnar slip away from him at the Pub, but this was getting out of hand. It may be time to retire the old demon.

It took much effort, but I reigned in my anguish and softened my approach. Through clenched, I addressed my loyal subject. "Devon, you were with Gunnar the most. You must have an idea of where he has taken her."

He stood and looked up at me, then cast his eyes downward. "I believe they went through the South exit to the Fifth Circle. Gunnar was friendly. Many demons enjoyed his company and engaged in conversation with him. I swear, Master, I did not hear him speak of the gateways in front of me. However, he had spoken to many traveling merchants. I guess he had formulated a plan from their travel tales."

If Gunnar weren't her brother, I'd hunt him down and burn him to ashes.

I paced, thinking over my next move. The South exit into the Fifth was not far. At this point, they probably had crossed over. From there, the nearest gateway would take them at least two weeks to reach on foot. Damnit, *Kenzie, did I anger you so much that you would run into danger?*

An unexpected voice interrupted my musings. "Pardon me, Master; no one answered, so I let myself in. I have news." Suran, the commander of my army, joined us on the terrace. I was so furious I hadn't been paying attention to my surroundings. I should have heard him enter my domain or, at the very least, sensed his presence. All these years of peace were making me soft.

"Clean up and stay close," I said to Cerai, Neo, and Devon.

I motioned Suran to follow me into the library, which was a mess. Suran looked around at the damage, but said nothing. He was a giant demon, my height with the head of a bull and a body as thick as it was wide. His nostrils flared, and the gold hoop in his nose lifted when he huffed.

Suran was my closest friend. We had known each other since we were boys and fought side by side throughout the years. He had helped me fight my siblings and my father. And he also helped me build the Fourth and bring peace to my domain. I trusted him even more than the others I left outside to clean up my mess.

I went straight to the bar cart and poured two glasses of Argon Silver.

Suran let out a low whistle as I handed him the glass. "That kind of day, huh?"

I scowled over the glass as I drank the demon whiskey. It burned my mouth and down my throat. I inhaled deeply, feeling the fire blaze through my veins. I topped off my glass and then sat in the same seat Kenzie had been in earlier.

"So, who'd you let beat you up?" Suran sat down across from me and pointed to my face.

A smile crept over my lips. The first time Kenzie had hit me, my magic healed the injury within hours. This time I willed my healing magic to leave the bruise alone. Kenzie's hit had been packed with a lot of power for someone so small. I was proud of her and proud to show off a battle scar. It would be gone by morning; in the meantime, I wore it like a badge of honor.

"Ah, I see. You let a woman do that to you." Suran nodded in approval. "You're in love with the Fae. Good for you."

He reached out his glass to me, and we tapped our glasses together. I took another swig of Argon and breathed through the burn.

"Alright, tell me what you did to make her hit you. And don't say you didn't do anything. And don't say you don't want to talk about it either." He leaned back in his chair and rested his feet on the coffee table.

I frowned at his perceptiveness and proceeded to tell him everything about Kenzie.

My asshole best friend chuckled when I was finished. "Wow, after all these years, Dash, you're still a dipshit when it comes to the ladies."

"Fuck off. I'm flying to the Fifth to bring her back. Are you coming with me or not?" I sipped my whiskey, letting the effects of the alcohol work their magic. The anguish I had felt simmered to annoyance.

"You will do no such thing unless you plan to take her back to the human realm. And that I wouldn't advise. Your father is moving fast. He's nearing the Third as we speak. You need to prepare for war."

I pinched the bridge of my nose. Why was my father such a royal fuck face?

"He's coming for her. The dragon flora cut her. He knows what she is. I was hoping to mark her to protect her from him."

"Did you tell her that?" Suran asked.

"No," I realized now that was a mistake. "Kenzie walked in here right after I heard the news that he had crossed into the Second. I reacted and spoke too quickly. And pissed her off in the process."

"Marking her would be the only way to keep her safe here and in the human realm. My father won't go to the mortal realm to chase her. And he can't track her yet. Her mate's magic burned the tracer embedded into her body by the dragon flora. But he can follow me anywhere. Fuck. I can't go after her." I scrubbed a hand down my face.

"I have to help her escape. But I can't send you or the Legion or anyone else. My father will know. I have to fight him, hold him here, and hope she can find her way home alone."

The thought of that made the demon whiskey bubble up in my stomach. I fought the urge to heave.

"You're right. Anyone belonging to the Fourth or who has any affiliation with you will be followed. And no one from the other Circles could be trusted to go against your father. Does she have anyone in her realm that could help? Any demon connections?" Suran made a valid point.

I shook my head. "No, but she is mated to a mage, a wolf, and a vampire. If they had a guide, they could walk into this realm, find her, and walk out. A sacrifice would have to be made."

"Well, there's your answer. If they love her, I assume they do since she's mated to them, they'll make the sacrifice. Now all you need to do is track them down."

"Yes, I can do that . . . somehow. In the meantime, prepare the Legion for war. My father is not allowed outside of the Fourth. We push back hard and send him packing." I finished my whiskey and went to work.

CHAPTER 35

KENZIE

Gunnar was optimistic that we were getting close to the gateway. According to his intel, he estimated it would take two weeks to get there on foot. He also learned that most demons walked short distances or teleported everywhere. And they could communicate over reasonably long distances telepathically. There was no need for cars or telephones. Lower caste demons didn't have those abilities. Those demons led difficult lives and were often abused, mistreated, and sometimes tortured for sport. They were enslaved. As appalling as that was, the most mind-blowing tidbit regarding lower caste demons was that they had been human, had died, and were sent here to live eternity in hell. The Dark Realm sucked, all of it except for the Fourth Circle.

Dash's domain did not suck. It was almost perfect. I couldn't begrudge him for his refined lifestyle. It came at a high cost, and he worked hard to keep it. A part of me wished I had made better use of my time there. Gunnar explored and gained a world of knowledge that would make a best-selling book. He didn't want to be here anymore than I had, yet he waited for me while I recuperated from our journey to the Fourth, the poisonous flower stint, and then again while I mourned Brody. During my downtime, he had studied and plotted, and schemed. He was the best big brother a girl could ask for.

Gunnar began to fidget. His gaze darted around us, and his head kept glancing over his shoulder.

I followed his gaze, and my eyes widened. Something was barreling straight for us. That was not good.

"Sandstorm," I muttered. "We need to find shelter."

"Are you sure that's what it is? It seems more . . . ominous. It's all black and gray." Gunnar squinted at the fast-moving cloud.

"Yep, just like the ground under our feet," I looked around and found nothing. We had been walking for miles in a desolate desert.

"We passed an outcropping of boulders about seventy yards or so back. What do you think?"

My shoulders slumped. I looked back the way we came and then toward the wall of sand. Neither option was ideal. "Lesser of two evils?"

Gunnar nodded, and we jogged back the way we came. As we ran, he handed me a few rags to be used as torches to cover my ears, nose, and mouth. We passed what would have been the seventy-yard mark and found nothing. We kept going, but soon the sandstorm had caught up with us. We found an outcropping of rocks, but it was no more than two feet high. It would provide no shelter.

The storm came, and Gunnar and I huddled, staying low to the rock. The force of the wind knocked me back, and Gunnar grasped my hand and held on as best as he could. His other hand slipped from the rock, and we both went flying. As the sand pelted our bodies, I held onto his wrists for dear life. I couldn't see a darn thing. We tumbled across the desert plains, somehow managing to stay together.

We stayed low to the ground. The wind howled, and sand whirled dizzyingly around our bodies. I grabbed Gunnar's arm, and he shielded my more petite body with his.

Sand started to pile on top of us. I panicked. If we were to be buried in all this sand, no one would find us, and we would die a slow, agonizing death.

I called on my magic and went with my instincts. I tried to shield our bodies, but the onslaught of sand and wind was relentless. Using my Fae magic, I created a swirl of wind just enough to ease the sting of the pelting sand. My magic struggled against the storm's force, but I pressed on and created a shield that extended from me and wrapped around Gunnar, effectively keeping the wind and sand away from our bodies.

During the entire journey in The Dark Realm, my Fae magic felt more robust, but now under this massive storm, my power waned. Sweat dripped down my back, and my body shook under the exertion.

"Hold on, Kenz. It's almost past us!" Gunnar shouted over the howling wind.

I ground my teeth and held onto my magic. The storm seemed to hover right above us. The wind roared as though it was a living thing, and the sand was its weapon. My resolve was crumbling in the never-ending storm.

And suddenly, the world went quiet.

CHAPTER 36

DASH

My staff did everything that needed to be done and then some. Devon, Neo, and Cerai were timid around me, and I was both proud and disappointed in myself. Power and authority were addictive drugs. And yet I didn't want to rule like my father; I didn't want to be anything like him. I would have to make amends, but it would have to wait. There was too much to prepare for.

Cerai brought me the clothes Kenzie wore before she left and the dress she'd worn on her first night here. Neither were washed, and her scent calmed me.

"Master, you may want to hide them in your personal quarters," she said with a bowed head. "I will erase all traces of her scent from the halls to confuse your father."

Cerai was a pixie. My father had destroyed her wing the last time he was here. She was just a child. Neo took a liking to her, so I allowed her to stay. Masking scent was tricky, but her meticulous cleaning skills, along with her pixie dust, were able to do the trick. I knew she had a hand in helping Gunnar and Kenzie escape without a trace. Kenzie had stood up to me on the pixie's behalf. My precious

Fae was fearless. No one had ever stood up to me, not even my former wives. No wonder I hadn't bonded with them.

Devon ran into my office out of breath, "Master," he was bent over at the waist, trying to collect his breath. "Master, there's something . . ." his breath came out in rapid gasps.

"Calm yourself, Devon." I stood up from behind the desk and went to the bar cart to pour a glass of water for him.

I handed it to him, and he gulped it down. "Thank you, Master, sir. There's a demon at one of the lounges. Come, you need to speak with him. He's an old, retired commander from the Fifth; it sounds like he knows the Mistress."

"Which lounge?" I growled.

"The Soggy Knickers," he muttered.

Of course. I hated that place, but every town needed a place designed for sex and titillation.

My wraith enveloped me, and I appeared at The Soggy Knickers.

Like the human realm, The Dark Realm had its share of brothels and exotic dancers. We were demons, and sex was part of our nature.

The Soggy Knickers was a seedy sex lounge. It wasn't human realm seedy, though I've been to those, and this wasn't as bad. Yet even the classiest brothel on earth couldn't compare. In the Fourth, this was the lowest caliber we had to offer. Some demons had baser desires, and so I allowed it.

I flashed into the entryway, and the madam approached me immediately. "Master Dash," she batted her lashes at me. One of her eight tentacles fanned herself, while one teasingly traced down my arm. I slapped that tentacle away.

"One of my men said there was a retired commander from the Fifth. Bring him to me." I stated.

She bowed her head, "He is at the bar. I'll bring him to you." She slithered away and quickly reappeared, dragging the man out by his tusk.

The madams here were not to be messed with.

I nodded my thanks, grabbed the commander by his tusk, and flashed back to my library. Devon still stood there.

"Yes, Master, yes, that's him." Devon pointed at my captive.

"Thank you, Devon. That will be all." I dismissed him.

His jaw dropped at my thanking him. *Damn it, Kenzie.* I was learning bad habits from her.

"Sit." I shoved my captive into a chair across from my desk. "What is this I hear about a Fae?"

"I . . . I never met a Fae." The captive's eyes enlarged.

He was hedging. I growled and let my shadows coalesce behind me.

"It's true, I swear. I never met her. Was told to find her, but we didn't. She must be dead. But her father will not accept it. I was tasked with finding a way here as we had already searched Five and Six, sir."

"Master. Here in my domain, you will address me as your Master. Who is this man? Her father? Tell me everything."

I sat and listened to Zed with restrained interest. He was indeed a retired military commander of the Fifth Circle and had almost lost his life battling against a formidable knight thousands of years ago. The warrior spared him in exchange for a favor owed to the knight or someone in his line. The knight had passed, and the favor was never called upon until recently. Kenzie was the great, great, great, I didn't know how many greats, but she was his granddaughter. And her father and grandmother called in the favor owed by Zed, the demon sitting across from me.

They hadn't found her because Kenzie and Gunnar had stumbled into my domain. Zed had no authority to come and go into the Fourth Circle. He was on a visitor visa, one he could have easily acquired while Kenzie's father was here. He was dragging out the process.

"Why not bring him here? You know the simple process of getting into the Fourth?" I eyed him curiously.

He squirmed in his seat. Then hid his face in his hands. His human form was impressive. He once had great power, but he was, as the humans say, elderly.

"Her mates are powerful, and I had hoped to strike a deal. I wanted to feel that power once again." He hung his head in shame. He should be ashamed.

My precious Fae's father was going out of his mind trying to find his daughter, and my evil father was coming to steal her from me or, worse, kill her to spite me. She could have been long gone before he even knew she was here.

"Take me to them. I need to speak with them now." I demanded.

"My power is not what it once was, Master. I cannot go to them. They must summon me."

Fuck I was afraid of that. It was ok. Jafir was still in the village, or at least he better be; he would get me there.

I gave Zed a menacing glare. "You will remain here. My staff will take you to the waiting area."

As soon as I said this, Neo appeared, as he always did whenever I needed him. He bowed to me and motioned for Zed to follow him.

Telepathically, I summoned Devon. He appeared in the doorway and bowed, "Master?"

"Find Jafir and bring him here," I commanded, and Devon shuffled away.

I sat behind my desk and looked at the damage I'd done when Kenzie was here. She hadn't flinched at my power display. If not mistaken, she looked amused.

That was over a week ago, almost two. She should have reached the gateway by now, but reports had come in about a storm that had raged across the desert plains. A storm the realm hadn't seen the likes of in over a thousand years.

I ran my tongue across my teeth, and anger laced with fear flared like an inferno in my blood. Kenzie could be wandering around the Fifth Circle lost. I wanted to find her and quickly.

Devon and Jafir appeared in my doorway.

"Master, as you requested," Devon bowed and exited the library.

Jafir strutted toward the bar cart and helped himself. He had an imposing human form. The women in that realm swooned in his presence. The women here did the same thing come to think of it.

"As I said earlier, Dash, the human, transitioned but is not fully formed yet. Give it some time," Jafir poured himself some Liquid Gold, then tipped his head as an offering to make one for me also.

I nodded and waited for him at my desk. "This isn't about the human. I need a guide to a specific location in the human realm."

He pursed his lips, "Where might that be?"

"Don't know the exact coordinates, but I have a houseguest that owes a mage family a favor. And I need to speak with them. After our conversation, I'll get myself back here, and I'll need you to guide a wolf, a vamp, and a mage to the Fifth."

He threw back his drink, slammed the glass down, and belched. Jafir had always been socially immature. It was part of his charm.

"That's a tall order, my friend. And I am supposed to be on vacation. But for you, why not! They will need to make a sacrifice to enter and exit, and even with that, they may not make it through alive."

CHAPTER 37

KENZIE

I had sand in crevices one should never have sand. And that wasn't the worst of it. Shielding us from the sandstorm zapped my magical energy and turned us around. We didn't know which direction to go. The Fifth Circle didn't have a rising sun or moon. The best Gunnar could do was guess what time it was and our location. And I offered zero assistance as I was challenged on both topics.

Exhaustion was bone-deep, but we needed to keep moving. We climbed upward to a windswept plateau hoping the height advantage would reveal something we could use to guide us.

From the view at the top of the dune, in every possible direction, were more mounds of sand and zero mountain peaks.

I tried my mage sight, but it was wonky. Fucking magic burn. I plopped down to recover. Gunnar sat beside me and rummaged through his bag. We still had some rations, dried meat, and carafes of water. There was hope.

"You saved us, Kenz. Thank you. I planned as best as possible, but a sandstorm, who would've thought?"

"You did great, Gunnar. And don't thank me yet. We still need to get out of this place." I took off my jacket and upturned the pockets to get out the sand. Then I did the same with my boots and socks and my jeans.

Gunnar de-sanded himself as well. "So, I say we wait right here until it gets dark. Maybe there will be lights that we could follow. We must regroup, find a village, and ask for directions."

"Sounds like an excellent plan." I sighed. I lay down on the sand and stared at the gray sky. It could be a long while until it got dark.

"What did Dash do? If you don't mind me asking?" Gunnar had laid down also.

"Oh, you know . . . offered me the one thing I can't have in exchange for me to remain his little prisoner," I quipped.

"Really? Hmmm. What did he offer?"

I shrugged. It was time to release that insecurity. "I can't have children, something to do with my uterus. Dash said he could heal me, but I'd have to remain in his private quarters."

"Well, that's shit."

"Tell me about it. He seemed nice, aside from kidnapping us.”

Gunnar snickered. "He was very generous, Kenz. He did all of that because he's in love with you. You know that, right?"

"Love is not locking someone in a cage. Love is not manipulating the other to do your will. Besides, I'm not interested."

"Don't be so hard on the guy. On top of all the things he did for both of us, he treated you with reverence and respect. I bet he's losing his mind right now, wondering if you're safe." He sat up and looked at me. "He practically became unhinged when that plant cut you. And after that portal incident . . . he was broken. Something I am sure he had never experienced firsthand."

"Every demon in the village both feared him and loved him. He's brought peace to a realm that had always been at war. There's darkness, sure, but as you could tell by the places you did see, it's nice, and everyone had a deep respect and fondness for him. He's insanely powerful." Gunnar continued.

"And you're the talk of the town. According to the gossip, he has been single for several decades. And then you come along and start throwing his money around." He laughed.

I rolled my eyes at the sky, then turned my head to face him. "I did that one time. He wasn't going to tip the waiter. Can you imagine?"

"Well, according to everyone I met, he never did until he met you. Did you see the amount of money he left at the wine bar? You have everyone singing your praises." Gunnar leaned back on the sand.

I contemplated Gunnar's words. He was right on many counts; Dash was good to me. Even in intimate moments, when I said no, he didn't force himself, and he could have. He was generous and tender when we were alone. There was no doubt the demon was on top of the power scale. I saw his temper when he lashed out at Cerai and again in his library when he burned a hole in the wall. And those were mere glimpses.

Despite that, I missed my men, my bestie, and even Bear. And Brody, I needed to be around those that knew and loved him just as much as I did. I needed to ensure his memory would live.

"I miss home. I would've stayed with Dash if it weren't for my life in our realm," I said in a soft voice.

"Thought so. It's ok, Kenz. If it's meant to be, it will work out somehow. Rest. We'll travel at nightfall."

Rest didn't come easily. I lay awake thinking about our time in the Fourth Circle. At the wine bar, I had concluded Gunnar was my half-brother. Curious to know if he had come to the same conclusion as I had, I proceeded to ask him personal questions. Yes, I was too chicken to come straight out and ask him.

"Tell me about your life, Gunnar."

And so he did. It was shameful I hadn't thought to ask before. He knew so much about me and all I knew was that Granny and Dad referred to him as a family friend.

According to Gunnar, his family had been friends with my family for generations. He had four sisters and one brother. At sixty-seven years old, he was the youngest and the only one in his family that didn't have children. He wasn't married and had recently broke up with a woman he'd been with for twenty years. When I asked why he didn't marry her, he said that she was human. Made sense considering how we supes lived much longer lives than humans did, not to mention our slow aging process. Gunnar looked to be in his late twenties like Stel and Caid.

His family were hedge witches specializing in healing. He could heal himself and knew a few spells and potions, but he wasn't proficient at them. He was a combat mage, Tier Six, one notch below my father. With this news, I was certain my assumption was correct.

He had learned combat magic from my father and grandmother. My father never mentioned Gunnar. Neither did my grandmother. I was sure my Granny knew; she knew everything. It was one of those scandalous family secrets. Gunnar was a love child that my father had hoped to remain hidden.

"Are you close to both of your parents?" I asked. What I really wanted to know was if his parents were still happily married, but that might be suspicious.

"I'm close to my mum. My father not as much. He and I have always had our differences. My combat mage abilities make me different from the rest of the family. But," he shrugged. "I am what I am. I decided long ago if he had a problem with how I turned out, then it was his cross to bear. Not mine."

Well, that sealed it. Mage magic was inherited. He was my father's son. Un-fucking-believable. Since it was my father's secret, I'd let him reveal it. Until then, I was content to play pretend.

"So there's this kid, in the pack. He's a wolf, about eighteen years old. I adopted him as my little brother because, as you know, I don't have siblings. But I've decided to adopt you too. As the older brother of course, since you're way older than me." I gave him a sidelong glance and grinned.

Gunnar laughed, which was a relief. "I feel the same way. It's kind of nice not being the baby of the family. Even though I'm not that much older than you."

"Yes, you are."

"Are you sure? I'm your brother. You don't have to lie about your age. Besides, it's kind of obvious with all the gray hair."

"I do not have gray hair!" I flicked sand at him.

"Well, you're right. I figured that was better than pointing out the wrinkles on your face."

"Fuuckk you!! I do not have wrinkles either, you shit!"

Gunnar rolled over on the sand, cackling.

"You know what, whatever. I know what you're doing. You're just trying to make yourself feel better because I'm a better merc."

"Whoa! Whoa! Whoa — wait one minute. I'm way better. My kill count tops yours by tons!"

"Over your long ass life, maybe, but not since we've been in The Dark Realm. I guarantee I've killed more demons than you."

Gunnar clutched his hand to his chest, feigning offense. "Bite your tongue, young miss. My kill count in this realm is way higher."

We both laughed at our ridiculous conversation, then fell silent.

"Have you been counting?" I asked, my tone serious.

"Maybe." Gunnar glanced at me, then shrugged. "Yes, I have. All mercs do. What's your number?"

"I'm not telling."

Gunnar gasped. "Fine, be that way."

I laid on the sand with my back facing him, knowing full well this was not the end of that topic. Mercs we were a competitive bunch. With a smile on my lips, I fell asleep.

CHAPTER 38
KENZIE

Gunnar was still sleeping when I roused, so I stepped away and relieved my bladder. My mates would pee themselves with laughter if they knew I'd popped a squat in the middle of The Dark Realm.

The thought made me smile as I climbed back up the dune. Gunnar was awake and asked, "What are you smiling at?"

"Just thinking about my guys." I gazed around me and saw a few dim lights in the distance. That was the only sign of civilization in this forsaken place. I motioned to Gunnar, and he stood up to look.

"Let's go ask for directions, then," he said.

We walked toward the lights until the sky lightened to a lighter gray. As soon as the sky lightened and we could no longer see the village ahead, we stopped to rest and then woke when it got dark and continued.

On the third cycle of the light gray sky, the village was within a few hours walk. We decided to skip the rest period and soldier on. By the time we reached the village, the sky had turned dark, and we were dragging our feet.

Unlike the Fourth Circle, there were no villagers moving about the little town. It seemed abandoned, which I hoped wasn't the case. We needed to replenish our supplies.

Desperate to get a couple hours of shut-eye, we ignored the dismal streets and sought a resting place.

Down a dark alley, a two-foot overhang provided shelter from what had turned out to be a cold drizzly night. It smelled like urine, but I was too tired to care. As soon my tired ass hit the ground, my eyes closed.

A whimper woke me. Gunnar was fast asleep, unbothered by the whining nearby. I got up and investigated, following the soft mewling down the alley and around the first corner. I searched, determined to find the source of that sad, scared sound.

Something tugged my elbow, and I spun around, slicing the air with my dagger. My attack missed Gunnar by scant millimeters.

"It's just me, Kenz," Gunnar whispered, his hands in front of him.

"Are you crazy? I almost killed you!"

"Sorry. I woke, and you were gone. What's going on?" he muttered.

"Shhh . . . listen," I sheathed my dagger.

The whimpering was louder; it was close. I followed the sound, which led behind a pile of trash to a little ball of fur. The tiny four-legged creature stumbled around in a circle. Probably a newborn, I knelt, placed my hand down, and it snuggled up to me. Poor little thing was shaking. I held it up and looked at it with my mage sight. Its coat was silky and black as night, and it had mismatched eyes, which reminded me of Dash. It had four sturdy legs, large floppy ears that pointed to a sharp triangle at the end, a stubby tail, and sharp teeth. I held it up to look at its gender bits. Male. He was adorable. I held him close to my body and petted it gently. How did something so cute end up here alone?

"Where's your mama, little one?" I cooed at the little puppy, then turned to Gunnar, "Water?" I asked in a soft voice.

He handed me a carafe. "I'll go look around."

I put the puppy down and poured water for him on my hands. The little one drank eagerly, peed, then snuggled around my boot.

Gunnar came back and shook his head. I handed back the carafe and thanked him. I picked up the puppy, laid it on my chest, and zipped up my jacket, and we started moving again.

We walked for hours and stayed on the outskirts of the sparse villages. It was quiet and deserted. Not that anyone would want to live in these places. But I guessed if your soul was sanctioned to hell, this was your fate. The thought made me cringe, and at the same time, I wished Dash were around to question him.

"You're going to keep a pet? From hell?" Gunnar asked breaking the silence.

"Well yeah, I'm not going to leave it here," I petted the puppy's head. "We need water, though."

We walked until we found suitable rest spots, taking turns keeping watch. Our supplies were nil, and we had no clue if we were going in the right direction.

Finally, we came upon a few demons with carts. They weren't the nice-smelling food carts in the Fourth, but it was a sign of life and Gunnar found someone that understood Gaelic. He confirmed we were heading toward the nearest gateway. The demon was nice enough to refill our carafes, even though he scowled and did so begrudgingly. We thanked him for his generosity and continue our journey.

Gunnar and I were sleep-deprived and hungry as we dragged our bodies through the gray terrain. My new puppy kept our morale high. He was a joy to have around and didn't need much, just water now and then. He bounced around with his tail wagging, and if something startled him, he'd transform into a puff of smoke, earning him his name "Smokey." And although his fur was black as a starless night sky, he was the candlelight that gave me hope to continue home.

CHAPTER 39
STELLAN

The phone call I'd had with Mr. Jameson nearly knocked me off my feet. It took a full heartbeat rotation to get my shit in gear and gather the other three . . . two men. Fuck. The loss of Brody still hurt like a motherfucker.

I sent a group text, gathered a few things in my room, and went downstairs.

"Are you for real?" Caid asked as he arrived in the living area.

I finished a bottle of water, then chucked the plastic in the recycle bin. "That's what he said. The demon they had been working with sent a message somehow. He requested a meeting at Kenzie's place at the Majestic. Mr. Jameson included. It's urgent."

"Alright, I'm ready. Erik?" Caid asked.

I checked my phone and hadn't received a response, so I dialed his number. It went straight to voicemail.

"No response. Should we go?" I asked my brother.

He nodded. "Erik will show up. He's been solid since he dreamwalked with Kenz."

Caid and I teleported to Vegas. We had time to kill, so we sorted ourselves before everyone arrived. I had just finished placing an order for food delivery when Mr. Jameson popped into the Penthouse.

"Where's the other one?" Kenzie's father asked.

I shrugged and looked at my phone messages and hadn't received anything. Then the doorbell rang. Caid answered and let Erik in.

Not sure why he teleported into the hallway, but at least he was here.

The doorbell rang again, and Caid signed for the food delivery.

"All right, since we're all here, this is what I know. The demon that owes us a favor appeared in our workshop with a message to meet here. That was the first time he had made contact with us. We usually do the summoning. He said Kenzie was found, and a demon lord wanted to speak with us directly about her whereabouts. And that's everything." Mr. Jameson put a fry in his mouth and chewed.

"How did he make contact with you?" Erik asked in a clear voice.

Mr. Jameson rubbed his temple. "Another demon, a reaper."

I stopped chewing my burger and stared at my mate's father.

"Come again?" Caid asked.

"A reaper. He had the full kit. Scythe and everything." Mr. Jameson had a solemn look on his face.

"Well, fuck, what does that mean?" I asked.

Mr. Jameson shrugged. "Son, your guess is as good as mine. That's why we're here. I suggest we not jump to any conclusions until the demon arrives."

I couldn't eat after that. I grabbed a bottle of whiskey and waited in Kenzie's room; it didn't seem right to drink in front of Erik since he had been sober.

Luckily, I didn't have to wait for very long. A loud pop rocked the Penthouse; I shifted and ran down the steps.

A bright light filled the living room. It smelled like cloves and cinnamon with a smidge of smoke. Once the light dissipated, a large male stood at the center. He was an inch or two taller than me but slimmer. At six feet five inches, I was used to being the big man in the room. I didn't quite like it. I growled.

He spun in place, taking in the room. Caid was vamped out, and magic crackled along Erik's arms. Mr. Jameson had his sword ready.

"Did you know that The Majestic, this very place, is neutral territory for demons? It's considered a vacation spot. We are allowed to come and go here as we please, and no one will raise an eyebrow. And Kenzie, my precious little Fae, owns this place. What are the odds? I can visit as often as I want to." The demon rambled on and started looking around the place. He wore an expensive-looking suit in all black.

"Where's my daughter?" Mr. Jameson asked, not missing a beat.

I shifted back to communicate with the demon. He noticed me and said, "I can communicate with your wolf."

"Sure. But that would be rude, since no one else can," I answered.

He smiled, and I could tell he was holding in a laugh.

I growled, and he shrugged, dismissing me. Motherfucker.

"I need your help to get Kenzie out of The Dark Realm," he said.

"Who the fuck are you?" Caid was beyond annoyed.

"Daywalker, very interesting," the demon rubbed his chin. "I'm . . . Dash. Kenzie was with me in the Fourth Circle and ran off with," he fixed his gaze on Mr. Jameson. "Her brother."

Mr. Jameson bristled.

He had confessed this secret to me when Gunnar and Kenzie had disappeared. She must've figured it out.

"Why didn't you bring them home? You have power. You could have brought them home." Kenzie's father shouted at the demon.

The demon looked thoughtful, then said, "Long story short, I wanted to keep her. But she wouldn't have it. So she left."

"And why can't you find her and bring her back now?" I stared at the demon.

"My father is coming to my realm. To find her. That's an even longer story." He waved his hand dismissively and went to stand at the window. "If I go after Kenzie, he will track me and find her. If he finds her, he will kill her, which would be kindness, or enslave her. I want you," he pointed at us with a twirl of his finger, "to find her and bring her back here. And I will deal with my father."

"Why should we trust you?" Erik asked.

The demon crossed his arms over his chest. "Do you have another option?"

That was the crux of it. We had tried to gain access to The Dark Realm and nothing had worked. The only other thing to do was speak with my brother's sire.

"How will this work? How soon can we go?" I asked, moving things along. If we could get our mate back, we needed to get going.

"Spoken like a true Alpha. Straight to the point. As soon as you can be ready."

"We'll do it. Whatever it is, we'll do it," Caid said.

"Let's go," Erik reaffirmed.

The demon smiled again, "Fair enough. You share a Fae bond, which will help you locate her. Going through to the other side will be jarring. And your most powerful magic might be suppressed, so prepare yourself."

I drew in a sharp inhale. "What the fuck does that mean?"

The demon sighed, "Unless you want to get stuck in The Dark Realm, you'll have to make a sacrifice. You won't be able to shift, and you won't have any sunlight to nourish you. You can drink demon blood. It won't have any adverse effects, but you may want to pack some reserves. Demons aren't easy to kill. And you," he pointed to Erik, "will not have access to your magic."

"What do you want? I don't believe you would do all this without wanting something in return. What's in it for you?" I asked.

The demon laughed. "I love Kenzie, which is why I wanted to keep her. And I believe she loves me, or at the very least, is interested in me. She just needs time to get to know me better. The Dark Realm boosts her power, and she could be Queen at my side. But . . . she chose you, which I will tolerate. I'm not sure why she wants to come back here. She was abducted under your watch."

He smoothed down his suit jacket. "You don't deserve her. And maybe I don't, either. But I am letting her go so she can be with you shits and waging war against my father to keep her safe. That is how much I love her. Prepare yourselves. Your guide will be here soon."

We watched the demon waltz upstairs, slack-jawed. Mr. Jameson followed the demon.

I gathered some things Kenzie may have missed while she was away. Caid ordered blood to take with us and some other essentials while Erik stocked up on spells and tonics.

Fifteen minutes later, the Grim8 Reaper, whose name was Jafir, showed up in the Penthouse.

"Master Dash, it's time," he said even though Dash was not in the room. Dash appeared a moment later, followed by Mr. Jameson.

"The transition is complete, Master." The Reaper bowed his head.

"Transition?" I squinted at Dash.

He looked at me, then back at the Reaper, then back at me.

"It's nothing. Any questions?" Dash asked us.

"If there's something else going on that we need to know, speak the fuck up. I don't want to be blindsided trying to keep my mate safe." Caid fumed.

Dash looked at the Reaper again and nodded. "Jafir will tell you when you get to The Dark Realm. I won't put you or Kenzie in any danger."

I looked at the two demons and threw up my hands.

"Fine. How do we get back?" I asked.

The Reaper pulled out a parchment.

"Directions to the gateway and the timeframe. Gateways move, so here are two. I'll review how to keep time in our realm on our way there," the Reaper said.

"Will Kenzie and Gunnar be able to walk out of The Dark Realm?" Erik asked.

"I will meet you at the gateway when it opens," the Reaper replied.

"As a Grim, he can move through our realm quickly and easily. And he'll be able to guide them out," Dash replied.

"Why couldn't they get out at the portal that opened here at the Catacombs?" Erik narrowed his eyes, his distrust of the demon clear.

"The demon that ran it wanted to enslave them rather than let them go." Dash rubbed his chin. "Any more questions?"

We shook our heads.

"Oh, one more thing, you never met me. Your ticket into The Dark Realm was all this guy, Jafir. If another demon asks, you never met me and have no idea who I am."

"Considering we don't know if Dash is your real name, that won't be hard to do." Caid rolled his eyes.

The Reaper growled as though offended. "This is Master Dashiele Morningstar, son of Lucifer himself. Show some respect."

Magic swirled through the room and then the world went black.

CHAPTER 40

KENZIE

Me, Gunnar, and Smokey continued walking through The Dark Realm, following the directions we'd received. It was hard to tell if we were going in the right direction. But it was all we had to go on.

The villages were far behind us now, which was just as well. Most of the demons we encountered were less than friendly, and we had to fight our way through. Again. The Fifth and Sixth Circles sucked donkey balls.

We sustained minor injuries, and it didn't help that we had run out of water days ago. We were back in the desert, walking along the gray sand.

There was a big part of me that missed Dash. It would have been easier to wait it out in the plush Fourth Circle until we found a demon to strike a deal with, but that was the pessimist in me talking. I pushed the negative self-talk out of my head and put one step in front of the other.

Out of nowhere, something hit Gunnar from behind, sending him twenty feet across the gray sand. Damn it, this was getting old. I unsheathed the sword Gunnar had lent me and held it out, ready to deal with the demon. It was small in stature and regarded me with beady eyes.

The demon lunged at me, and I parried to my right, swung my sword, slicing his arm. Black blood seeped out of the wound. The demon flinched back, cradling his injured arm. He growled, showing me his monstrous teeth. I aimed my sword, and he cringed. His reaction made me pause. *This was different.* Most demons we'd encountered hit first and not once had I seen one flinch.

The demon growled, doing his best to look intimidating, but his trembling body gave him away. I sheathed the sword.

"Do you speak English?" I asked in my best soothing voice.

He snarled and puffed out his chest. Ok, guess not.

Smokey peeped his little head out of my jacket and growled at the demon. It was the cutest thing.

The demon didn't think so. It looked affright, dropped a satchel to the ground, and hightailed in the direction we were headed.

"Look at you, you little badass," I cooed at Smokey. He yawned.

Gunnar dusted himself off, looking put out. The cowardly demon had laid him out pretty good. I cleared my throat, doing my best to stifle the giggles bursting inside me.

He huffed as he picked up the satchel the demon had left behind and opened them. In the satchel were a couple gourds filled with liquid.

Gunnar popped the cork, sniffed, and then tipped it over, spilling clear liquid droplets on his palm.

"Don't drink that! It could be poison or pee," I warned him.

"Smells like water, looks like water. Let's give it to your hellhound." He reached his palm out to Smokey.

"Hey! No animal testing on my puppy!" I turned away from him, but it was too late. Smokey lapped up the liquid.

I held my breath waiting for a calamity to happen. Nothing. The puppy seemed fine, and I sighed in relief.

Smokey wanted more. So Gunnar poured more into his palm for him.

"It's just water, Kenz." Gunnar took a swig, then held out the gourd to me. As soon as my fingers brushed the water jug, he swiped it away from me and said, "What's your number?"

I chuckled. "Give."

He handed me the water and eyed me while I drank.

After swallowing, I said, "Ok, on three, we'll both say our number."

Gunnar smiled and nodded.

"One, two, three . . ." I said.

"One hundred thousand!" He shouted.

"You're such a liar!" I smacked his arm.

"And you're a cheater!" He took the gourd from me, laughing as we walked onward.

So this is what it's like to have a brother? I smiled despite his juvenile pranks.

Thanks to the demon, we had enough water to last a few days. I couldn't have been more grateful.

We continued trudging along through the sand for a long while when something warm bloomed in my chest. I came to a stop and let Smokey out of his hiding place, thinking he had peed on me. Smokey whined, voicing his displeasure when I put him down. I checked my clothing. No pee. Weird.

"You ok?" Gunnar narrowed his eyes at me.

"Um...not sure," I rubbed my chest, "something is different." The warmth in my chest started to tingle. "I'm having a heart attack," I said to Gunnar.

He frowned and then grabbed my wrist. "Your pulse is fine. What does the pain feel like?

I shook my head. "No, not painful. It . . . it's warm, and it tingles a little."

"If it were a heart attack, it would be painful like your chest was caving in. Do you want to rest a moment?" he asked.

"No. I'm good." I rubbed at my chest again and used my magic to probe at the spot that tingled. It sparked and startled me. Stel? It couldn't be.

Smokey pawed at my boots. I picked him up and placed him in his hiding place. The Fifth Circle was desolate. There was no sign of life or landscape to marvel at, just a gray desert. If it weren't for the water we had gotten from the demon, we would have died from dehydration.

We continued walking while the warm tingly sensation in my chest grew stronger and stronger. It felt like pack magic, and I'd hoped it meant we were getting closer to a gateway. Unsure of the source, I hadn't mentioned it to Gunnar. There was no need to get him excited about something that may not be true.

After some time, I let Smokey down, and he went running and jumping alongside me, eating insects. He would find a scorpion, smash it with his paws, then bring it to me. I shook my head, declining his offering, and he gulped it down and ran to find something else. Always running a few feet ahead, then running back. He was freaking adorable.

In the distance, we noticed a village of some sort. Gunnar and I sighed in relief. I couldn't make out much, but I had hoped we'd find someone to guide us in the right direction.

Smokey suddenly ran back, leaped into my arms, and burrowed into my jacket. Something scared him. I zipped up my jacket, securing him in place, and drew my sword. Gunnar drew his.

There was nothing around us, and the village was still about a half mile away. I turned on my mage sight and got nothing. Gunnar shook his head; he got nothing either.

As we got closer to the village, we heard shouting and crying. The pleas for mercy kicked in my protective instincts, and I ran toward the sound with my brother right behind me.

We were in a residential area. Small one-story huts clustered together made up a neighborhood with a makeshift town square in the middle. We stuck to the outskirts, not wanting to draw attention until I heard crying and a menacing voice I had recognized.

I marched into the town square. Demons of all shapes and sizes gathered around to gawk at the scene. My eyes bugged out of my head at what was before me. Motherfucker.

The Rogue had a demon by his neck screaming obscenities, striking it with his fists.

I recognized the small demon. He was the one that floored Gunnar, the same one that Smokey scared away. The one that had left his gourds of water, which saved our lives.

The Rogue didn't notice us until I pressed the tip of my sword against his neck.

"That's enough. Release him," I said in a calm voice.

"You! You're . . . you're alive," he stuttered and whipped his head back and forth between Gunnar and me.

"Of course we are; we're not easy to kill." I slid the tip of the sword under his jaw and nicked his skin. "Release him."

I tugged on the demon's arm with my free hand and pushed him behind me.

"He stole from me," the Rogue stated with his chin up. "He is a weak low. He shall be punished."

"No. Your days of punishing people are fucking over."

"No? How dare you?"

"You brought me here against my will. You've been terrorizing the magical community for your selfish gains, and you have the audacity to say, how dare I? You know what fuck you. I have had enough. I thought we needed you to get us out of this shithole, but not anymore. Your psychopathic rantings end now."

I rotated my wrist, ready to lop off his head, but a firm grasp steadied my arm.

"Easy, sweetness, we need him for questioning," a raspy voice stated behind me.

My vamp appeared in front of me and knocked out the Rogue. My knees gave out.

CHAPTER 41
KENZIE

Stel wrapped an arm around my torso, holding me up, his muscular body pressed against my back. Caid strode up and knelt before me, pressing his head into my belly. Erik stood beside me, his head burrowing in the crook of my neck.

I reached one arm to hook around Stel's neck and the other around Caid's head. Tears streamed down my face. Was I dreamwalking again?

"Are you . . . are you real?" I whispered.

Caid tipped his head to face me, "We're real, love."

"We've missed you. So fucking much," Stel kissed me all over the side of my dirt-streaked face.

My neck felt wet. I placed a kiss on Erik's dusty hair. He didn't say a word.

We stood there glued together for a long, needed moment until someone cleared their throat.

Stel captured my lips with his, then stepped back. Caid stood and kissed me on the mouth; his tongue darted between my lips. He pressed his forehead against mine, and then he released me.

Erik clung to me. I turned to face him and wrapped my arms around his middle. People were talking, but I tuned them out. My magic man needed this moment, and I did too. A torrent of emotions rolled from him. Relief, sorrow, happiness, and despair. Lust.

I pulled away from him and looked at his tear-streaked face. He kept his eyes closed, and I rose on my tiptoes to kiss each one. And then his lips. His mouth responded to mine. I suckled his lips, swallowing his sobs. We broke our kiss but remained in each other's arms.

"I love you," I whispered.

His turquoise eyes gleamed at me. "I love you more."

He released me, and Caid took his place. Caid crushed me to his chest, then startled, taking a step back.

"What the fuck?" He unzipped my jacket, and Smokey's head peeked out.

Stel looked over my shoulder and growled. Smokey whimpered.

I bopped Stel on the head, "Hey! Don't scare my puppy, you big bully."

Caid gave me a dry look, "You have a new pet?" He peered at Smokey. "Is that a hellhound?"

Stel reached into my jacket and pulled my puppy out by the scruff of his neck. "This is a hellhound. A runt."

"Stop, both of you. Smokey was lost, and now he's mine." I took Smokey away from Stel and cradled the puppy, who licked my jaw, and I beamed down at him.

"Ahem!" Gunnar cleared his throat. "We have company."

I glanced at Gunnar, who was now holding the sword he'd lent me. *Did I drop my sword?* I was the worst merc ever.

Once Smokey was secured in my jacket, I grasped Erik's hand. We were surrounded by about two dozen demons, including the demon I had saved from the Rogue.

"Hey, are you okay?" I asked the demon.

"Thank you, Mistress," the demon said in perfect English. "I am Milo."

"Thank you, Miss," came from another voice in the crowd, then another, and another.

Before I knew it, the crowd voiced their thanks and moved to surround us. Their gratitude was humbling and a bit overwhelming. I could only imagine what the Rogue had done to these demons.

Smokey peeked out of my jacket and growled at the crowd. The crowd stopped and dropped to their knees.

"Milo," I turned to the demon the Rogue had been punishing. "Can you explain what's happening right now?"

"Mistress, you . . . You've tamed a hound," he stammered.

"I'm not sure he's tame, but okay. What does that mean?"

"Hounds are guardians of The Dark Realm. The evil mage killed its mother and her pups; this one got away somehow. They are never so docile. But this one likes you. You deserve respect for taming the hound and saving us," Milo explained.

"Okay. Can you tell everyone they don't need to thank me, and they can go on their way?" I motioned toward the crowd.

"They mean you no harm, Mistress. They want to pay their respects for dealing with the evil mage."

"Well," I looked around, unsure of where to begin. "Thank you all for being respectful. Please stand and go about your day as usual."

The crowd bowed and dispersed, all except Milo. He stood near me with his head down. Erik put an arm around my waist and kissed the side of my face. I smiled and leaned into him.

"Milo, you dropped your water gourds, which saved our lives. We owe you our gratitude," I said to the demon.

"Oh no, Mistress, thank you. You spared my life twice. It would be my pleasure to service you."

Stel and Caid growled. Erik smiled. Milo shrunk back.

I reached out to grasp Stel's hand, "My name is Kenzie. These are my mates Erik, Stellan, and Caid." I pointed at Gunnar. "And this guy is my brother, Gunnar. It's nice to meet you, and sorry about the sword thing." I motioned to the slice on his shoulder that had already formed a scab.

"No, no, Mistress. It is a pleasure to receive such a wound from one so noble and fierce. I shall wear the scar with pride."

Weirdo.

"Okay, well, we need some help. But can you give us a minute?" I asked Milo.

He nodded, and I turned to my men.

"How did you get here, and why are you here? I am happy to see you, but I don't understand. And please tell me you know where the gateway is; I want to go home."

"Long story, love." Caid kissed my lips.

"Milo, is there somewhere we can sit and have some privacy?" Stel asked the demon.

"Of course, anything the Mistress needs." Milo bowed.

Gunnar found a cart resembling a wheelbarrow while Caid pulled out a roll of duct tape from his backpack. He taped the Rogue's mouth, wrists, and ankles and threw him in the cart. Milo motioned to a thick, limbed demon nearby. As though the Rogue weighed nothing, the giant demon wheeled the tied-up Rogue alongside us as we followed Milo to a hut, which he said was his.

The huts here were in the shape of mushroom heads. Some were round, and some had sharp points. All of them were in varying colors that were dull from age or weather.

Milo said the demon that wheeled him would watch over our prisoner until we were ready for him. He led us to a green-colored mushroom and motioned with his webbed hand to follow him.

Before stepping into Milo's mushroom house, Stel grabbed my hand. "We just need a minute," he said to the others and the demon. He reached into my jacket, picked up Smokey, and then set him on the ground.

Stel led me toward the side of the mushroom house. Smokey followed behind us, exploring as we went.

Stel backed me to the wall and leaned in. "I've missed you, sweetness." His deep raspy voice sent tantalizing shivers through me.

He dropped his backpack. My sword clamored to the ground.

His hungry mouth found mine. His lips were hot and desperate.

I breathed him in as he stole my breath.

He palmed my breasts, kneading them through my clothes. The need to feel his skin on me, in me, was so great. I tuned out the voices of passersby. Nothing mattered except my wolf and me.

I pulled on the waistband of his jeans, unbuckling his belt. Then tore off my jacket and top.

I reached down to untie my boots, then kicked them off — one foot and the other. Stel latched onto my taut nipple. I gasped.

He tugged off my pants and panties in one movement. I kicked them off and let them lay in the dirt while Stel pushed his jeans down, freeing his rigid cock. I groaned at the sight of his enormous member.

I climbed his body, impatient to feel him inside me. I hooked my ankles behind his back while he dragged his tip up and down my wet slit.

"Now, Stel. I want you right now."

He speared my core with his massive cock and growled. My nails dug into his scalp, and I bit his lip; blood filled my mouth.

He rocked into me nice and slow, allowing me to adjust. I suckled his lip, soothing the puncture I'd made. My eyes opened, and I stared into his, love and lust reflecting in our gaze.

His hips moved faster and harder. My back scraped against the wall behind me. A wave of exhilarating pleasure rolled up and down my spine and then pooled in my core, rising higher with every thrust. The suckling sound of our joined bodies filled my ears, the sweetest melody.

My sensory nerves were on fire with pleasure. Stellan gripped my thighs while he pumped into me, slamming my body into the wall. His lips fastened to the mark he had left on my shoulder. Ecstasy exploded through me. Stars swam in my vision. Stel didn't stop; his thrusts became more frantic. My pussy clamped down.

"Oh fuck," he moaned, and his body jerked as he released himself inside me. "I love you, Kenzie. Never leave me again."

I kissed my wolf, making promises I had every intention of keeping.

CHAPTER 42

KENZIE

After Stel and I got reacquainted, we picked up Smokey and went into the mushroom.

The interior opened up to a living room that had Moroccan-style floor seating. The ceilings were high with holes in them which served as windows providing circulation and light. Milo had a few belongings and kept his home neat and organized. I felt terrible as we were covered with dust, grime, and blood. Milo didn't seem to mind one bit.

Gunnar, Erik, and Caid were seated on the colorful cushions strewn about the stone floor. I released Stel's hand and went to sit between Caid and Erik. Stel decided to sit between my legs. It had been so long that I clung to them as tightly as they clung to me.

Milo brought in cups of water and a bowl of milk for Smokey. I wasn't sure what kind of milk it was, but my puppy lapped it. He had his muzzle deep in the bowl, drinking and blowing bubbles simultaneously. We all laughed. Then Smokey lifted his cute little face, snarled, then went back to drinking his milk.

"Mistress, our Chief will want to speak with you. Make yourself at home. There is a bathroom there, and I will be back for you shortly." Milo scampered away as quickly as he had when he ran into Gunnar a few days ago.

"Tell me everything," I told my men.

"Long story short, your demon found your family, asked to meet with us at the Majestic, and made arrangements for us to come through and find you," Caid started.

"Dash is at war with his father, or he would have done it himself. The poison you were inflicted with came from a plant his father created. It was designed to kill its victims and allowed his father to learn what you are and track you. Our magic had burned through the poison, but by then, he already knew you were at Dash's and was on his way to come for you when you left." Stel rested his chin on my thigh.

"He brought us here, and we've been looking for you for who knows how long. Seems like weeks, but here it's hard to tell." Erik's hand squeezed mine.

"A few days ago, I felt our bond and knew we were going in the right direction. We kept following it until we found you in the square," Stel added.

"That's all great, but how do we get out of here?" Gunnar said. "No offense, but I'm with Kenzie. We want to go home."

"I'm sorry. Have you guys met?" I pointed between Gunnar and the guys. They gave non-committal grunts and nods.

"Dash gave us a map. Although, it would be good to have a guide. Maybe Milo?" Caid replied.

"We'll all get through, right? None of us are stuck here?" I asked them.

"Of course, sweetness, we had to make small sacrifices to get here. I don't have access to my wolf, but I am not helpless." He turned to face me, showed me the dagger I gave him as a gift, and smiled. "This thing cuts through demon skin like butter."

I winked at my wolf, and then I turned to face Caid.

"Because there is no sun, I need to consume blood. But I brought human blood with me, and we've had a few skirmishes on our way here, and it turns out demon blood is not so bad." Caid gave me a sly smile.

The thought of him drinking demon blood made my tummy curdle. Then I realized what was missing.

"I don't have my magic. Not all of it, anyway. I can use spells, and I have tonics and potions." Erik leaned over and kissed my cheek.

Milo returned and said, "Mistress, the Chief insists on meeting you. He wants to honor you with a feast."

"Well, um, that is incredibly kind of him, but we're trying to get out of here. My companions and I are weary. We want so much to go home."

"Yes, yes, Mistress, the Chief will help you, but first come, the feast will commence momentarily."

I looked across from me at Gunnar. He shrugged, "We need the help, Kenz. Let's meet the Chief and go from there."

The Chief's home was a few doors down from Milo's and was the only red-colored mushroom house in the village.

Milo introduced us to the Chief, bowed, and left, saying he would help prepare for the feast while the large-limbed demon happily watched over the still-unconscious Rogue.

As it turned out, the Chief was an elderly, stout fellow. Like Milo, he was four feet tall but where Milo was slender, Chief Hobs was round. His wiry white beard fell to the floor, brushing the ground as he walked about.

His home looked like a mushroom, like the others, but it was much more extensive.

At the entryway, there were two stairways, one leading upward toward the ceiling, lined with bookshelves. And another that went down. We descended the stairs to what the Chief said was the main living area.

The spacious room was cozy and offered several mismatched chairs. I sat between Stel and Erik on a distressed leather sofa while Caid took the seat on the floor between my legs. Gunnar perused the shelves while Smokey explored the demon's home like he owned the place.

My puppy sniffed here and there, and I crossed my fingers, hoping he wouldn't pee on anything. Satisfied the place was safe, Smokey leaped into my arms.

"Kenzie, you will keep the hound, yes?" Chief Hobs asked, keeping a wary eye on Smokey.

"I am. He was wandering around alone and scared. He protected me and I protected him. He is now mine." Smokey rolled on his back and I rubbed his belly.

"Good." His stiff posture relaxed. "I understand you need to get through a gateway posthaste and I will help by offering a guide. The nearest is set to open in two days. It will take you only a short time to reach it, but I suggest you leave at first light. Tonight you rest, and we will honor you for saving us from that menacing man.

"What was he doing here?" I asked.

"He made a deal with Mammon. Thus he traversed between realms often. He was cruel and wanted to use my people as his test subjects. Mammon is a mid-level demon, he doesn't care for us lows, especially the ones here. He would not offer protection, so the mage came and did as he pleased. We are a peaceful bunch here. Many were discarded after service to their demon lords. And had come to settle here for a life of peace. We stay amongst ourselves. The mage thought we were his to abuse. Months ago, he was on the brink of death, and I healed him. There were times I wish I hadn't. But it is my nature."

"I'm sorry, did you say months ago?" My hand paused over Smokey's belly, and he whined. Stel looked down at him and growled.

Chief Hobs nodded, "Yes, two months ago."

I looked over at Gunnar, horrified. "Two months, meant what at home?"

"Love, you've been gone for almost four months," Caid answered.

"Fuck," Gunnar muttered.

I squeezed Erik's hand and leaned my head on Stel's shoulder. So much had to have happened. It was much too long to be away from the men in my life and my business and fuck!! It wasn't just about my mates, although I missed them terribly. But there was also Bear and Tris. And my Dad had a lot of explaining to do.

I wanted to go home.

"Not to worry, Mistress, your mates are here, and you will have proper help to get you home. All of you," Chief Hobs said, and then a bell rang. "Ah, your private quarters are ready. I will take you there myself, and then we shall go to the feast! We have prepared a delicious meal to honor you."

As we left his grand mushroom house, the Chief stopped and asked, "What will you do with him?" He pointed at the unconscious Rogue.

I wanted to kill him, but Stel had prevented me from doing so for a reason, so I looked to him for answers.

"He needs to answer some questions, then we will kill him," Stel grabbed my hand and started forward.

"Oh good! Would you like to do that now? Killing him at the feast would be a great honor for the festivities."

"Yes." We all said at the same time. We were all dying to rid the realms of this dick face.

Caid woke the Rogue with a hard slap to the face. The Rogue jolted awake and tried to wiggle free of his bindings. Caid tore the tape off, ripping his skin and pulling out the hairs of his mustache.

The Rogue screamed in pain, and I smiled with delight. Being in The Dark Realm was making me crazy, or crazier.

Stel smacked the Rogue in the face. "Who are you working with?" Stel asked.

The Rogue's face twisted with contempt, "No one! Just the demon, Mammon."

"Who is continuing your experiments?" Stel asked and delivered another slap across the Rogue's face again. The slaps were probably unnecessary, but I understood his need to hurt the asshat.

"I don't know!" The Rogue said.

"Ok, this is going to take too long," Caid said. "I could glamour him, although my vamp abilities are weird here."

"I got this," Erik pulled a vial from his backpack, checked the label, and smiled.

"Truth potion." He winked at me.

Caid pulled the Rogue's hair back and pried his jaw open while Erik dumped the potion down his throat. Caid forcibly snapped his jaw closed and forced the Rogue to swallow.

Stel rounded on the Rogue and said, "Tell us everything about the experiments you were doing on the supernatural communities."

Luckily, Chief had the wherewithal to provide us with parchment, ink pot, and quill. Gunnar and I did our best to write down everything we could. The Rogue had plenty to say. We had names, phone numbers, spell ingredients, and directions. We even got his personal info, including address, birth date, and password, and he gave us everything we needed. After hours of writing, my body shook with anger.

The Rogue's experiments were further along than we had anticipated. We had already dismantled two of his facilities. One was BRS in California, and the other was a facility I had found in Germany while searching for Bear.

He had two more partners, as he called them. A corporation based in Canada and another partner in Mexico City. Fuck my life.

"One more thing," I said to the Rogue. "You mentioned when we were in the warehouse in Germany that I had enemies. Someone had willingly provided you with info on me. Who was this someone?"

"The she-wolf," he replied in a hoarse voice.

"Which one?" I wasn't being obtuse; I had two she-wolves gunning for me. I had had a run-in with Sandy, one of the wolves I had met in Vegas. In her humble opinion, I wasn't good enough for the Alpha's sons. And the other was Stel's pregnant ex. They weren't together when he got her pregnant or when Stel and I had met. Still, she hated me with a holy vengeance.

"The pregnant one," the Rogue replied.

Caid cursed. Erik gasped. Stel growled.

"I swear that fucking she-wolf is in love with me." I shook my head thinking about what a pain in the ass Christine had been since we'd met.

The guys chuckled, and we all filed out to head to the feast.

CHAPTER 43

KENZIE

Questioning the Rogue took longer than expected, so we didn't have time to freshen up before the feast.

The Chief brought us to their place of worship, a short walk from his home. Here the villagers paid homage to Lucifer. Erik, Stel, and Caid hissed at the mention of their God's name.

"Not to worry, he won't show up here," Chief Hobs assured us.

I gave my men a watchful glance, then turned to pay attention to the Chief as he walked around the garden.

The garden was the first and only garden we had come across in Fifth Circle. When I asked Chief about this, he said all of Lucifer's temples were beautiful abundant gardens. His home was in the First Circle, in the heart of The Dark Realm, and was twice the size of Earth. The Chief continued explaining that there were wondrous creatures, abundant fauna and flora, and many oceans. His palace was made of gold, and he was the most beautiful, most fierce creature in all the realms. I wasn't planning to visit, so I took his word for it. But it made me wonder about Dash.

"Have you been to Fourth Circle?" I asked the Chief. Gunnar's ears perked up, and he stared at the Chief with the same curiosity I had.

"Oh no, that belongs to the Dark Prince. Lucifer's youngest and favorite son. Very powerful that one, but temperamental if the stories hold any truth to them. Lucifer has had many children over the eons, and Dashiele is the only one to withstand his father's wrath, making him the treasured one." The Chief said all this in a matter-of-fact tone and continued strolling toward the garden's center.

Gunnar and I looked at each other, horrified. *Fuck.* He stood beside me and said, "Did we just escape from the Prince of fucking Hell?"

I swallowed hard. Then Stel pressed his body against my back and massaged my shoulders. "It's ok, sweetness. We'll talk more about him later."

I turned around, pressed my face into Stel's muscular strength, and breathed in deeply. He reached into my jacket and pulled out a whiny Smokey. I held onto my wolf with my entire body soaking up his strength.

"Mistress, are you unwell?" Milo asked beside me.

"I'm fine," I said, releasing Stel.

"I heard you mention the Fourth Circle and brought you this. A refreshing beverage from a fruit only grown in the Prince's domain. You'll like it, and it will restore your energies." Milo said in a small voice.

Requiem fruit. I took the offered cup, sniffed the contents, and then took a sip. After drinking, I smiled. "Delicious."

Milo beamed and promised to save all of the Requiem drink for us, and he walked off with a big smile.

The center of the garden had been set up for the feast. Tables were covered with food, and the demons were laughing and drinking merrily. Chief explained each food item as we walked by. Unlike the Fourth Circle, these were all delicacies of The Dark Realm. It smelled delicious, but nothing looked familiar.

After hearing about Dash's lineage, I wasn't famished, even though I should have been. I ate the bread and fruit and stayed clear of the mystery meat. The Fourth Circle drink was just as delicious as I had remembered, and I was thankful for the beverage. The guys ate like scavengers, which pleased the Chief.

Toward the end of the evening, the Chief gathered everyone's attention, "We are gathered this evening to honor our guests from the human realm who has stopped the evil mage's acts of violence on our people."

The demons cheered.

"Our guests have further honored us by offering to kill our enemy here, on these hallowed grounds!"

There were no more than thirty demons at this gathering, but it sounded like thousands were here when they started cheering.

Erik, Caid, Stel, and Gunnar gathered around me, blocking me from my view of the Chief.

"Kenzie, love, this is your kill, but . . ." Caid held my hand.

Stel grasped the other and finished what his brother was trying to say, "But I don't want you . . . I don't think you should be the one to do it. I would be honored to be the one to make this . . . sacrifice."

Gunnar nodded, "It shouldn't be you, Kenz, all things considered."

They were worried about what this would mean regarding Dash's father. For once in my life, I didn't argue. I had no problems taking a life, and the asshole had it coming. But I believed every word Dash said about his father and had no desire to sacrifice anyone on temple grounds dedicated to the God of The Dark Realm. But I didn't want my guys to do it either.

"Me!" said Milo beside us. He waved his hand in the air excitedly. "Me, me, me, I want to do it!"

"Milo, please . . . we don't condone acts of violence here. I know you were a favorite target of this mage, but this is the Mistress's decision. She chooses to be the executioner or appoint an executioner," the Chief said.

The entire crowd was silent, waiting with anticipation. Milo stared at me with pleading eyes, his hand still in the air. I went to stand next to him.

"Killing him may not give you peace Milo," I said softly. "Are you sure this is what you want?"

"Yes, Mistress. He had tormented endlessly. It will be a great honor, and I will be a hero in this village." Milo continued to wave his hand above his head.

I plucked his hand from the air and addressed the crowd, "I've chosen an executioner."

The crowd roared and chanted Milo's name. With the same speed I witnessed when he ran into Gunnar, he rushed up to the Rogue and pulled out the fucker's heart.

Whoa! I didn't think the little demon had it in him.

Milo held up the heart and bit into it. The other demons hoisted him on their shoulders and paraded around the feast, chanting his name.

Shortly after the sacrifice, the Chief escorted us to our guest quarters. I was grateful to leave the feast. I was exhausted and had enough of watching the demons cut the Rogue into pieces. The Chief said it was an honor as they would use the parts as food or spells. That was more info than I needed, and I was glad I hadn't eaten much.

At the far end of the village, we ended up at another mushroom hut. The Chief said it was reserved for esteemed guests traveling to the gateway.

The interior was much like the Chief's: two sets of stairs, tall ceilings and mismatched chairs. In the back of the dwelling was a small kitchenette with carafes filled with water, Requiem juice, and some milk for Smokey, who slept soundly in my jacket.

From the kitchen, it split in two directions into two separate rooms.

"The largest room is to the right. Mistress, if it pleases you, Abba here can cleanse your clothes while you bathe. They will be clean and dry for you in the morning." Chief told me while a female demon beside him curtsied.

"That is very generous. Thank you," I replied but stayed put. I was reluctant to leave my men.

"Go, love. Relax a bit; we'll join you in a few moments." Caid kissed my temple.

"Ok," I said, but hesitated.

Stel pressed his chest to my back and squeezed me from behind while Erik tipped my face up to meet his.

"See you in a minute, beautiful." Erik brushed my nose with his.

I looked over at Gunnar, and he nodded. It seemed like the men wanted to discuss something privately, or they wanted me to have a moment of peace. Maybe both.

CHAPTER 44

KENZIE

I followed Abba into the room, which was larger than I expected. The queen-sized bed sat close to the floor and had been covered with a soft, peach-colored blanket. My eyelids drooped. Exhaustion was catching up to me.

After settling a sleeping Smokey on a pillow, I used the facilities and went out a side door that revealed an outdoor shower. The tranquil setup released my accumulated tension since we'd left the Fourth Circle.

Water flowed down black porous rocks and pooled into a shallow basin. Steam rose from the water as though it was a natural hot spring. There was a lantern that cast playful shadows over the miniature waterfall. It was a little slice of heaven after being in a desolate desert for so long.

Abba stood in the corner of the outside bathroom, waiting for me to undress so she could wash my clothes. Lord knows they needed it. I quickly undressed and handed the filthy clothing to her, not wanting to delay her any further. She bowed her head and exited the way we came.

The water was hot, almost scalding. I let the events of the entire journey leave me like the dirt that ran down my body. Four fucking months.

I heard someone moving around the bathroom and smiled, knowing it was Erik. My vamp and my wolf were sneaky; they never made a sound. Erik joined me in the shower moments later. He turned me to face him, his lips fastened to mine, and his hands roamed over my body.

The exhaustion I had felt left me, leaving only pleasure in its wake.

"I missed you, Kenzie. So much." My body trembled. His lips trailed a scorching path from my neck down to my breasts. He laved the mark Stel had left during a dreamwalk.

He continued leaving fiery kisses down to my navel. He got on his knees and hooked one of my legs on his shoulders, spreading my pussy for him.

I should have been mortified, disgusted. I was a rank mess. The evidence of constant fighting, walking for days in the desert, and my quick interlude with Stel hadn't been washed away. But Erik didn't seem to care.

"You're so beautiful," He said, staring at my core.

Then he swallowed my pussy lips whole, spreading them apart with his tongue.

I braced a hand on his head and writhed against his mouth. He suckled my clit and groaned, sending sweet vibrations all over my cunt.

The onslaught of vibrations made my hips rock, fucking his face.

Erik sucked harder, his tongue probing my entrance. He slid in a finger, and I shuddered, coming all over his lips.

I was panting, and my body trembled, but he was just getting started. Erik turned me around and pressed me against the shower wall. He eased my hips back, bending me at the waist, and tapped my foot, spreading them apart.

He glided his fingers between my folds, then threaded his cock into me nice and slow.

I braced my hands on the wall before me while pushing back, urging him to fuck me harder. He gripped my ass and plowed into me. His thrusts were so deep I ached for more. He reached around and massaged my clit; another climax swelled inside me.

"Oh fuck, Kenz," he growled. He was reaching his peak.

My body rocked over his cock, matching his thrusts. He slapped my ass. The sting of pain unraveled me. I came undone. Mewling. Breathless. With a forceful grunt, he emptied himself, his body pushing mine against the shower wall.

He covered my body with his. Both of us gasping for air.

"Are you ok?" Erik asked.

"Mmmhmm." I turned my head, allowing him to kiss my cheek.

"I, we should probably let you rest. But we've been losing our minds without you." He pulled out and helped me stand.

"I wouldn't want it any other way." I leaned against his chest.

"Well, that's good because Caid will be here in a minute."

Not even ten seconds later, Caid waltzed into the shower.

He moved behind me and placed a kiss on my shoulder.

I smiled and held onto Erik. Erik smiled down at me.

"I love you. I'll let you two have your moment."

He gave me gentle lingering kisses, then released me to Caid.

I wrapped my arms around Caid's waist and smooshed my face into his chest.

A familiar smell permeated the air. I pulled away from him, swiping the water away from my eyes.

He held a familiar travel-sized bottle of my favorite shampoo. I grinned at my vamp.

"Let me take care of you, love."

Caid washed my hair, massaging my scalp. Then he scrubbed my body clean; leaving kisses on my skin as he lathered me with soap. His hands stroked my tired, sore muscles while the water rinsed me clean. I quivered under his ministrations.

And then I returned the favor. Sort of. I ran the bar of soap over his shoulders and the rigid plains of his muscular chest. I flicked my tongue over his nipple. Then moved my soapy hands down to his solid abdomen.

I had meant to wash his back but got distracted by the swollen cock pressed against my belly. I got on my knees, paying special attention to this particular appendage. He gasped.

"Love, I'm supposed to be the one taking care of you." His voice was breathless.

"You are. I've missed sucking cock," I purred and took him in my mouth.

His breath hitched.

His salty seed coated my tongue. I worked his shaft and massaged his balls.

I stroked his long shaft, guiding him deeper down my throat.

Caid growled. He picked me up and carried me out of the shower, propping my ass on the bathroom sink.

His mouth crushed mine, and at the same time, his cock sank into my throbbing hole.

I hung on to him for dear life while he pummeled my pussy.

He yanked my hair, exposing my neck, leaving light feathery kisses on the mark he had left there.

"I love you," I said between breaths.

He sucked hard on the mark he left on my neck. Pure bliss swallowed me whole. I was done. I slumped in Caid's arms, gasping for breath, then passed out.

A moment later, I was on a soft bed, snuggled up to my wolf. I searched for Caid, who was against my back, and my magic man, who was lying horizontally on the foot of the bed.

I let out a grateful sigh and let blessed sleep take me.

CHAPTER 45

KENZIE

The guys woke early and were ready to go. I took another shower and dressed in my now-clean clothes.

Gunnar looked well-rested and eager to get moving. I couldn't blame him; I was also sick of The Dark Realm.

Chief Hobs brought over bread, dried meat, extra carafes of water, and Requiem juice for us to take on our journey. Milo and Gle, — the giant demon that stood guard over the Rogue while he was trussed, were also ready to take us to the gateway.

I hugged Chief Hobs when we left, and he had made me promise to come by and see him next time I was in The Dark Realm. Honestly, I hoped never to be back, but then again, there was Dash. A part of me wanted to see him. I pushed that thought out of my head as quickly as it entered, annoyed with myself.

The first day of travel was easy-breezy. With my guys at my side, I had no reservations about who or what would come at us next. It almost felt like we were purposely in a strange realm and casually making our way home.

My heart still ached over losing Brody. His absence was keenly felt. It took immense effort to keep his loss from overwhelming me. He should be with us.

During our journey, my men had filled us in on what had transpired since Gunnar, and I got abducted. My father had come to the Fifth and Sixth Circles for a month trying to find us. That made me feel all warm and fuzzy. He cared; he really cared.

Tris was handling my business. And Bear was staying at Jameson Castle. Erik said they had searched for his mother and sister who were still alive but hadn't found anything.

"So, how are the baby mamas and the babies," I asked. It was a subject they were avoiding.

Erik cleared his throat. Caid grimaced. And Stellan looked impassive.

"What's going on, guys? Talk to me," I pressed.

"Nothing, sweetness," Stel said.

"You're lying." I stopped walking until he turned to face me.

"It's nothing, and I don't want to upset you."

"Too late. I'm pissed." I kicked the gray desert sand for added emphasis.

"Ok, it's great news. I am not the father of Christine's baby. Yay," Stel said, trying to make a joke of the situation.

I rolled my eyes. "That's not even remotely funny."

"She lied, sweetness." His tone was serious this time. "She falsified the reports, had them changed, and forced the ultrasound nurse in the clinic to corroborate her story."

I stopped dead in my tracks. "That doesn't make one lick of sense. How and why would Christine do that?"

"Photoshop. And she threatened the nurse." Erik tugged my hand, urging me to keep walking.

"Seriously? How did you find out?" I couldn't believe it.

"The nurse's cousin told us. Cristela is her name; she was caring for Carlos." Caid answered. "We have the real test reports and a video of Christine threatening the nurse."

Motherfucker. After everything she put me through. Put Stel through.

"Stel, wait." He stopped and turned to face me.

I jumped into his arms and held him tight. "I'm sorry. I'm sorry I forced you to get involved. I never in a million years would have asked you to go to those stupid appointments if I had an inkling of what she was capable of."

"Thank you, sweetness, but it's not on you. It's all her. And, well, it gets worse. We had a way to get here sooner by summoning a demon. She stole the parchment that was needed to do the summoning."

He set me down on my feet and pulled me into his body as we walked.

"What? What demon??"

Caid and Erik walked alongside Stel and me.

"Simone's girlfriend had a spell or something to summon some demon. Her girlfriend had her stuff in Simone's room, which got stolen. Christine's scent was in the room, and she disappeared."

"Son of a bitch! Wait. Simone has a girlfriend." I almost stumbled at the thought. I didn't realize she was a lesbian.

Caid just nodded, and Erik chuckled.

"Why do you think she was always flirting with you, Kenz? She's into the ladies."

The guys laughed.

"You guys have a fascinating life." Gunnar chuckled.

It wasn't funny, but it sure was interesting. My poor wolf. He had been excited to be a father. And I had ignited that excitement. He insisted from day one that the child wasn't his. Fucking Christine. And I was pissed at myself for sticking my nose in his business. *Never again, Kenz.*

Stel would've been a great father. He still could. I leaned into his body and thought about Dash's offer. Had I known what was going on back at the ranch, I would have given his offer some thought.

I fell silent, seriously considering it as we continued. If it were possible to give Stel a baby, I would do it. Somehow, I'd negotiate something with Dash. The demon prince cared about me, or so I thought. Either way, I was a businesswoman. I would figure it out.

We walked on till it got dark and camped out on the sand. The guys insisted that I sleep while they took turns keeping watch. I refused and insisted I could and would pull my weight. Stel gave in, which meant I could ride his dick while everyone else slept. Caid woke up, of course, and did some insisting of his own. After being away from them for so long, I didn't mind one bit. The journey was tiring, but I had been able to sleep soundly until Erik woke me for another round. I was tender in all the right places, and I loved it.

The second day was uneventful as the first. When we arrived at the village, it was deserted. Stel questioned Milo about it. The demon just scratched his head. He hadn't expected it to be empty either.

According to Chief Hobs, the town should have been much like his own, a town of worship. There were no worshippers, and it looked to have been abandoned recently.

My skin crawled. There was something not right about this.

CHAPTER 46
DASH

"Master," Neo bowed, "the Legion is ready."

I nodded and flashed out to the northeast corner of the Fourth. Suran was waiting for me, the Legion at his back. We rallied the army in preparation for this, and they were ravenous for blood.

Before they were in sight, I could feel the surge of my father's army heading straight for us. What an asshole. I knew the minute Kenzie was cut by that fucking flower of his that he would be interested in her. I had hoped to keep her safely hidden in my personal quarters.

But I had offended my precious Fae, and she ran away from me. I had it coming; I should have explained the dangers and given the gift freely. Now I needed to make amends for my mistakes. Getting her mates here to find her, keep her safe, and take her home was the best I could do. I hoped they didn't fuck this up.

Suran and I stood on the front lines, and Jafir appeared on my other side. The three of us had been friends all our lives. Despite everything that we went through, we had each other's back. And days like these, I was ever so grateful.

"Thank you both for being here," I muttered. I could feel them both looking at me.

"The Fae has changed you." Suran slapped my back with a meaty paw. "About time. And no thanks needed; I was getting bored and fat."

Jafir and I chuckled.

"Love is an odd look on you, my friend. It'll take some time to get used to." Jafir grinned. "But I like it, and besides, we can't have Suran getting any bigger."

That was the last time we'd exchange pleasantries. My father's army surged forward, not missing a beat. There were no gentlemanly negotiations between us. He didn't even stop to have a conversation about Kenzie or, at the very least, tell me what the fuck he was doing here.

I blasted my way directly to him, killing demons as I went. I used my magic and my sword. It was absolute carnage.

In the middle of the bloody battlefield, I faced my father. We circled one another. He twirled his sword, and I mirrored his movements. He smirked and feigned a lunge. He parried.

"I'm not here to fight you, son." He smirked and blocked my strikes.

I clenched my jaw and ducked a strike aimed at my head. I laughed and spread my arms wide, "it sure looks like you're trying to kill me."

He paused and bent over laughing. "Oh, my son, I am trying to make you stronger."

I huffed and sent a stream of hellfire straight at him. The hellfire consumed him, and he brushed it off as though he was picking lint off his favorite coat.

"Good hit, but . . . it's me, and it will take more than that to be rid of me."

I sent a barrage of hellfire and even ran my sword through him; the bastard laughed harder. Ahh fuck, this was going to be a never-ending battle.

"What the fuck do you want?" I glared at the God of The Dark Realm.

He dusted off his burnt clothes, and unfurled his wings, the edges charred from my hellfire, "Isn't it obvious? I want you to be better. And you've improved. I'll give you that. But I need more. I need you to be better. Better than me."

He sent a stream of fire straight at me, but it didn't burn. His fiery magic surrounded me and created a prison of flames.

My father stood in front of the flames and said, "If it takes killing everyone you love over and over again, I will do it until your power exceeds mine. Show me what you're made of. You know where to find me."

My father and his army disappeared.

Kenzie.

I slammed my body against the flaming bars of my prison, singeing my body in the process. Suran and Jafir came to me and circled the bars trying to release me. But this was my puzzle to solve. In the meantime, I needed to ensure Kenzie's safety.

"Go! Find Kenzie!! She needs help; my father is on his way to her," I barked out orders, but they didn't move.

"GO!"

Suran and Jafir left with a hundred soldiers. The others that were left gathered the dead and cleared the battlefield.

I paced in my cell, racking my brain over what to do. My father was the lord of hell and a right prick. He was the most powerful being here and had created this realm. *What the fuck did he want?*

"Master," Devon stood on the other side of the flaming bars. "Your father is more powerful than you, but . . . you are clever. Instead of fighting him with strength, fight him with intelligence."

Devon had a point. I couldn't free myself with brute strength. I sat in the middle of my prison and focused, studying the magic. There had to be a way to unravel it. As I studied the construct, its simplicity made me shake my head. It couldn't be that simple, and if I were wrong, it would burn me alive.

For Kenzie, the risk was worth it.

I changed into my wraith form and approached the flaming prison bars. Little by little, my shadow slipped past the bars. My father's fire singed my wraith. I kept going — a little more. I forced myself through. Almost there.

An electrical jolt knocked me back. My vision swam, and darkness threatened to overwhelm me. I ground my teeth, my breathing ragged. Fuck.

My father used hellfire and fire. Fire was an element of nature, and hellfire was a part of me. I blew out a breath and began calling the fire to me. The slow process was like sucking in a deep breath. And it burned like a son of a bitch. My insides were boiling, but as I inhaled the flames, my prison bars began dissipating. My body melted like a candlestick; it was agonizing. I screamed. I persisted, using my pain as the catalyst to keep going. My eyeballs were melting, and I could barely see anything. My prison was reduced to hellfire. The flames consumed me entirely, but my human form was already healing, and I had my wits about me. My brain was functioning, and my soul was still intact. If I hadn't been killed by now, I could survive this. I focused on the hellfire and molded it to my will, rebuilding my body inch by inch and clenching my teeth through the pain.

The pain receded, or perhaps I went numb all over. Either way, I could focus a bit more on the prison made up of hellfire.

This should have been easier. If only I could have shifted. I called on my beast and tried shifting. Nothing happened. I cursed with frustration.

I'm a spell breaker I can do this. With a deep breath, I calmed my heart rate. The inner workings of the magic unraveled piece by piece. *Motherfucker, it can't be.* I stood and sliced my hand with the dagger in my boot. Blood pooled in my palm. I stuck my bloodied hand in the flames of hellfire and chanted a simple nursery rhyme my mother had taught me as a child.

The fiery prison vanished with a loud hiss.
I didn't waste any time and headed to the Fifth Circle.
I'm coming, Kenzie.

CHAPTER 47

KENZIE

The ghost town made us all fidgety. We tried to relax, but something about the entire situation made my hackles rise.

There was a massive stone archway in the middle of the square, which according to Milo, was precisely where the gateway would open. At the appointed time, it would light up, and we'd be able to see the human realm on the other side.

We sat on benches no more than forty yards away from the arches, and then the ground rumbled. Afraid the quake was about to split the dirt under our feet and swallow us, we ran from it, putting more distance between us and the gateway.

The dust settled as soon as the earthquake ceased, and everything went silent. The archway stood a hundred and thirty yards away. And the ground seemed undisturbed despite the ferocious rumbling.

"What the fuck, Milo?" I shouted.

Stel and Caid stood on either side of me, and Gunnar was in front of us, sword at the ready.

He looked around bewildered, "The Dark Lord is coming! Quickly to the gateway."

As soon as the words left Milo's mouth, a horde of demons appeared and blocked our pathway to the gateway. *Aww, shit.*

A demon in human form casually strolled through the army, making his way toward us as though he had all the time in the world. His hair was cropped short, and he wore a scowl. He wasn't much taller than me and had a sword strapped to his back. I sensed he kept his magic hidden, just like I did in the human realm. Hmmm . . . that was troubling. But there was no doubt this was not the king or lord of the realm.

"How much longer until the gateway opens, Milo?" I asked our demon guide, who was kneeling on the sand.

He tipped his head to the sky, then turned to me and said, "Fifteen minutes, Mistress. It will remain open for five minutes after that. But you cannot leave."

I wasn't sure if that was human or dark realm minutes, but it didn't matter; we were getting out of there.

"Fuck that," I muttered. "Be prepared to fight our way through. I'll magic shield a pathway directly to that gateway as soon as it opens."

"Will that work?" Gunnar asked.

I shrugged, "If you have a better idea, I'm all ears."

The brothers eyed each other over my head and nodded while Erik shrugged his shoulders.

I searched for my magic and felt it rise within me. I kept it hidden like Mr. Demon, who stopped ten feet in front of us.

"You're not allowed to leave," Mr. Demon said in perfect English. "The Dark Lord will be here shortly to deal with you."

As if we were going to wait for this Dark Lord.

"Milo, thank you for getting us this far. You may want to get out of here before your lord shows up." I glanced at the demon.

"Thank you, Mistress, for saving me. I wish there were more I could do." Milo said in a shaky voice, and then he sped off. Gle, the lumbering giant, followed behind him.

Erik stood off to the side, prepping some spells. A few feet away, Gunnar rolled and twirled his sword around, warming up his wrists. Caid winked at me, and I was wrenched off my feet into Stel's arms. "Stay close to Caid; I'll be right behind you." He pressed his lips to mine and kept us locked together for a minute.

Stel released me, and I pulled Smokey out of my jacket and set him down. "Alright, puppy, this is going to get a little dicey. I need you to do that smoke thing and stay out of trouble, ok?"

The hound regarded me with his tongue hanging out and his tail wagging. He took on his smoke form and vanished. It hurt my heart to let him go, but I didn't want him to get stabbed or trampled.

The gateway lit up between the archway. It shimmered with a brilliant golden light, a familiar earthy terrain beyond it.

"Here we go." I gathered my magic and blasted through the demons, killing them on contact.

We ran. Gunnar ran through first, swinging his sword and cutting down anyone daring to get close. Caid right behind him. Erik was beside me, throwing spell bombs at the demons.

I concentrated on shielding us the best I could. My magic always provided a protective shield around me; all I needed was to extend the protection, which I had done before. I raised my shield to Stel as he was behind me, then stretched it as far as I could to cover Erik, Caid, and Gunnar.

We pushed forward, determined to get to the gateway. There were just too many of them. The demons came from us at all angles. Gunnar was upfront, swinging like a maniac. Caid and Erik took care of the demon horde pressing in on us from the sides while Stel practically walked backward, taking out demons. It was an effective effort, but we were outnumbered.

"Kenz! We need your fire," Stel shouted.

I nodded, pumped extra magic into the shield to keep us safe, and then called my Fae magic. Flames surged up my arms. "Duck!"

The guys hit the ground as I spun in place, sending a blast of fire all around us. Demons screamed, some fell to the ground, and the rest backed away. "Let's go!" I screamed.

We sprinted toward the gateway. My magic was waning, but I pushed forward with determination. A demon clipped my ankle and caused me to face plant into the sand. The unexpected stumble caused me to lose concentration on my magic, and I felt the protective shield slip.

Stel stomped the hand that grasped my ankle and sliced clean through the demon while Caid picked me up and kept running.

Reinstating my shield was not working as efficiently as I had hoped. My magical reserves were low, and I was jostled in Caid's arms as he ran. Without his vamp powers, he was not nearly as fast or agile. But he was still strong, and he kept me in his arms.

Gunnar got hit with an arrow in his thigh. He went down. Caid managed to haul him up with one hand, dragging him as he kept running.

Stel took me from his brother in one seamless move and kept running. Caid held Gunnar under his arm while Erik provided cover with his spells.

I tapped Stel several times, telling him to let me down, and then the ground rumbled, and we all toppled over. Stel rolled and kept my body covered with his. Beneath him, I took a few precious seconds to shield us, then wiggled under him to find Caid and Gunnar. They were on the ground a few feet away from us. Their bodies had gone completely still.

Stel shook his head and refocused. I motioned him to where his brother and mine were, and we crawled to them. They were both conscious, slow to get up, but still alive. I let out an audible sigh and realized we had company.

Another horde of demons had shown up. They wore an emblem on their chest that resembled a backward capital R. Requiem Square. Dash had sent help. His army fought the demons that blocked us from the gateway.

I turned my back to the fighting and looked around for the gateway.

"Kenzie? Kenzie!!" Stel shouted, "Are you ok?"

I nodded and glanced at the gateway. Stel followed my gaze. Caid and Gunnar sat up and turned to where Stel and I had been staring.

At the arches in front of the gateway was the most beautiful being I had ever encountered. He was huge, twelve feet tall, and his impressive wingspan thirty feet across blocked the gateway. He emitted a golden light so bright I squinted to shield my eyes.

He floated in front of the gateway, and his golden eyes stared into my soul. His power, dark and galvanizing, pressed on my shoulders.

I curled in on myself, wanting to hide, which was useless because he had found his target. Me.

Caid, Erik, Stel, and Gunnar stood and placed me behind them. The king, no, he was no king; he was a God. The God of Hell smirked. The battle raged around us. The demons content on killing each other hadn't spared us a single glance in our direction.

Nervous energy bubbled up inside me. I wanted to run, wanted to hide, wanted to do something. Gunnar was favoring one leg, and on autopilot, I used my magic to sterilize the slice and stem the blood flow.

"Kenzie? Stop. You don't need to worry about that right now," Gunnar placed a hand on my shoulder.

I shrugged him off, "I need to do something." I ripped the hem of his shirt and tied it around the wound. It was a shitty job, but it stopped bleeding and hopefully wouldn't get infected.

The Lord of Hell studied us as though we were interesting little ants. He hadn't said a word. His unwavering gaze held me captive.

I bounced on my toes. Anxiety pooled in my belly. *What the fuck is he waiting for?*

I couldn't take it anymore; his presence alone made me twitchy.

"Fuck this. I can't just stand here," I pushed my way past my mates and pointed my dagger at the fallen angel. "Hey, you! Move it! You're in our way."

He tipped his head to the side and smiled. Oh fuck, what did I just do? I straightened my spine and stepped forward. His wings folded in, and he gracefully floated down to the sand. The gateway was still open. I wanted to go home desperately but knew Dark Lord asshole was here for me.

"I'll create a distraction, and you guys get through that gateway," I stated.

"We're not going anywhere without you, Kenzie," Erik said beside me.

Stel pressed his body into my back and said, "Not a chance, sweetness."

"He's not taking you from us." Caid blocked my path.

"Fuck that, Sis." Gunnar had his sword ready.

I rolled my eyes, although none of them could see. It was assuring to have them at my back, but I needed to end this. "He's here for me. Let me negotiate your freedom."

Stel wrapped his muscular arms around me and held me tight, "Not happening, Kenzie. We all go, or we all stay."

For a millisecond, my body slumped in his arms; I loved my men so much. And I was not about to give them up.

I drew a deep breath and straightened my spine.

CHAPTER 48
DASH

I soared in the air, flying as fast as I could. The ground blurred as I sped by. The roars of battle reached my ears. I was close and realized my error. The gateway was on the hallowed ground dedicated to my father. Fuck. No wonder he had found her so easily.

I barreled down to the battlefield in my dragon form, letting out a war cry. My soldiers cheered as they saw me coming. I breathed hellfire on my father's troops and circled to the gateway where he stood. He didn't even bother to look up at me. He was solely focused on Kenzie, which was not a good sign.

Her back was straight, and she glanced my way, but she kept a watchful eye on my father.

Gunnar stared at me as though he recognized me and then mouthed my name. Kenzie's head snapped in my direction, and a part of me swooned at having her attention.

My father took advantage of her distraction and flashed. He grabbed her and then vanished out of the way.

NO! My dragon roared. Fury rose within me.

Kenzie's mates frantically searched for her, but she was gone.

I searched the air and the ground but didn't find them. My father wouldn't go far. He wanted to taunt me, of that, I was sure.

I touched the ground sending a plume of sand all around me. Kenzie's mates were frantic trying to find her, but I knew my father. He wanted to torture me in every way possible.

My father reappeared as soon as I shifted, and Kenzie lay limp in his arms.

"She has nothing to do with this." I pointed at him. "Let her go."

"I think she has everything to do with this, son." He glanced down to look at her. "She's your one true mate, after all. But, if you want her, you'll have to prove it. All of you."

My father smirked at her mates. Fuck, he was going to kill them just for fun.

Suddenly, Kenzie rolled to the ground, and her dagger was out and dripping with blood. Her body was poised to strike, her dagger ready.

My father eyed the wound that struck his heart. Black blood bloomed on his pristine white shirt. Even a Fae blade wouldn't cause fatal damage, but it would slow him down.

"Scratch what I said. I think I will keep her for myself." My father tore his shirt off to reveal his wound closing.

I moved to stand between her and my father while her mates surrounded her. All of us were ready to battle to the death.

My father chuckled, "Five of you then? Well, it hardly seems fair. Here, let me help."

With a flourish of his hand, magic washed over Stellan, giving him access to his wolf. He shifted back and forth in quick succession, testing it out, and growled. My father did the same for Caid. The daywalker changed into his vampire form. Fangs and claws extended, and he snarled. The Lord of Hell snapped his fingers, and magic danced on Erik's arms. The mage called on his mage powers and let them pool in his palms.

"There. Now, no one has any excuses," my father said. He

summoned his power, and the ground pitched and heaved, as though we were on a boat in a turbulent sea.

Kenzie pushed me aside and made a few arcane gestures. A well of magic erupted out of her, and then she sunk her fists into the ground. The quake rolled out straight toward my father and split open under his feet. He gasped in surprise and snapped his wings before being swallowed up.

Like a psycho, he tossed his head back and laughed. He threw magic bolts at her mates, making them scatter out of the way. I went left while Kenzie went right, using our magic to shield them as best as possible.

While my father was distracted, Erik threw magic streams at him, knocking him off his aim. That pissed him off. A bow and arrow appeared in his hands, and he aimed it at the mage.

Kenzie ran to protect her mate and straight into an arrow made of Lucifer's hellfire.

CHAPTER 49
KENZIE

A bow and arrow made of hellfire magically appeared in Dash's father's hands and he took aim at my mate.

Nope. Not today, demon!

With magic-enhanced speed, I ran toward Erik, rammed into his body, knocking him out of death's path, and ran into it myself.

I had never imagined my life would end like this. Shot in the heart by an arrow crafted of hellfire made by Lucifer, the Dark Lord of Hell.

At first, my Fae magic struggled against it, trying to heal the injury. My entire life, I had been protected from bodily harm. If it had been fire, my magic would have prevailed.

I felt the sharp sting as the arrow pierced my skin then came the blistering pain as it entered and went right through my heart. My magic surged, trying to repair the damage, but the hellfire overrode my magic.

Agony engulfed me. Then the pain seized as soon as it had started. And all that was left was nothing. I floated in the abyss, a dark weightless void.

In the void, a whisper from a familiar voice filled my ears.

Oh no, you don't, Kenzie baby, it's not time yet.

The voice was deep and comforting, and I froze in the abyss, hoping to hear it again. But it was silent, and I had resigned to it being just a distant memory.

CHAPTER 50
STELLAN

Everything had happened fast and yet in slow motion at the same time.

My mate watched the god of darkness point his bow and arrow at Erik. Kenzie used her magic enhanced speed to run over and protect him. I chased after her, and so did Caid. But my brother and I were too far away.

Kenzie pushed Erik out of the way, and the arrow went straight through her heart.

I felt her die the moment it happened. As though the same arrow had pierced me. I stumbled, losing my footing, and then got back up and sprinted to her lifeless body.

Her eyes were vacant as I cradled her in my arms. Blood blossomed from the middle of her chest; the hellfire hadn't spread. But the arrow had gone straight through.

"Kenzie, stay with me." I moved strands of hair away from her beautiful face.

Dash's smug father floated above us and looked at his son, "If you truly love her . . . save her . . . all of you."

And then the fucker disappeared into the sky, and his army vanished.

I stared down at my mate and had no idea what to do next. There had to be a solution. It couldn't end this way. Lucifer said we truly loved her; we could save her. I had to try something.

"Do something!" Caid yelled at Dash, who was pacing and screaming obscenities at the sky.

I pressed my lips to hers and had hoped to transfer pack energy to her lifeless form. Nothing happened. My connection to the pack was weak. Fuck. I glanced at the portal as it blinked out. I needed to get to the other side.

"Erik!!" I screamed and hadn't needed to do that. He was sitting right next to me. Sobbing over Kenzie's dead body.

"Erik, can you reopen the portal?" I asked. My throat was raw from screaming or crying.

"I . . . I don't know." Erik stammered as he stroked Kenzie's face. He closed her eyes which was appropriate, but the gesture made my heart skip a beat.

"Try Erik. Please, I need access to my pack magic to transfer to her." I said in a gentler albeit desperate tone.

"You think that will work?" he asked as he got up.

"It's worth a shot." I kissed Kenzie's forehead.

"What are you doing?" Caid asked as he knelt next to me.

"Trying to transfer pack magic. Try your blood." I said to my brother. He nodded and knelt at her other side.

Caid took his dagger, the one Kenz had given him, and slit his wrist. He pressed it to Kenzie's lips, and nothing happened.

"Love, please drink," Caid whispered. With his thumb, he parted her lips and dribbled blood in her mouth.

But Kenzie didn't drink.

Erik came up beside us and shook his head. "I can't. The portal is rejecting my magic. Let me try something else."

He closed his eyes and summoned his magic. His hand glowed,

and he placed them on the wound on Kenzie's chest. A brilliant gold light sunk into the gaping hole.

I held my breath in anticipation. But nothing happened. Everything so far wasn't working. Please, I prayed. And the glow of Erik's magic fizzled out.

Erik gritted his teeth and tried again. His magic disappeared completely. He slammed his fists into the sand below us and cursed.

It was as if Kenzie was rejecting our magic. As though she was gone from us for good and wanted nothing to do with us. The three of us hung our heads, and then I looked up at Dash.

He was tugging at his black hair, pacing.

"Dash! Get your ass over here and help us." That got the demon's attention. He shuffled over to us and knelt at Kenzie's feet.

I moved around to kneel at Kenzie's head so he could get closer to her.

"I'm sorry, Kenzie. I tried to keep you safe from him." He kissed her lips.

"Your father said if we truly loved her, we could bring her back. What did he mean?" I said to the demon, which got his attention.

"You need to infuse your magic into her." He said.

"We already tried that! I don't have access to my pack's magic. She's not taking in Caid's blood. And she's not accepting Erik's magic. You try." I scowled at the demon.

If he was her true mate, he could bring her back to the land of the living. I'd be ok with that as long as she was still around. Sharing her with the demon would be better than visiting a hole in the ground.

Dash rolled his neck, and then he summoned his magic. A cloud of violet laced with silver sprung from his hands and surrounded his being, then wrapped around Kenzie's body. Like Erik's magic, it seemed to sink into her for a few moments, and then it disappeared.

"Fuck! We need more help. Her soul is at the precipice between here and the hereafter." Dash said.

His words were like a knife to my heart. Despair threatened to drown me, and it took all of my willpower to keep my head above water.

Please, Kenzie, stay with me.

CHAPTER 51
KENZIE

I was floating in a sea of silky cobwebs. The strands of webs were soft yet sturdy. It provided comfort and strength. It was pleasant, and I knew I could stay here forever.

"Stay with me, Kenzie baby."

It was Brody's voice, but it couldn't be. I had witnessed his death.

Brody wasn't here, and neither were my other mates. I missed them and glanced over my shoulder, but they weren't there. I ignored the pain in my heart and continued floating in the abyss.

Someone or something shoved me, and I was wrenched into darkness. The abyss was black and icy cold. There was nothing around me, yet the cold scratched at my being. I did not want to be there. I tried to get out. I had to get out.

I spun in place and couldn't see a thing. Frustrated and scared, I willed myself to calm down and remembered my magic. I reached for it and found nothing. It had always been with me. Was it gone? Why would it be gone? I panicked. I was still stuck in the dark abyss of nothingness and no magic to help me escape.

Disturbing awareness settled in, and I realized there was no pain.

No. It can't be.

My physical self, my body, was broken. No. Not broken dead.

Oh, this was not good.

It seemed like an excellent time to hyperventilate, yet I had no lungs to breathe.

I willed my consciousness to relax and focus on my mates. I thought of my brilliant magic man, my protective wolf, and my ever-loyal vampire. And I thought of my charming human with those dimples that made me swoon.

Something pinched at my center, and then I was wrenched backward and found myself standing over my lifeless body between Stel, Caid, and Erik.

They were screaming angry words at one another, yet they seemed sad.

Stel's brow was bunched up in a scowl as Dash spoke to him.

Caid clenched his jaw and squeezed my hand.

Erik rocked back and forth; his eyes tinged with red.

My men were mourning me. And it broke my heart to see them so sad.

Dash was pacing and cursing the sky. He was furious.

Smokey sniffed at my body until Gunnar picked him up and sat next to Caid.

Stel had been speaking, and I strained to listen to his words, yet it was like he was on mute.

Something tugged on me, and then I was forced back into my body, and my sense of hearing returned.

"I don't have access to my pack's magic. She's not taking in Caid's blood. And she's not accepting Erik's magic. You try."

Stel had been speaking about me. They were trying to revive me. And I wasn't accepting it. Why wouldn't I take it? I loved them. I belonged to them; they belonged to me.

Stel cradled my head in his lap. I was looking up at him through closed eyes.

Dash paced a few feet away, pulling on his hair.

Something else garnered my attention. It was bright, warm, and inviting. It beckoned me, and I went after it. The bright light was so close I could feel its warmth, but before I could reach it, something tugged on my being and held me still.

"Oh no, you don't, beautiful. Not yet." My focus whipped around toward that familiar voice again.

I'd recognized this man anywhere, even though, at that moment, he seemed completely different.

He was dressed in all black: jeans, a button-down, and a long trench coat. Like an apparition, his form shimmered.

"Brody baby!" I gasped.

"Hi, Kenzie baby. Get back here." His hand extended toward me.

Hesitantly, I reached out to him. And then his body surrounded my spirit self.

"Time for you to go back, beautiful," he said to me.

"You died," I said.

"You did, too. Well almost. But it's ok. I'm taking you back."

"What about you? Come with me."

"I'll always be with you, Kenzie. But, if you cross the veil, you will be lost to all of us."

"I don't understand, Brody baby."

"You'll understand soon. Just focus on me, and don't let go."

He caressed my spirit self, and I rubbed against him like a cat. He shimmered again, vanished out of sight, and reappeared at the foot of my physical body.

Stel, Erik, and Caid stared at Brody. Their mouths hanging open.

"Fucking finally!" Dash growled out. "I was beginning to think you failed."

"She's here, she was almost gone, but she's come back. Right Kenz?" Brody looked at me again, and then I understood. He wanted me to go back to my physical body.

I stood at my foot, looking down, and noticed a tendril of silver wrapped around my ankle and extended out toward Brody's wrist. His armband, the one he had given me, bound me to him.

In his other hand, he gripped a scythe. Confused, I looked between him and the weapon. What the fuck? Is he? Did my human transform into a Reaper? Is that possible?

"We are bound, you and me. And because it is a Fae bond, I will always come back to you. It may be some time until I see you again, but soon, baby. I promise. But that will only happen if you go back." His head tipped to my body, which was laid out and lifeless. "I promise, Kenzie baby. I'll be back. Come on. It's time."

I nodded and sunk back into my body, but nothing happened. I lay there and waited. My men argued.

"Nothing's changed!" Caid said to Brody.

"I've secured her spirit self to her body. That's as much as I know. I just started this gig remember?" Brody replied.

"We need to get her to the other side of the portal. I can't access pack magic from this side," Stel said.

"Dash, reopen that damned portal. If your father can shut it down, you can open it." Erik chimed in.

"Fuck. It's worth a try. Everybody get ready to jump through. You too, Brody." Dash strode to the arches and called on his magic while Stel carried me.

He held my lifeless body in his arms while my spirit self walked behind him. I hopped back into my body, but my soul didn't want to stick.

Dash's demon magic surged as he chanted. Sweat poured down his temples. His eyes glowed. His power sparked my Fae magic. Finally. I sighed as my magic rose to meet his.

The portal opened with an audible snap. Dash yelled, "Go, go, go!"

Stel carried me through first, followed by Caid, and then Gunnar ran through holding Smokey. Erik went through next, and then Brody and Dash.

Stel carefully laid me on the ground and pressed his lips to mine. A surge of magic swarmed through me. I reveled in his magic, strong, sure, and confident.

Then Erik placed his hands on my stomach. His magic brushed up against my own. My wolf and mage's magic danced under my skin.

Stel was breathless when he released me, but his magic stayed with me, and so did Erik's.

Caid kissed me and parted my lips with his tongue. Then he sliced his wrist and dribbled his blood into my mouth. A pool of blood trickled down my throat. His blood sizzled in my veins.

Their powerful magic swirled through me, and love poured into my body. Stel's magic was strong and steady. Erik's magic sparked and challenged me. Caid's magic was like a fire that swam through my blood. Brody's Reaper magic anchored me right where I was meant to be on the side of the living. And then there was Gunnar; he hadn't touched me, hadn't offered up his magic, but his presence was the familial support I had longed for all my life.

Oxygen filled my lungs, and my sensory nerves switched on.

"That's it, sweetness, breathe." Stel's raspy voice came in loud and clear.

Pain bloomed in my chest. My body convulsed.

"Oh shit! We need to tend to the wound." Erik said.

The hellfire damage to my chest set my insides afire. I couldn't hang on. I didn't want to. I recoiled from the pain and searched for the bright light.

"Stop it, Kenzie baby! Just hang on." Brody pleaded.

I slipped out of my physical form. The pain was too much.

I didn't go far. Couldn't. Brody's magic anchored me to my body.

"Kenzie, hey, look at me." Dash got my attention. "I'm not sure how I'm able to see your spirit right now but stop trying to float away. Stay with your body."

"No, it hurts. I can't."

"Your men need you to stay. I need you. Don't force my hand."

"Stop bossing me around."

"We're losing her!" Erik cried.

Someone thumped my chest. I floated away and watched the scene unfold.

"Dash, do something! You're a demon, for fucks sake. Your father is the God of Darkness. He said if you loved her, you could save her!" Stel shouted.

Dash scrubbed a hand down his face. "She's going to hate me. But it will bring her back. I can bind her to me."

"Do it, Dash! She's slipping!" Brody growled. He had both hands over my ankle. The armband glowed with a silver light.

"Forgive me, Kenzie," Dash whispered into my ear and brushed his lips over mine.

He took my dagger from the holster on my hip and sliced his wrist. His blood dripped into my mouth while he placed his other hand over the wound.

He started chanting. Power rose around him and seeped into my body. His voice grew louder, his violet magic swirled between us.

Something stirred in my chest. My spirit-self got sucked into my body.

Dash's power enveloped me. My skin heated, and my heart rate galloped. Scorching heat sizzled on my spine, and my back arched.

And then the world went quiet.

CHAPTER 52
KENZIE

I was nestled in soft pelts of fur and all alone. Panic prickled all over my skin. I turned my head, and the familiar scent of my wolf drifted into my nostrils. I was wearing his hoodie. I searched for my mate bonds and found them in my chest, solid and steady. All worries and panic left me; I was safe, and so were my mates.

I stretched my stiff body, then slowly rose as I searched the foreign room. The stone floors were cold under my feet. A few bags in the corner told me my guys were indeed there. I smiled and went to the large picture window opposite the bed. The scenery reflected a night, dark sky overlooking a tumultuous ocean. Scotland, perhaps. It was too dark to be sure. I sighed when I found the bathroom.

The hot water ran down my body as I inspected the wound on my chest. A rigid pink line marked where the hellfire had entered, piercing my heart. That sucked. I leaned against the shower wall and closed my eyes, recalling the events after Lucifer's hellfire struck me. Brody. A tear trickled down my cheeks. *Was that real?*

A moment later, I felt someone enter the shower.

"Hi, Kenzie baby," Brody said from behind me. His warm breath fanned across my neck.

His hands reached around my waist, and his chin rested on my shoulder.

"Brody baby?" I squeezed my eyes shut. *I'm dreaming of being with my men. This must be the afterlife.*

"I'm here, baby. Look at me."

I turned in his arms, kept my eyes closed, and ran my hands from his chest to his neck to touch his face. I felt a dimple, and my lids fluttered open.

"Hi." He beamed at me.

"Please tell me you're real, and I'm not dreaming," I gasped.

"I'm here, babe."

I clung to his chest and sobbed.

"Shh. It's ok. I'm different, but I'm here. Do you remember seeing me in the in-between?"

"Do you mean when I died? Was that . . . was that real?" I muttered into his chest.

"Yes, all of that happened."

I tilted my head to face him. "You saved me."

He flashed me a smile. "I helped. It was a team Kenzie effort."

"So you're not dead?" I ran my hands over the hard planes of his shoulders and chest. His skin was warm, and he smelled the same as I remembered.

"Technically, yes. But as a reaper, I still have my human form, which means everyone will assume I'm alive. I guess I'm a supe now."

I left a lingering kiss on his chest, flicking out my tongue to taste his skin. He tasted like my Brody. His body quivered under my touch. I placed kisses all over his skin. Eager to touch, to taste, every inch of him.

His breathing quickened. His rigid cock pressed against my stomach.

I reached down and palmed his cock, reveling at his enormous size. I took him into both hands and pumped him up and down, making him groan.

"Fuck, I missed you." His voice was husky.

He hoisted me up, and my legs wrapped around his torso. He leaned me against the wall and clamped his mouth onto one nipple. His tip pressed at my entrance. My pussy pulsated, begging him to fill me. Slowly, he pushed in; my core ached at being stretched. I kissed him fiercely as he buried himself in me. He drove his cock into my wet cunt harder and faster, slamming me into the tiles behind me. My orgasm rolled through me, my walls squeezing his cock. He kept pumping, bucking his hips until he spent himself inside me.

After Brody and I remained in the shower making up for lost time, we lay on the soft pelts, wrapped in each other's arms, as he explained his new existence as a Grim Reaper.

"After dying in the Catacombs, I woke up days later in the in-between, where my father greeted me. He's a reaper. I guess it's a family thing. He filled me in on our legacy and said this is my existence from here on out. As I understand it, the basics are, I have two forms, this one," he waved a hand down the length of his body. "And my reaper form, which I transform to when I'm out reaping souls."

He sat up, and his form shimmered. He wore a dark robe with a hood that hid his face. A scythe was strapped at his back.

I got closer and inspected his form. *Whoa!* "This is impressive, Brody baby."

"It's all so weird. Normally as a new reaper, I'd have to stay in The Dark Realm until after training, which can take years. Demon years. I have yet to learn the time difference. But, yeah, the reason I'm here is because of you. When I woke and found my dad, I also noticed this connection and knew it was you and you were close. We had to speak with the Reaper Council, which was how I learned about our Fae bond. Because of your lineage and our bond, we're," Brody scratched his head. "I don't know the right word, but I can find you anywhere, in any realm."

"We're tethered to one another, like a lifeline. Sort of like the marks from Caid and Stel. And Erik, with his magic," I offered.

"Yes, tethered, that's exactly it. Our souls are tethered. After we had discovered that part, I felt your soul leave your body and freaked the fuck out. I hadn't known what to do except follow that connection."

"The hereafter, correct?" I nodded.

"Some call it the abyss or the veil. Or the in-between. But, yeah, you pain in the ass. You were trying to float away. Once your soul passed through the veil, I wouldn't have been able to bring you back."

It was my turn to laugh. "I wasn't trying to run away from you."

"I know, babe, I know, but you scared the shit out of me. Again. No surprises there."

"Hey! At least I'm consistent," I teased.

"Don't push it, Kenz. I swear, after you got teleported to The Dark Realm, I had fantastical ideas of locking you up somehow so that you couldn't leave, or get hurt, and no one would be able to take you from me ever again." He drew me in, tightly burying his face in my neck.

I stroked his hair. "I'm here, Brody. I'm not going anywhere. It's ok. I'm ok."

I held him tightly, comforting him as best as I could.

"I love you. And thank you for loving me. Because of your love, I can be here in this Realm with you and the guys. Almost like I hadn't died. Thankfully the guys were too messed up after that night in the Catacombs; they hadn't reported me dead. For the most part, I can resume living in a sense."

"That's convenient. Yay for me." I smiled at him. I had seen him die and mourned his passing. Never in a million years could I have asked for a better outcome.

"Well, not so fast. I still have Reaper training and my duties there. During that time, I'll be gone most days and might be back on the weekends or something like that. After training is complete, I'll be able to be here with you, and work is more of an on-call kind of thing.

"Ok, not the best news ever, but I'll take it. I'd rather have this reaper version of you than none at all. How long is training?" I asked.

"A year. I'll have a couple of days a month to return to you," he replied.

"A whole year? What the hell?" I exclaimed. I had been away from my mates for four months. One year was going to be awful.

"I know, it sucks, but it seems there are many things to learn. It's kind of like a military boot camp for reapers." He smirked.

"Well, I suppose I shouldn't complain. I'm glad you're here. I thought I'd lost you." I climbed onto his lap.

He rolled us over and laid us back on the pelt-covered bed. Brody's hands were working the buttons of my jeans, and then Smokey leaped onto his back. Brody jumped up in surprise, his scythe appearing in his hands.

"Fuck!" He shook his head, each breath hard and fast. "I almost reaped your hellhound."

Smokey whimpered and burrowed his little body under my hoodie. I laughed.

"Not funny, babe," Brody huffed.

I continued laughing. "Hey, you scared my puppy, and now he won't come out, which means no more sexy time."

The corners of Brody's lips turned up even though he was trying to fight it.

"Come on; the guys and your family are waiting. And I'm not needed back in The Dark Realm for at least another week." He held out his hand.

"How'd you swing the time off so soon in your new job?" I stood up with his help.

"My father. Guess it helps to be the son of the man in charge. He's dying to meet you, by the way."

I paused on the stairwell outside the bedroom door and thought about it — a reaper for a father-in-law. My life was so freaking crazy.

Brody urged me forward, and we descended into an empty sitting room.

"The guys are in the castle proper. Granny had us stay here. She thought you'd like it," he said as he led me outside.

I set Smokey on ground allowing him to relieve himself. Brody noticed me shivering, and draped an arm around my body. The walk to the castle proper was thankfully short. I looked behind me at the turret where we had been. It was a recent addition. How Jameson Castle was able to change according to my grandmother's wishes was unknown to me. I made a mental note to ensure she and my father divulged any other family secrets I should know about.

Once inside the castle, Smokey ran ahead, and we found Erik, Caid, and Stel in the library. No Dash.

Erik greeted me with a tight squeeze. I hugged him back and breathed him in.

"Kenzie, you died saving me." His voice was soft. "I can't express how grateful I am. I don't deserve you."

He drew away from me and stared into my eyes. "Don't die, Kenzie. Please. Never again. Promise me."

"Ok, never again." I nodded.

He kissed me deeply before releasing me.

CHAPTER 53
KENZIE

Stel scooped me up into his arms. I wrapped my legs around his waist, threaded my fingers behind his neck, and leaned in for a kiss.

Smokey nipped at his heels.

"The puppy needs to learn some manners, Kenz," Stel said in his Alpha voice, which made Smokey hang his head.

"Stop scaring the puppy, Stel." I smiled as he set me on my feet.

"Don't let Stel fool you, love. He loves the pup. Smokey has been following him around like Stel's his daddy." Caid chided, then kissed my cheek.

"Where's Bear?" I asked.

"He tried to stay awake for you, but Granny told him to go to bed. You'll find him in the same wing as your old bedroom," Caid told me.

"And Gunnar is with your father, sweetness. I believe they went to his study." Stel moved over to a table strewn with paperwork.

I peeked at what they were working on.

"We're planning to deal with the people who worked with the Rogue," Erik said.

"Do you guys want help?" I asked.

"No." All four of my men said at the same time.

I smiled. I was pleased to see them working together again.

"Go up and visit Bear, love. We'll have some food prepared for you," Caid assured me.

"Sounds good. I'll leave you to your plotting." I turned to leave, then glanced over my shoulder to ask about Dash, but decided against it.

Stel was behind me a split second later.

"He had to go back to the Fourth Circle, sweetness. He'll be back by morning."

"Are you and the guys okay with having Dash around?" I turned around to face him.

"Yeah, we talked about it and we're good. Yes, we were pissed he didn't bring you home earlier, but he protected and cared for you while you were in his domain. And he brought you back to life. You were dead, Kenz. We're all just glad to have you home." He kissed my forehead.

I leaned into his body and murmured a thank you. And then I went to find Bear, with Smokey following behind me.

On my way to visit Bear, I ran into Granny.

"Granddaughter, I'm happy to see you home, alive and well." She embraced me.

I lingered in her arms longer than usual. Hugging wasn't our thing.

"It's great to see you, Granny. I'm relieved to be home," I replied.

"Are you looking for your father or Theodore?" she asked.

I smiled at her. Only my Granny would insist on using formal names. I wonder how the kid felt about that.

"Bear. Thank you for looking after him." I hooked my arm with hers as we walked down the long hallway.

"He's a good boy. And I must admit, although I hated that you were gone, it was nice to have these halls filled with people again." She patted my hand.

I glanced at her and silently vowed to visit more often. It had to be lonely in this vast place, all by her lonesome.

"Fourth door on the right," She directed me. "I'll see you in the morning, child."

"Goodnight, Granny. I love you."

"I love you too, Mac." She kissed my cheeks and went in the opposite direction, her robes swishing around her.

I stopped in my old room first. It hadn't changed since I was eight; although it seemed as though someone had recently slept here. I glanced at the stuffed animals on the bed, grabbed the white wolf, and snuggled the treasured toy. It even had Stel's baby blues. *He was mine before we even met.*

My backpack, the one I had lost before getting sucked into a portal by the Rogue, was sitting on my desk. I searched the pockets and found Bear's father's dog tags. I slipped the memento into my pocket, picked up Smokey, and went to Bear's room.

He was sound asleep when I peeked in. I didn't want to disturb him, so I quietly went in and placed a kiss on his forehead. Smokey leaned over and licked his cheek. I loved this puppy so much.

Before I stepped out of his room, Bear woke up. "Ms. Kenzie?" he sat up and rubbed his eyes.

"Hi, Bear. Sorry to wake you," I whispered.

He stumbled out of bed and hurried toward me. I kept one arm on Smokey and wrapped the other around Bear. He had gotten taller.

"How are you holding up, kid?"

He sniffled. "I was worried about you."

"I know. I'm sorry."

"You can't leave me again. I . . . I have no . . . no one." He wiped his tear-streaked face with the hem of his shirt.

"Hey, look at me." I hooked his chin gently to have him look up at me. "Bear, you always have me. And my family is your family. We're not going anywhere."

He nodded and hugged me again.

Smokey pawed at his head, wanting attention.

"You do have a puppy!" His eyes sparkled.

"This is Smokey. I found him, and he's ours now. Isn't he cute?"

Smokey licked Bear's face, making him giggle. We sat on the floor of his room, talking and playing with the new puppy.

He told me about keeping up with his studies via the tutor Granny hired, and how he continued working with Clay. He seemed to enjoy all of it but was also excited to live with me in Texas.

The guys had been in touch with the authorities to find his mother and his sister's bodies with no luck. Bear had been told they were killed but hadn't seen them die. Perhaps they were still alive. I wouldn't dare give him false hope, but finding answers was at the top of my to-do list.

"Oh, before I forget," I pulled the dog tags out of my pocket. "These belong to you."

His lips trembled, and his eyes welled up. He was trying so hard to hold in tears.

"I, um . . . found them and didn't have a chance to give them back to you."

He didn't take the dog tags from my hand. He just stared at them.

I placed the chain around his neck, and he let the tears go.

"Thank you," he murmured.

I scooted closer to him, keeping my back propped against the bed, and draped an arm around his shoulders.

He rested his head on my lap and sobbed. I petted his hair while Smokey cuddled his side.

Poor kid. I didn't have any words, so I let him cry himself to sleep.

Stel peeked in. I smiled at my wolf, grateful he was there to help me get the kid off the floor.

He gently picked up Bear and placed him in bed. I tucked Bear under the covers and placed Smokey next to him.

"Keep him safe, puppy. Come find me in the morning."

Stel grasped my hand and led me out of the room.

"Are you ok?" he asked me, keeping his voice low.

"Yeah. Poor kid. I'd like to find his mom and sister. I know the result may not be good, but it would be good to give him some closure. I think." I snuggled into his body.

"You're probably right, sweetness. I'll help in any way I can. He's ours, Kenz. We'll take care of him no matter what."

"I love you, big fella."

CHAPTER 54

KENZIE

After spending a leisurely morning between the sheets with my mates, we went into the castle proper, looking for food. My father, Gunnar, and Bear stood in front of the dining hall. A swathe of inky dark locks caught my attention. I halted mid-step, unsure how to address the demon looking straight at me.

Stel and Caid pressed their bodies to mine, one on each side.

"Talk to him, sweetness," Stel whispered and kissed my neck.

Caid tipped my head to gaze into my eyes. "I love you."

I shivered, missing the warmth of their bodies as soon as they walked away. Brody and Erik followed them, leaving me alone with the demon prince.

Dash casually strode his way over, and for the first time since meeting him, I felt unsure of myself. I fidgeted nervously, not sure what to do with my hands, and I shifted my weight on my feet. The last time I'd seen him in Requiem Manor, I punched him in the face. And then I remembered the ultimatum he had given me and the showdown with his father, which had killed me. I narrowed my eyes at Dash as he approached.

He smiled and extended his hand, "May I have a word, precious Fae?"

I nodded and led him through the castle's front door, taking a path down to the rocky shores.

"Are you well?" he asked.

"Umm . . . considering your father killed me with a hellfire arrow, I'm excellent." I glanced at him, and his smile grew wider. I forgot how much he liked it when I got snippy at him. Come to think of it, most, if not all, of my men liked it when I got a little, or a lot, feisty. *Why was that?* I wondered.

"Glad you're back to yourself," Dash said with too much smile in his voice. He noticed me glaring at him, and he sucked in his cheek as though trying to hide his glee.

"What exactly is it that you find funny?" I paused on the path and crossed my arms over my chest. He helped save my life; perhaps I should have been offering gratitude, yet I was annoyed.

Dash faced me and held his hands in the air. "No offense, Kenzie, it's just . . . you're . . . challenging. I can tell by the torment in your eyes you want to thank me for helping to save you, yet you're still pissed for putting you in a position that got you killed."

"And for trying to manipulate me by giving me the most fucked up ultimatum and for kidnapping Gunnar and me, and then not helping us get through a gateway to bring us back here much sooner. And let me see, what else can I add to the list?" I was fuming. It wouldn't surprise me if steam were shooting out of my ears.

"Yes, all of that too. But in my defense, I set up meetings with demon guides, but you got poisoned. And then I tried again, but there was that incident with Brody. And as far as the gateway, I didn't know I had the power to do what I did. I'd never tried. Never had the incentive until then."

He had a point. I had been laid up during most of my visit.

"I'm not sure I'm ready to forgive you or if I'll ever be able to," I replied.

"Good," he nodded. "I want the chance to prove . . . how much you mean to me. I am well aware you have four mates already. And your life is with them, and my life is in a whole other realm. But, if you let me, I can earn your trust, forgiveness, and love."

Dash dropped his chin to his chest, and his shoulders sagged.

I wanted to reach out and wrap my arms around him. But I decided against it and continued walking.

After a few moments of tense silence, he said, "Talk to me, Kenzie, please."

The silent treatment was my go-to place. And it made my men crazy. I wasn't a good communicator, and I could thank my father for that trait. But I had been on the receiving end of the silent treatment, and it downright sucked balls. I needed to make a conscious decision to be different, to treat the people I loved differently.

I blew out a deep breath. "I don't understand. I suppose I don't know you well enough to know your motivation for what you're asking. Or maybe I do, and I don't know what to do with it. You're a demon, and well, I'm not prejudiced or anything, but there are so many unknowns."

I sighed. "To be honest, Dash, you intrigue me. But I don't know if I am intrigued because you're so different. Or if it is an intrigue that is soul-deep. I have four men in my life whom I love deeply. Is there room in my heart, life, and bed for another? Perhaps but I'm not certain."

At some point, while we strolled, our hands clasped together. And somewhere along my tirade, my body leaned into his. We reached the top of the pathway down to the beach and gazed at the sea for a moment. The castle was not far behind us, and we were well within the wards that protected and concealed the entire property. It was close enough to home yet far enough to give us privacy.

Dash curled his arm around my waist and pressed his chest against my back.

I leaned into him and placed my arms on his.

"It's beautiful here, and you have plenty of love and support. I can see why you like it so much. And also how foolish it was for me to keep you from all of it. But the way I feel about you is sealed. I knew you were mine when I laid eyes on you, and I am yours." His lips grazed my cheek, then my jaw and my neck. Every touch sizzled and sparked.

"Being with you feels good; it feels right." I squeezed his arms and sighed. "But I won't leave here, ever. I can't live with you in The Dark Realm. And I won't ask you to leave your people in the Fourth vulnerable."

"I'm not asking you to do either, precious Fae."

I turned in his arms to face him. "What are you asking, Dash?"

My hands glided up his chest to his neck, and my fingers toyed with the collar of his coat.

"Let me explain, and maybe that will help you understand my actions."

He turned me around and led me to a rock with a flat-ish surface. He sat down and then positioned me to sit between his legs.

"As you know, I had three wives and a dozen children. My father slaughtered every one of them, and I swore I wouldn't take any more wives from that moment on."

I remembered the story and nodded.

"I didn't mention that I could have saved one of my wives if I had claimed her as my mate just as your wolf and vamp have done with you. But I didn't, because although I loved all of them, I had never been in love with any of them. Unfortunately, the children were caught in the crossfire because my father didn't care. He could have spared them, but when it comes to my father, it is always a learning lesson."

I shook my head. "Your father is a colossal asshole."

He chuckled, "Yes, yes, he is. Anyway, as you know, I was content with my bachelor lifestyle until you stumbled into my Circle. I knew he'd come for you when the dragon flora poison got into your system. Perhaps I should have told you. But I didn't want to scare you. One touch from that poison was all it took to get a read on you. He knew what you were, and he came for you. I do not have the power to heal or protect anyone from my father's poison. And that was the reason I made the proposition. No matter how long he searched, he wouldn't have found you in my private quarters. It's a pocket dimension that he cannot infiltrate. I would have kept you there for a thousand years if that's what it took for him to tire of searching for you. Yes, in hindsight, that was an error on my part."

He drew his arms around me a little tighter. "I realized my error, but it was too late. You and Gunnar were gone. The best I could do to keep you safe was to have your mates find you and bring you here while I prepped my army to take on my father. That didn't work as well as I had hoped. He knew the moment you were at the gateway and teleported out while caging me in a fiery prison before he left. I freed myself and got to you just as the battle turned."

"My father pushed me to open the gateway and claim you. Doing all of that increased my power range and saved you. While you were resting, I went back and spoke with my father. He is proud of me. Go figure. And has promised me peace for at least one hundred years."

"Just like that? Your power increased, and now he's happy and has agreed to leave you and everyone in the Fourth alone?" I asked.

"Yes. He believes in . . . what do humans call it? Tough love?" He rested his chin on my shoulder.

"That's so messed up. But I will not waste my time analyzing the Lord of Hell." I rearranged myself to sit between his legs again, facing him directly with my legs draped outside his.

"How is this supposed to work for us, Dash? I live here. I can't leave my men." I gazed into his eyes.

"Right now, I need to get back and put things in order. Also, a lot has changed in terms of my power spectrum. I need to get back to fully understanding things. After that, I can spend more time here. When and if you're ready, we can visit The Dark Realm. As my mate, you can come and go anytime you want. And your men are welcome to come with you. No sacrifice is needed. And you'll be able to visit Brody."

Visiting Brody got my attention. The Fourth Circle was fascinating and worth exploring under the right circumstances. And everything thus far sounded reasonable.

"What's the catch? What do you want in return?" I asked my demon.

"We are bonded now, Kenzie. You know how bonds work with the supernatural; it's the same with me. I am yours now, and you are mine. And before you ask, you having other mates is not an issue. My sister has twelve," he said with a shrug of his shoulder. "The difference between your other mates and me is the rune on your back."

I glanced back, curious, which was silly. I didn't have a mirror.

Dash chuckled. "I'll show it to you later. Also, I am dominant as far as magical powers go. Thus you'll feel a power boost. And, being born in The Dark Realm makes me a demon, as you know. Being Lucifer's son makes me a demi-god. And now that we are bound together, and my blood is in your veins, you are now god-touched."

"Wait? What the actual fuck does that mean?"

"You're still you. Just sturdier. The meaning of the mate bond for demons is to have someone we can live with for all time. My father is older than the earth's sun. He's alone. He's had countless wives and children and has immense power. However, despite all of that, he lives a lonely existence. He doesn't want that for me. He sensed you and I had a bond and forced it to happen much sooner than it would have," he replied.

"What would have happened if we didn't bond the way we did?" I asked curiously.

"At the gateway? You would have died and crossed over the veil. I would have found my way to you if it weren't a life-or-death situation. Maybe not immediately, but somehow I would have found you again." He kissed my knuckles.

"And is this what you want? You want me for the rest of your life?" I traced my thumb over his lips.

"One thousand percent yes. I wouldn't have been able to bond with you if it wasn't meant to be." He caressed my cheek. "Also,

Kenzie, what I said about healing your womb is still available to you should you want it. As a gift. No strings attached."

I was stunned. If it were possible, hell, yes, I'd want it. But I didn't dare say it out loud, too afraid I'd scare the opportunity away. And then I thought of Stellan.

"Are you certain you could heal me?" I spoke past the lump in my throat.

"It's an easy fix for me, Kenzie. I guarantee it can be done. I'd rather do it in The Dark Realm at Requiem because my power is different here. But yes, anytime you're ready."

"What will happen to me? Is it painful? Will I be able to get pregnant right away?"

"I suspect you may feel some discomfort, and you will need some time to relax while your body adjusts, but that should be all. And you should be able to conceive right away. Are you anxious?" His gaze lingered on my lips.

"Umm . . . somewhat." I nodded.

"Ah, the wolf. You want to give him something that was taken away."

"Yes. I forced Stel and Caid to get involved with the baby mamas. I wanted them to experience everything fatherhood had to offer since it was something I couldn't give them. Stel was certain the child wasn't his. Once we got the test results, he looked forward to becoming a father. And now . . . I know he's disappointed. I hate that fatherhood was dangled before him and then taken away. If I can make him a father, I want to do it."

"You are selfless and honorable, Kenzie. We are all so lucky to have you as our mate. It would be my pleasure to heal you whenever you're ready." He cupped my face with his hands.

"Thank you, Dash. Not just yet. I want to speak with Stel and the other guys first. And umm . . . please don't mention this to them. This is a lot to unpack. I am overwhelmed with information. And I've missed so much time here. I have a lot of catching up to do." I leaned into his hand and closed my eyes. My brain was overloaded.

Dash's lips brushed mine. "It's ok, Kenzie. Take your time. We have forever."

I surrendered to his kiss savoring the smokey taste of his soft lips. He swept his tongue through my mouth, and I climbed onto his lap. His hands roamed my back, then cupped my ass. I moaned. My heart raced, and my skin prickled with arousal.

He groaned, then released me. "I want you, but not here, not now, but soon. Today is about you reuniting with the people who have missed you. We will have our moment."

I pressed my forehead against his. "Ok, soon, yes?"

"Very soon. I need to get back to Requiem for a few days. I'll come back, my precious Fae." He kissed my jaw down to my neck.

"Right now? You're leaving right now?" I tilted my head, granting him more access.

"Unless you'd rather I stay?" His lips lingered under my left earlobe.

"Yes. I want you to meet Tris and return to the ranch with us." I moved to get off his lap, but he held me firmly on his lap.

"I'm happy to do anything you ask, my precious Fae." He pulled me in for another deep kiss making me swoon.

"Come on, let's get you inside." He rose with me, still clinging to his body, and set me down on my feet.

"Thank you for everything you did for me, Gunnar, and my mates. You did more than help." I snuggled into his side.

"You're welcome, Kenzie. I would do anything for you." He kissed the top of my head, and we walked back to the castle.

CHAPTER 55
KENZIE

On our way back to the castle Dash and I ran into Bear, who was playing tug with Smokey. As soon as the puppy saw me, he jumped into my arms.

"Hi, puppy. I missed you too."

Smokey licked my chin.

"Is this ok?" I asked Dash. "Keeping the hellhound here with me?"

"Hounds are my father's guards. This one is a runt, so he is better off with you. Plus, he has bonded to Stel. He will be a fierce protector to you and yours. And I think your ward has found a new companion." Dash glanced at Bear as he approached us.

Smokey yawned and closed his eyes.

"Hi, Bear." I draped an arm over the kid when he came to stand beside me. "Have you met Dash?"

Bear nodded, shook the demon's hand, and said, "I'm going to pack my things. Stel said we're going to Texas today."

I ruffled his hair, then he ran ahead of us.

In the castle, Dash went to hang out with Gunnar and my four mates in the library. I set Smokey on a pillow next to Stel, left the men to bond, and went to find my father.

On my way out, Gunnar said aloud, "My number is still way higher than yours."

"Keep dreaming, big bro," I said while exiting the library.

Gunnar's laughter followed me down the hall.

At the entrance to my father's study, I knocked on the open door before crossing the threshold.

"Come in, Mac." He met me in the middle of the room and wrapped me in a hug. "It's good to have you home."

"Thank you, it's good to be home. And thank you for looking after Bear and helping the guys."

"These people are important to you. And that means they are important to us. You are very fortunate to have so many who care for you. Oh, here, before I forget."

My father pulled out a phone from his desk and sat down. "Same number as before. It is enchanted, allowing us to communicate. It would have been interesting if it worked in The Dark Realm, but I understand yours was lost. You'll need to sync your info."

"Thank you." I took the phone.

Four months ago, I wouldn't have been caught dead without it. Now that it was back in my hand, I almost wished I didn't need it.

"So I heard you went to The Dark Realm to search for us?" I sat in the chair opposite him.

"I did, and I don't know how you two survived down there. I am glad you're safe." He scratched his beard.

"I couldn't have done it without Gunnar," I said.

We sat in silence for a brief but tense-laden moment.

"Why didn't you tell me about him?" I blurted

Dad didn't respond at first. He ran his hand through his hair, making it stand up all over the place. He looked tormented, and I almost felt bad. But . . . I deserved answers, so I pressed.

"Dad?" I leaned forward and placed my elbows on the desk.

He stared off into space for a moment.

"I loved your mom. She was the only woman I have ever loved. You remind me so much of her it hurts. She just left. And I didn't know how to raise you. I did the best that I could. I know you don't love the merc life; I never held it against you. It was just something I thought we could do together . . . common ground. This is hard to say to you, Mackenzie."

"I don't understand. Dad, I figured my resemblance to mom was a bit of an obstacle for you, which I get. In all honesty, I've never held it against you. But what does that have to do with Gunnar?"

"He's your brother." His shoulders slumped.

"Yes, I figured that out. Why didn't you tell me?" I raised my chin.

"His mother and I were together for many years, off and on, until she got married. Years later, she was separated, and we got back together. Anyways, she worked things out with her husband. I didn't know she was pregnant or had a child till much later. Things were working out with them, so I left things alone."

"Fuck. Does Gunnar know?" I asked incredulously.

"Stop swearing. Yes, I told him. When you got back." My father nodded. "He has a good relationship with his family. I didn't want to throw a wrench in their happy life with this news. If his mother wanted him to know, she would have told him. But your wolf figured things out, and I thought I should say something, considering every-thing you've been through."

"Well, shit," I stood near the small fireplace.

"Stop swearing, Mac." He scowled at me.

"Are you sure?" I asked.

He nodded and came over to stand beside me. "His mother came to me for help with his combat mage training. I had a hunch and got a DNA test. Years later, I met your mother and didn't mention it until she was pregnant with you. She was six months pregnant when I mentioned it, and she was livid. Eventually, her anger simmered. However, I believe it may have been one of the reasons she left."

"Bloody fucking hell," I muttered.

"Mac, seriously. Can you refrain from cursing for one conversation?"

"Umm, no fucking way. You're dropping bombs on me and saying a shitload of curse words is my payback. Fuck."

And then I started laughing. I was giving my father a hard time and purposely taking it too far.

"You're impossible." My father rolled his eyes and sat in his favorite chair near the fireplace. I went to a cabinet opposite his desk and poured two glasses of whiskey.

I handed one to him and sat across from him.

"Are you disappointed in me? Mad?"

"Disappointed . . . no. You're almost five hundred years old, Dad, and I'm an adult. I know full well you have a past. I would never hold it against you. Mad? No, not at all; Gunnar was your burden. As far as my mother . . . that's some shit." I snickered when he shook his head.

"I would like to think she wouldn't have left an infant because of something that had happened in your past, but if she did, that is her burden. I don't hold any of it against you," I said with sincerity.

"How are you so level-headed about things? Most children would admonish their parents for withholding this kind of info." He asked.

"I'm not going to lie, Dad; I wish we communicated more. But you'll always be my father, no matter what. And the way I see it, I'd rather be happy with our time than waste it being mad or disappointed. Plus, I like Gunnar. I couldn't have made it through The Dark Realm without him." I shrugged.

"I don't deserve you, Mackenzie, but I am so happy and proud to have you as my daughter. And I am happy you and your brother have found each other."

Smokey bounded into the study and pawed my toes. I picked up my puppy and stood.

"Only you would bring home a hellhound and keep it as a pet." We clinked our glasses together and took a swig.

"Children!" Granny appeared in the study. "Brunch is ready. Make yourselves presentable."

I giggled, and my father rolled his eyes. My Granny hadn't lost her touch when it came to scolding my father.

"I promise to stay in touch more often, Mac." My father hugged me.

"Me too, Dad." We hugged it out and went to join the others gathered in the dining hall.

It felt like a new beginning.

CHAPTER 56
KENZIE

Later that day, my five men and I took Bear and Smokey to the ranch in Texas via a portal. Dash agreed to stay another night, for which I was grateful as he seemed to be getting along with everyone just fine. Plus, I was reluctant to let him go.

Tris and Robert met up with us at the ranch. I didn't hold back the tears when I saw my bestie.

"Damnit, Kenz. That was the scariest four months of my life. If Caid didn't tell me about the dream walking, I'd have killed myself." Tris told me.

"He told you about that?" This was surprising, although, it shouldn't have been. Tris knew all about my lovers over the years. And out of all my mates, Caid would be the one to speak freely, no abridged version necessary.

I glanced at my vamp, and he winked at me.

"Of course he did. And he didn't leave anything out," Tris chided me. "Tell me about The Dark Realm."

Tris linked his arm with mine, and we exited the back door to sit by the lake. It was chilly, so I remembered to grab a couple of blankets before we headed out, and Tris remembered to grab some purple stuff – the wine we had bought at the bazaar in Vegas months ago and a couple of glasses.

I told him everything about the Rogue, my time in the Fifth and Sixth Circle, Requiem Square, discovering I had a brother, and Dash.

"You have five mates?" he squealed.

Out of everything that had happened, I knew my bestie would be most interested in the demon.

"I'm glad you got to meet him before he left." I glanced back at the house, wondering what my demon was up to.

"He's hot, like the rest of them. But he's different. There's something . . . devilish about him. What's he like in bed?"

"We haven't had sex yet," I replied in a small voice.

"What?!" Tris nearly jumped out of his seat. "How could you control yourself around that man?"

I doubled over laughing.

"Girl, you need to kick all those people out of your house and ride that beast."

I couldn't stop laughing.

Robert, Tris' boyfriend, came to join us.

He kissed Tris on his cheek and sat down with another bottle of purple stuff.

"I can hear you two cackling from inside the house. Which is saying something considering I don't have supernatural hearing." He refilled our glasses with a generous-sized pour.

I got my giggles under control and thanked him.

"And while I am glad you two are having a fabulous reunion. It's been hours, and your mates are getting testy. So, I volunteered to come out here and bring up serious matters. Like . . . business."

"Boo!" I cried.

"Yeah, boooo!!" Tris joined me, and we both started laughing again.

"I give up." Robert threw his hands in the air. "Dinner is almost ready. Get your asses in the house and join the rest of us."

He took a couple of steps away, then turned back and grabbed the bottle of wine. "No more wine for you until you've had food."

Tris smacked his ass as he walked away, and we laughed some more. Robert shook his head, a big smile on his face.

I watched my bestie watch his love walk away, a wistful smile on his face.

"Sometimes, I don't know how he puts up with me." Tris turned to face me and clasped his hands over mine. "I think . . . I think I'm going to ask him to marry me."

I wrapped my arms around him and gave him a tight squeeze.

"That would be amazing, Tris. Did you get a ring?" I asked when we settled back on the chairs.

"No, not yet. I've been waiting for you. Maybe you can go with me to shop for rings?"

"I would love to. Tell me everything about you."

He updated me on his life. Which mostly revolved around my disappearance. It was both flattering and embarrassing at the same time. Tris was the rock in my world. I depended on him so much. However, I felt like I had abandoned him, which I needed to compensate.

"Tris, how are we going to do this?" I asked, leaning on his shoulder. "I have my mates and will probably live here full-time. And you're getting married."

"Well, first, Robert hasn't said yes."

"He will."

"Yeah, I know, but . . . regardless. We'll move here. He and I have already discussed it. He can work anywhere. And with teleporting and private jets, we can go back and forth if we need to." He rested his head against mine.

"What do you think about selling Whimsy Skinceuticals?" I asked. Whimsy was my skincare product line, and Tris handled all of the admin for the business and was a shareholder.

"Let's do it. I figured that's where things were headed after you started selling off your investment properties. I think it's a good idea.

We can come up with another business plan here. How about a bar? Or maybe a medispa?"

I laughed. "Both are very different business models, but why not? Let's do it!"

Our wine glasses were empty then, so we had no choice but to return to the house.

I was surprised to find Uncle B sitting at the kitchen counter, drinking a beer with Brody.

"Hi, Uncle B." I hugged him. "When'd you get here?"

"This long ago," he held up his half-filled beer bottle. "Clay and I did the portal thing, thanks to Erik."

I left him with Brody and went to say hello to Clay, my tech mage and one of Bear's tutors. I found them busy playing a video game in the entertainment room. Smokey was lying on a pillow, chomping on a monstrous bone. Bear and Clay pretty much ignored me. Like all gamers, they were hyper-focused on the screen in front of them, so I left them to kill bad guys and went to see if I could help in the kitchen.

The guys had taken care of prepping dinner. Since there wasn't anything for me to do, I grabbed another bottle of purple stuff and went to sit with Tris in the living room. I was about to sit and relax when the doorbell rang.

Carlos and his nurse waited on the front stoop.

"Hi Kenzie, glad you're back. Do you remember Cristela?"

"I do. Nice to see you again. Come on in." I ushered them inside. "Wow, Carlos, you look great."

Carlos was a billionaire entrepreneur who had been involved with the Rogue mess. Stel had brought him back to the ranch to detox, and it worked. He no longer had pale skin or a gaunt face. Detox served him well, or perhaps it was his new love interest.

"Thanks, I feel better. I look forward to helping more with magic tech and some other business ventures with you and the pack."

"Sounds great to me. Let's make sure to talk more about that soon," I replied as the doorbell rang again. "Make yourselves at home."

At the door, this time, was a wolf shifter which I had adopted as my little brother, and an unfamiliar young female. I pulled Jason in for a hug.

"Hi, little brother," I said, trying not to get choked up.

"Hi, Sis. I missed you." He patted my back and released me. "This is Gemma. Gem, this is my sister, Kenzie."

Gem had long black hair, black eyes, and porcelain skin. She reminded me of Simone, except for her Asian eyes. I shook her hand and went to answer the door again.

My father, grandmother, and brother entered. My mouth dropped.

"I'm stunned. Why are you at the door? You're welcome in my home anytime. You never have to knock." I hugged all three of them.

"We wouldn't miss your homecoming party for anything, Mac." My grandmother kissed both of my cheeks. "And it's good for me to get out once in a while."

"I'm grateful to have you here, Granny. All of you." I said to my family.

Erik approached us and offered to show them around when the doorbell rang again.

"Alphas!" I hugged Stel and Caid's parents. "Why are you knocking? You never need to knock."

"Of course we do, Kenzie. This is your home; we respect your privacy." Alpha Reese smiled.

"Welcome home, daughter." Lila, his wife, hugged me back

Caid met us at the entryway and offered to introduce his parents to my family.

I walked with them into the house and then turned back toward the front door even though the bell didn't ring.

"That's everybody, sweetness," Stel stepped behind me and placed a hand on my waist.

"This is amazing, Stel. Everyone I care about is here. Thank you," I turned in his arms and tiptoed to kiss him on his lips.

"We're all happy to have you home." Stel pulled me into the party.

I gazed at all the people that have come to mean so much to me.

"I'm happy to be home. I've missed everyone."

I turned toward the door again.

"Everything ok, precious Fae?" Dash asked me.

Unconsciously I leaned in and kissed him on the mouth, still holding Stel's hand. Stel smiled at us, and I glanced at the door again.

"Yes, I think so. I'll be right back." I released Stel's hand, and both men followed me to the door.

Stel got in front of me and swung the door open, shielding me from whatever I had sensed outside. I peeked around his muscular torso. Dash held me back, then Stel sniffed the air and frowned.

"I smell wolves, but there are a lot of wolves here," Dash said beside me.

"It's Aunt Mimi." Stel glanced at me. "She'll appear when she wants to be seen. But if you want, sweetness, I can bring her here."

"Umm, no, it's ok; I'll just go out for a moment and see if she'll come to me. You guys stay here. I'll be ok."

I ducked away from my men and went outside. I looked left and then right and saw movement behind the hedges on the side of the house.

"Hi, Aunt Mimi," I said to the reclusive wolf. I extended my hand. "Join us, please."

Slowly, she came out of her hiding place and pressed her head against my chest; her face nuzzled into my bosom. Stel and Dash were beside me.

"I'm happy to see you again, too." I patted her back.

"Hi, Aunt Mimi," Stel said, and she released me to cup his cheek with a calloused hand.

Then she noticed the demon and did the same thing.

"Pleasure to meet you, revered seer." Dash bowed his head.

"The Dark One brought the Fae home. I said so." She turned to face me again, and I guided her to the house.

She hooked her arm with mine, took a couple of steps, and then stopped on the path. I glanced at her and then at the house. We had an audience, and they were making her nervous.

Lila saved the day by ushering everyone inside, including Dash and Stel, while she and I coaxed Mimi closer to the door.

Aunt Mimi remained silent, took two more steps, and then stopped walking again to stare at me. She placed her hand on my tummy and hummed happily.

"Babies." She smiled at me.

My mouth hung open.

And then she shuffled away quicker than I thought she could.

Lila tried to stop her, and I was too stunned to stay a word or move.

"Kenzie? Are you?"

I shook my head.

"But it's possible?" Her eyebrows arched.

I nodded.

She hugged me, and I held on tight.

"How is this possible?" Lila asked when she released me.

"Dash," I whispered. I hadn't spoken with the guys about this new revelation and didn't want anyone to overhear our conversation.

"Come." she guided me to the SUV she and her husband arrived in.

We got in the truck, and she turned on the engine, and the radio, then said, "Ok, we should be ok to speak now." She smiled at me.

"Do you always leave your keys in the ignition?" I asked.

"Yes, we leave the keys on pack property and never lock the doors. It's an Alpha thing."

She waved her hand dismissing the topic. "Don't keep me in

suspense, Kenzie. I'm dying to hear about everything." Lila prodded with a smile.

I gave her a brief synopsis of my time in The Dark Realm and told her everything about Dash's offer to heal my womb.

"This is amazing news! But since we're having this conversation in private, I'm guessing you haven't discussed this with your mates."

"Correct. I want this and will have it done, but I just got back. And I don't want to give Stel false hope after everything."

"That's understandable. Your men were a wreck without you, so I'm sure they will be selfish with your time for a while. There's no need to rush, Kenzie." she patted my hand.

My Alpha mom-in-law was right, and I was grateful to have a woman in which to confide.

"Oh, here comes my husband. We should join the others before everyone comes out looking for us." She turned off the engine, and we both hopped out of the truck.

"Is everything ok?" Alpha Reese extended his hand toward his wife.

"Just a little girl talk," she smiled and accepted his hand.

Caid was suddenly beside me, showing off his vamp speed.

The Alphas went inside the house while Caid paused on the steps and turned me to face him.

"Love, I'm glad you and mom had girl talk, but we all get a little crazy if we don't know where you are."

I nodded, understanding him completely. My absence and near-death experience made my men even more protective than they already were. "I'm here, Caid. Everything is ok." I leaned into his body.

My other four men were waiting for us in the entryway. We need time to adjust. I gave each of them assuring hugs and kisses, and we rejoined the party.

Some things needed to be addressed. Taking out the Rogue's partners were on the top of the list, Brody and Dash would be leaving soon; Caid's baby mama was due in a couple weeks, and I was sure we hadn't heard the last from Stel's crazy ex. Plus, we needed to get Bear settled, and there was a mountain of business matters I had to handle. I sighed, feeling the weight of our responsibilities settling on my shoulders.

Stel took a seat at the kitchen counter and extended his hand to me. I grasped his hand and perched on his lap. His strength had always been reassuring, and at the moment, it served as a reminder the long to-do list wasn't mine to conquer alone. I had five men who adored me, and we had the love and support of family and friends.

I vowed to be present in that very moment and reminded myself – *One day at a time, Kenz.*

ACKNOWLEDGMENTS

A quick shout out to all the wonderful women who help make this book possible. Self-publishing takes a village and I couldn't have done it without a team of beta readers, proof readers, my editor and my character artist. Thank you all for accompanying me along this journey.

Author's Note

Thank you for choosing Kenzie's story! I hope you enjoyed it. Please leave a review as I'd greatly appreciate your feedback. As a new author I am whole heartedly interested in what my readers have to say. Your feedback helps me hone my craft and publish books you'll enjoy reading. Follow me on TikTok or visit my website to sign up for my free newsletter. Be the first to know about book release dates, free books, promo boxes and merch coming out soon!

Website: genaviecastle.com

THE PLAYERS

These characters make an appearance in The Kenzie Chronicles Books 1 & 2. For some characters roles may change in Book 3.

Mackenzie Jameson – Combat Mage and Half Fae, Business woman, former mercenary. Raised by her father. Mother was Fae, she disappeared after Kenzie was born. Kenzie in first book has trouble using her Fae magic.

Stellan Reese – Wolf Beta Republic of Texas Pack; Kenzie's mate

Caid Reese – Daywalker, Adopted son of Alpha Reese Republic of Texas Pack, Master Vampire of Austin Seethe; Kenzie's mate

Brody Knight – Human, CEO of Knight and Associates – Private investigator and personal bodyguard services; Kenzie's mate

Erik Reynolds – Powerful mage; Kenzie's mate and magic tutor

Tristan Banks – Kenzie's best friend and business partner

Robert – Tristan's boyfriend and Kenzie's business attorney

Mathieu Jameson – Kenzie's father, Legendary combat mage

Granny Jameson – Kenzie's grandmother, Combat mage

Uncle Brian – aka Uncle B – Mathieu's buddy from the military, Kenzie's handler when she was a merc for PG (Praetorian Group)

Theodore Bear Stevens – Kenzie's neighbor/ward, Tech mage

Clay – Tech mage specializing in technology; Bear's tech mage tutor

Gunnar Quinn – Mathieu's illegitimate son; Kenzie's half brother

The Republic Pack of Texas – Shifters

Joseph Reese – Alpha, Stellan and Caid's father

Lila Reese – Alpha, Wife of Joseph, Stellan and Caid's father

Stellan and Caid – Betas; Kenzie's mates

Aunt Mimi – Joseph Reese's sister, wolf shifter, seer. Recluse.

Jason – Wolf shifter, Kenzie adopts him as a little brother

JT – Wolf shifter

Mark – Panther shifter

Warren – Coyote shifter

Sandy – Wolf shifter

Stedman – Bear shifter

Christine Simpson – Wolf Shifter, Stel's ex and baby mama, Book 2

Simone – Daywalker, Caid's ex and baby mama

The Villains –

The Rogue aka Malcolm Johnson – Powerful mage, using dark magic.

William Bates – Co-Owner of BioRegenerative Services (BRS), Ordered the hit on Stellan and Caid

Carlos DeRosa – Owner of BioRegenerative Services (BRS), Stel spares his life, helps him detox from excessive drug use. He agrees to help Kenzie and the pack in exchange.

Avery Knox – Attorney for BRS, tried to get manipulate Kenzie. She didn't take the bait. He was killed by someone else and left info for Kenzie in a safety deposit box giving her info on the Rogue's experiments.

ALSO BY GENAVIE CASTLE

The Kenzie Chronicles - Series Complete

Fae Magic, Book One

Fae Blood, Book Two

Fae Bonds, Book Three

Fae Chaos, Book Four

~

Banished, An Elemental Kingdom Novel

~

Pure Blood Duet - Series complete

Chained

Unchained

~

The Sentinels Series

Nightmare Girl, Book One

Brother's Sins, Book Two

Family Rules, Book Three

~

Midway Mystics Collection

The Seduction of Duality, A Dr. Jekyll & Mr. Hyde Retelling

Book Two - Available 2026